SWE

Sweet Secrets

MARTIN EDWARDS

UPFRONT PUBLISHING
LEICESTERSHIRE

Sweet Secrets
Copyright © Martin Edwards 2003

All rights reserved

No part of this book may be reproduced in any form by
photocopying or by any electronic or mechanical means,
including information storage or retrieval systems,
without permission in writing from both the copyright
owner and the publisher of this book.

ISBN 1-84426-161-1

First published 2003 by
UPFRONT PUBLISHING LTD
Leicestershire

Typeset in Bembo by
Bookcraft Ltd, Stroud, Gloucestershire
Printed by Lightning Source

Contents

Coffer Jam	1
Like Father Like Son	3
Bitter Discovery	16
Chinatown	28
True Love of Money	37
Playing Cards	50
Plane, Pain, Plan	63
Sweet Dreams	65
Singapore Sling	74
Armless and Legless	87
Thai Dreams	98
Golf Balls	103
All the Fee in China	108
Swiss Roll	117
Singing for Supper	125
Rats	133
Roller Coaster	141
Hot Stuff	152
Back Trap	166
On the Road Again	174
Sea Sore	188

Flour Power	199
Hot Shot	206
Morning Calls	207
Courtesy of Her Majesty	215
Water Bugs	225

Coffer Jam

Bangkok, Wednesday, 31 May 1995

The young policeman stared at the stalled car blocking the midday traffic. He sighed, climbed down stiffly from his small bandstand in the middle of the junction and walked officiously towards the motionless Mercedes.

His black leather jackboots shimmered as they crunched the small stones on the hot tarmac. As he neared the car he stopped and squinted through his fake Ray-Bans. His body tensed and the hairs on the back of his neck bristled. There was something odd about the stationary car… but what?

The tropical sun beat down on his white motorcycle helmet and the dust from the cars, buses and trucks attacked his eyes and throat. He remembered what his instructor had told him on the first day of his basic training. Bangkok could be a dangerous city. He had to be extremely careful. His right hand moved down slowly to his waist. He checked the revolver belted to his side. Gently he unbuckled the leather safety strap. He cursed quietly, longing for the blaring horns of the blocked cars to stop, and ached to be at home again with his family upcountry beside the cool rice paddies.

He moved forward cautiously, his eyes fixed on the motionless vehicle. Suddenly, he realised what was worrying him. The car wasn't stalled… its engine was running, yet it wasn't moving.

Sweat dribbled down the small of his back. He tightened his grip on the revolver, moved slowly to within five yards of the motionless car and stopped again.

The darkened windows were crazed as if hit by a sharp stone. The policeman went cold and shivered despite the stifling heat. He edged forward carefully and saw that the car's rear windows were punctured with small neat holes. He turned sideways,

1

Coffer Jam

shuffled up to the back window and pushed gently against it with the heel of his left hand. His right hand tensed around the secure, smooth, wooden handle of his revolver. The crazed glass bowed but did not break. He waited. Nothing except sun, dust and noise. He held his breath, then gingerly pushed harder. Nothing... harder still...

Suddenly the glass shattered and a blast of cold air hit the young policeman's face as he stared wide-eyed inside the car. Crimson blood oozed over the new white leather upholstery. A fine-boned girl, a middle-aged Thai-Chinese man and his driver bled peacefully like ripped rag dolls.

The young policeman recoiled in horror and retched over the outside of the shiny Mercedes. Inside, a Chinese love song was still lilting from the car's CD player...

Like Father Like Son

Jakarta, Thursday, 13 April 1995

'Where the hell's Akbar?' grumbled the Minister of Agriculture, staring angrily at the empty space, which should have been occupied by his new white ministerial Mercedes.

The hot afternoon sun beat down on the portly Dr Amin. He felt his temperature rising rapidly as a result of both the sunshine and his anger at the missing car. He turned to his aide. 'Osman, go and find the lazy bugger. Unfortunately we haven't got all day.'

Osman scurried back into the bleak Ministry building, looking around wildly and hoping against hope to find the missing Akbar lurking somewhere near the entrance. Dr Amin exhaled noisily. His right foot started tapping in annoyance. He felt his blood pressure rising. He tried to calm himself, mindful of his doctor's recent advice about being at a dangerous age and avoiding stress. The Minister added muttering to his outward signs of anger. He began to sweat.

Thirty seconds after Osman's departure the ministerial car roared round the corner into the driveway and drew up sharply in front of the tapping, muttering, sweating Minister. Akbar jumped out of the car, smiled broadly, and graciously opened the back door for his perspiring boss. Dr Amin glared angrily at Akbar but said nothing. It was not done for a Government Minister to reveal basic emotions in front of a mere driver. Instead Dr Amin sank, silently seething, into the crunching new leather of the back seat of his Mercedes and waited for Osman to return.

Five minutes passed. Finally Osman ran out of the Ministry building looking hot and bothered. He saw the shining car, with the cool, smiling Akbar sitting in it, and clenched his fists. Osman too climbed grumpily and silently into the car. Akbar however did not open the door for Osman, who sat in the front next to the still smiling driver. Osman's only face-saving device was to ignore

3

Like Father Like Son

Akbar totally in an attempt to establish the social gulf between the two of them. Sensing victory, Akbar gunned the car's engine as if to make up for the time lost waiting for the sweating aide and threw the car into gear.

The Mercedes roared down the driveway, waking up the security guard dozing happily in the post-lunch sunshine as it swept out through the Ministry's grand rusty gates. The guard was draped like a worn overcoat over the uncomfortable, metal folding chair that was his daytime home. His rice-tight potbelly undulated gently to the rhythm of his open-mouthed, contented breathing and his arms dangled like aerial roots by his side. His too-tight uniform jacket ballooned open between the buttons that strained valiantly to tether it, revealing harlequins of a grubby, off-white sweatshirt beneath. The disturbed guard staggered sleepily to his feet and slopped a bleary-eyed ragged salute at the back of the passing car, which, by that time, had already pulled away from the Ministry and begun to weave its way through the busy Jakarta afternoon traffic.

'Some guard... any gangster would bloody well have to wake him up to get arrested,' grumbled the bad-tempered Dr Amin, still mopping small beads of sweat from his nut-brown brow.

The Minister lay back, sniffed deeply and savoured once again the new upholstery smell of his latest toy. His smooth forehead furrowed. How long would the toy remain his after the meeting that was about to take place? He stared out of the window, trying to take his mind off such a depressing thought.

Outside the cool, quiet Mercedes, a tangle of battered trucks, shining limousines, and noisy mopeds straining under the weight of whole families, jostled for space along the boulevard that glimmered in the heat of the sweaty, tropical afternoon sun. The roads in Jakarta never seemed quite wide enough to cope with the flow of daytime traffic that teemed down them.

Crowds of skinny, honey-brown people picked their way along the deformed dusty pavements and past street vendors who sold everything from baseball caps to noodles and cigarettes from three-wheeled carts.

The crowded boulevards and sidewalks were bordered by shiny, modern glass-clad skyscrapers. Outside each building was a

Like Father Like Son

shrill whistle-blowing uniformed guard, waving his arms in an authoritative and agitated manner at traffic, which, to a large part, ignored him. To complete the chaos, a loudspeaker boomed echoing instructions to snoozing or gossiping drivers to come and collect their masters. A typical Jakarta afternoon scene.

Dr Amin began to shiver. The car's air conditioning worked effectively even in the tropical heat and humidity. His patience finally broke.

'Akbar, are you now trying to freeze us to death having first kept us waiting for such a hell of a long time in the heat?'

The smiling obliging Akbar mumbled some soothing words. The Minister must be under severe stress to reveal this much emotion. With masterful arrogance he twiddled some knobs on the car's dashboard with one hand to appease his irate boss, while simultaneously giving little jabs and tugs to the steering wheel with the other as they continued to swerve in and out of the dense Jakarta traffic.

Deep down, Dr Amin wondered whether it was more the thought of the coming meeting than the temperature inside the car that was giving him the shivers. He looked at Osman, who was still sweating profusely from his abortive search for the driver.

'Did I ever tell you about my early life?' he asked.

Osman coughed nervously, thought frantically but said nothing. There had to be a way of answering the Minister that would not appear rude yet might save him from yet another repetition of the well-worn story.

Happily the Minister did not seem to expect an immediate response and continued talking as the car screeched up to some traffic lights and Akbar arched his back and stretched his arms as if having completed the hill climb stage of a rally. A crowd of grubby youths dressed in bedraggled short-sleeved shirts, long trousers and scuffed leather shoes with no socks immediately surrounded it and pressed a selection of gaudily wrapped goods against the car's rear window.

Dr Amin stared at the gaggle. 'Look at them. What sort of life do they have to look forward to? Trying to sell magazines they can't read and cigarettes the likes of which they've probably been

Like Father Like Son

smoking since they turned six.'

The street kids were wary and showed a degree of respect towards the Minister's car that was not normally present in their daily selling. They knew from the small flag mast at the front of the car that it contained a Government dignitary and that the occupant was not just some rich Chinese businessman on his way to make yet another million. Although, surprisingly, the car did not have the normal motorcycle outriders that carved a way for it through the dense Jakarta traffic, it still represented Authority. And Authority could easily cause problems for street vendors if it was upset.

Authority, in this instance in the form of Dr Amin, was definitely upset. He was not, however, in the mood to take out his bad humour on a gaggle of street kids. He had deliberately refused the official escort for this journey. Firstly, it made a hell of a row with its sirens blaring. Secondly, he needed the maximum time to think about his case. If he had analysed it, there was probably a third, more psychological reason. The longer he could delay the meeting, the happier he would be.

Dr Amin sighed and waived dismissively at the street kids who obediently ran off to pester other waiting cars. He looked at them weaving like needles in and out of the threads of jammed vehicles. They were inhaling sufficient carbon monoxide to make it a race against time whether the exhaust fumes or the local Kretek clove cigarettes first broke their health.

Dr Amin sighed again. 'You know, Osman, these kids remind me more than anything that I am a Minister in the government of a third world country.'

It also reminded Dr Amin of the type of life he might have been living had he not been blessed with significantly above-average intelligence. He could still hear his old Dutch-trained teacher complaining: 'Amin Bin Ahmed, you are capable of achieving good results. You must do better than this.' At least Dr Amin had something to be thankful to the Dutch for.

His mind drifted back to his early village life, during which he had worked so hard to make it to university in Surabaya. He thought of his concern when, as a seventeen-year-old, he had set off with his father, Ahmed Bin Mohammed, on the journey east

Like Father Like Son

from his home village of Banding to Surabaya, Indonesia's second largest city seething with over three million inhabitants.

He remembered his timid question to this father: 'Father, I am afraid. Do you think I deserve to go to Surabaya? Do you think I will do well enough not to bring shame on our family?'

Dr Amin turned again to Osman. 'Do you realise it took me several days at that time to travel to university in Surabaya?'

Osman groaned quietly to himself. He was definitely going to hear the story again. The way the traffic was looking today they would be lucky if it didn't take several days to reach the Presidential Palace. That left plenty of time for the Minister of Agriculture to reminisce. Osman tried to think of an appropriate response. He had to express enough interest to make sure Dr Amin continued, yet not so much concern that he would be trapped into a conversation.

'Sir, from Banding that must be a journey of... of... 600 miles. That was a long way to travel in 1950.'

Dr Amin looked sternly at his aide. 'Actually it's 800 miles. And in 1950 I was only ten. I might look incredibly ancient to you, Osman, but I'm not that old!'

Osman flushed. 'I'm sorry, sir... er... sometimes my mental arithmetic is... um... a bit rusty.'

Dr Amin's face clouded. 'Don't talk to me about bad maths. That's part of the reason we are in this bloody mess. Luckily for you, it was the maths of our agronomists and not yours that got us here.'

Dr Amin sat back in a deliberate effort to relax, and let his mind drift once again to his early youth.

'My father and I set off in mid August. I can see it now. The two of us in a bullock cart, creaking and bumping along dusty tracks. It was as well university started in late August, since the tracks became impassable quagmires once the monsoon rains arrived in November. As my father and I neared the city the tracks improved a little and soon a thin ribbon of pitted, potholed tarmac led the way to the city. When we reached the ribbon we were able to flag down the decrepit bus that was to be our home for the next twenty-four hours.'

Dr Amin remembered how the bus had creaked, lurched and

7

Like Father Like Son

ground its way, with only the briefest of stops, to Surabaya. There it would pause for two hours before starting its torturous overloaded return trip.

It was a miracle that the bus moved at all. The body leaned drunkenly because of the vehicle's broken springs and was held together with wire and layers of gaudy gloss paint liberally splashed on now and again during the two-hour pause at either end of the journey. No glass remained in any of the windows. This had been broken long ago, either by debris thrown up from the road during its interminable trips or by passengers hauling themselves and their belongings onto its roof. The roof served as the second deck and was usually fully occupied as the poor beast approached or departed from its main destinations. None of the interior fittings remained, having been either broken off due to normal wear and tear or removed by bored passengers to be kept as souvenirs of momentous voyages.

During its first life in Holland the bus had been equipped with the normal rudimentary gauges and dials that one would expect to find in a public conveyance. Although the instruments were still physically present they had stopped working long ago. Instead, like nurses stranded in the bush, the two drivers worked with the minimum of technical support and relied instead on their intimate knowledge of the tormented sounds that the bus made under various driving conditions to determine which noise was normal and which warned of a potential disaster. Under the constant care of the drivers and wreathed in black diesel fumes, the ancient vehicle swayed along the byways of Java in a majestic ramshackle style reminiscent of a grander youth.

It was only by imposing on her a regime of perpetual motion that the poor old lady was prevented from collapsing. If she had ever been allowed to rest for any more than two hours it was a certainty that she would never move again.

In truth the bus should have been scrapped years ago. Indeed, in most countries it would have been. However, in the Indonesia of that time, it rendered a vital daily service for the inhabitants of one of the most populous and poor countries in the world.

★

Like Father Like Son

Dr Amin had fallen silent. Osman thought he ought to say something to show he was still interested and to restart the familiar tale. They were still forty minutes away from the Palace and it was better for him that his boss relaxed in history than started quizzing him about facts and figures for the upcoming meeting.

'Your father must have been a very special person, sir. I mean, to spend so much time and effort promoting your education like that.'

Dr Amin smiled at Osman. He was happy that the young man, who at times reminded him of himself in his youth, should be so observant.

'Osman, you're right. My father was an extremely special man.'

At the time, young Amin Bin Ahmed had suspected the trip to Surabaya was as much of an experience and a nightmare for the father as it was for the son. However, a respect for his elders, and a desire to avoid being given a pinch for insolence, had prevented young Amin from asking too many indiscreet questions. His father was a serious man in his late thirties who did not like to have his motives or actions questioned. Over the years Amin Bin Ahmed had learned to tread carefully as far as certain subjects were concerned.

Dr Amin continued, 'He was for the most part an even-tempered, peaceful man, content to grow his basic crop of tobacco and maize on our small-holding. He visited the mosque when required and brought up our family of five children in the best manner possible. But you know, inside him he was a bit of a revolutionary.'

Osman turned round and looked at Dr Amin with genuine interest. He had not heard this part of the story before. 'How do you mean... a revolutionary, sir?'

Dr Amin chuckled. 'Well, only a minor revolutionary, but a revolutionary nevertheless. Anyway, that's a story for another journey. At that time our main family problem wasn't revolution, it was how to get me to university in Surabaya.'

Osman sighed quietly. No creaking family skeletons had been laid bare and he was still in for the next instalment of the normal

9

Like Father Like Son

saga.

Dr Amin remained silent for a few minutes. He thought about the great care with which his father had rounded up the clothing necessary for a trip of such importance from his numerous next of kin. Between all the families they had managed to assemble a trousseau, which in retrospect would have been better suited to a circus act than to a momentous journey. At the time, however, it seemed sufficiently coordinated and grand to give Ahmed Bin Mohammed the status deserved by a father taking his eldest son to university in Surabaya. It was a shame, nevertheless, that the members of his family who had contributed clothing could not have been slightly more uniform in terms of their build and fashion sense.

Having been installed in Surabaya, the young Amin Bin Ahmed had waved bravely to his departing father, not realising that he would never again see the small wiry Javanese man dressed like a circus clown. Even now, thirty-eight years later, a lump came to the throat of Amin Bin Ahmed, now Dr Amin, as he sat in his ministerial car remembering the event.

At the time, Amin had realised the material and emotional sacrifice his parents were making in releasing a strong son from the traditional bonds of the family smallholding. He had resolved then and there not to disappoint them.

Osman grew tired of waiting for his boss to continue. He coughed respectfully. 'What happened then, sir?'

'Uh?' Dr Amin stirred from his dreaming. 'Oh yes,' he continued, 'I worked hard at Surabaya University. The course work was no problem and I was soon able to fill in the gaps in my knowledge left by my old teacher in Banding. At the end of four years I graduated with first class honours.'

Dr Amin paused and cleared his throat. 'I believe my father would have been proud of me. But he didn't live long enough to find out.'

Osman thought of his own father who was still working for a local bank. He must be about the same age as the Minister's father was when he died. Osman turned to look at the Minister.

'But your father must still have been a relatively young man, sir. How did he come to pass away at such an early age?'

Like Father Like Son

'A good question, Osman. He died at the age of forty-two, of hard work and bad medical care. Can you believe that at that time they were unable to treat the malaria which was endemic on Java?' Dr Amin paused, then continued slowly, 'I returned home to Banding to bury him.'

Osman turned away to look out of the window and to avoid embarrassing the Minister, who wiped a tear from his eye.

Dr Amin waited a while to regain his composure, and then continued.

'As the eldest son, my rightful place upon the death of my father was at home. I should have been working in the fields and doing my best to look after the rest of the family. But the extended family decided that this was not to be. I was to continue my education by taking a Masters degree at Jakarta University. After this, as a highly educated man, I would surely find a way of repaying their investment.'

Dr Amin grunted again, only this time in satisfaction. 'And that my boy, is how I came to Jakarta.'

Osman glanced surreptitiously at his watch and then at the traffic jam. At least another fifteen minutes to go. He had better keep the conversation going.

'Can you tell me again, sir, about how you defeated communism.'

Osman tried to sound sincere but felt he wasn't succeeding. In fact, he was genuinely interested in this part of the story. Each time he heard it, he noted another detail about how his boss had survived Indonesia's revolution and how he had gone on to become one of the country's most influential Ministers. Osman knew he was working with one of Indonesia's living legends.

Dr Amin smiled wistfully, not reading any cynicism into Osman's request. He puffed his chest out ever so slightly so that, for once, it almost projected further than his stomach and continued talking.

'Well, I don't think I defeated it single-handedly Osman... but I like to think I did my bit.' Dr Amin felt again how good it was to have a surrogate son now that his own boy Nirwan was away most of the time at college in the States. He had always felt guilty that he had not spent more time with Nirwan. Although Osman

Like Father Like Son

was not his own flesh and blood, talking to him like this somehow made Dr Amin feel less bad about the lack of attention he had paid to his own son as he was growing up.

'When I arrived in Jakarta in 1961, although it wasn't as much of a change as going from Banding to Surabaya a few years earlier, it was still quite a culture shock for a young country boy.'

Osman laughed reverentially at the idea of his Minister as a country boy.

'Oh yes, I was still very much a country boy at heart,' continued Dr Amin, happy that Osman should find this hard to believe. 'But as soon as I arrived in Jakarta, I knew I was at the centre of the social unrest that was going on at the time.'

'How do you mean, sir? Was it to do with the damn Chinese?' To Osman, as with many ethnic Indonesians, the damn Chinese were always to blame somewhere along the line.

'No, no... Well, not only them.' Dr Amin shook his head carefully. He did not want to disturb his carefully slicked-down hair and release his black Indonesian curls to their natural condition before his important meeting. 'No, just think what was happening at the time. For a start, Sukarno had dissolved parliament. That was one of those events that had really upset my father.'

Osman looked puzzled. From his perspective, dissolving the sort of parliament that he was used to in Indonesia was no big deal. Perhaps the boss's father really had been a revolutionary.

'So if it wasn't the Chinese then it must have been the Communists, sir?' Osman had been well drilled in the sources of all civil unrest in Indonesia.

'Exactly!' barked Dr Amin. 'The bloody Commies... Akbar, watch out! You damned nearly knocked that young lad off his Honda... he doesn't look like either a Chinese or a Commie!'

Akbar, who had been paying too much attention to the story being told by his boss, muttered some apologetic curses and concentrated harder on weaving through the traffic while still keeping an ear open for the story.

Dr Amin took up his tale again. 'You see, Osman, there was a growing Communist movement within the university. I was approached to join it as soon as I arrived there.'

12

Like Father Like Son

Osman's jaw dropped. 'But... er... you didn't, sir...?'

'No, of course not, you stupid boy,' snapped Dr Amin, all ideas of surrogate fatherhood disappearing fast. To have a Communist connection of any description was a stigma that you carried with you for life in Indonesia. You certainly didn't get to be a Government Minister if you had associated with them.

'You know what that would mean! No, no, I can assure you that even without the impact of my father's political ideas I didn't think communism was right for Indonesia. Look at it this way. My father's only crime was to be born a peasant in a country where basic medical care was still lacking for all but the rich and privileged. At the end of the day he paid for this with his life. If, with all the disadvantages he had, my father could still reject communism then I definitely should.'

'So what did you do, sir?' said Osman, sounding suitably contrite.

Dr Amin looked unnaturally coy. 'Well, I suppose in a way I started my own resistance movement.'

Osman looked startled.

'Don't look like that, Osman. All I did was to mix politics with my studies for the next four years.'

'But that must have been incredibly exciting, sir... I mean, being a revolutionary.' Having failed to find out much about the father on this score, perhaps the story of the son would be more revealing.

'I wouldn't put it quite like that,' said Dr Amin, still nervous about being branded as an agitator even so many years after the event. 'The most immediate result was that my studies suffered... my thesis that should have taken two years was still not finished after four. But in a way you're right... I soon learned a hell of a lot about politics.'

'Was it all cloak and dagger work, sir?' said Osman, still sticking to his image of his boss as a cross between Robin Hood and a character in a le Carré novel.

Dr Amin toyed with the idea of stringing along both Osman and Akbar with tales of extraordinary bravery and subterfuge. After all, his image could do with some upgrading. What better than to be a closet national hero? But then he thought better of it.

13

Like Father Like Son

Anyway, the reality was quite brave enough.

'I started to speak quite frequently at the open-air night-time rallies. The more I spoke, the more I tried to convince people to resist the Commies. I'm not sure exactly what the people thought, but the crowds started growing. People came to listen…' Dr Amin chuckled to himself… *despite being bitten to death by the night-time insects.*

Osman cringed involuntarily. 'Is that where you met the President, sir?'

'Well, not exactly met the President, Osman… but in a way you're right,' continued Dr Amin. There was no need to shatter too many illusions.

'The President once told me that the first time he saw me was at one of those rallies. At the time he was still a young army commander and he used to attend some of the gatherings dressed as a civilian to try and see how much popular support there was for the anti-communist movement. I don't remember seeing him at all. Anyway, he must have decided that there was enough grass roots support because when the Commies finally staged the coup to overthrow President Sukarno, it was Suharto who lead the counter attack.'

'And that was pretty bloody, wasn't it, sir?' said Osman, egging on Dr Amin. Only five minutes more to go.

'Yes… at least half a million suspected Commies killed off and the same number thrown into jail. I don't think the total figure has ever been verified. Thousands more of them fled to Eastern Europe to join Indonesian friends already studying there on scholarships given by Sukarno. I think that the backlash against the Commies was much stronger than they'd ever anticipated. And they paid for it. Many died, and a whole load of the prominent ones remained locked up in jail for years. Some of them are still there.'

'And that's when President Suharto took office, sir, and asked you to join him?'

'Yes, Osman, you know most of the story already. The President's a man with a long memory and believes in repaying a debt. As he built his Government President Suharto rewarded those who had supported him during the struggle. And, by

14

Like Father Like Son

continuing to support old people for the next thirty years, he's made his old friends into some of the wealthiest people in the world.'

'And a lot of them are Chinese. I bet some of them are worth millions,' said Osman with an uncharacteristic show of bitterness as he thought of his father working for a Chinese-owned bank.

'Millions... you've got to be kidding! Billions more like,' added Dr Amin who too was thinking about money. About how, by comparison, he had not become unnaturally wealthy. Or indeed rich at all by wealthy Indonesian standards. He had, however, benefited from having been identified by Suharto as an active supporter of his cause and had been asked to restructure the Ministry of Agriculture. A job for which he had seemed ideally suited given his agricultural roots and his undoubted intelligence and academic training. His reward for sorting out the Ministry was to be sponsored for two years to study for a PhD at Harvard.

And so the pattern for his life was set. The result being that on this April afternoon in 1995, at the age of fifty-five, Amin Bin Ahmed from Banding – now Dr Amin Bin Ahmed, Minister of Agriculture – found himself sitting in his new ministerial car on the way to what he knew would be an extraordinarily difficult meeting with His Excellency, Suharto, President of the Republic of Indonesia.

Bitter Discovery

Jakarta, Thursday, 13 April 1995

'Well, my son, what is of such importance that it deserves a special audience with the President of the Republic of Indonesia?'

The old man stared down at Dr Amin from behind his massive, ornately carved teak desk, mounted like a pagoda on top of a teak podium. He continued talking without inviting Amin to move from his inferior spot in front of the platform.

'I can only presume it must be such excessively good news that you can't wait to share it with me.' The old man paused, giggled rather nastily and then continued. 'Or perhaps so terrible that you dare not keep it to yourself!'

The President smiled at his own joke while Dr Amin gulped at the accuracy of the President's comments and began to sweat.

Suharto was dressed, as was Dr Amin, in the formal, open-necked, quasi-military tunic top that was the hallmark of Indonesian politicians. The main difference was that Dr Amin's tunic top was charcoal grey and that worn by His Excellency General Suharto off-white. A colour that no one but the President was allowed to wear.

President Suharto looked tanned and fit and, with his balding head fringed with wispy white hair, the old man had all the outward appearances of a kindly old uncle. His moon-like face was clean-shaven and without wrinkles except for a few around the eyes which could have been caused by smiling. He glanced at Dr Amin standing reverentially before and below the Presidential Desk. President Suharto removed his metal-framed glasses and focused closely on Dr Amin, who did not react.

'Amin, are you with me?' snapped the kindly uncle.

Dr Amin was not. His mind had once again escaped to the mists of Surabaya and to the journey through life that had brought him to the Presidential Palace and today's fateful audience.

The old uncle's irate voice drifted into Dr Amin's consciousness... 'Amin, are you with me?'

Dr Amin jumped out of his safe dream world and smiled deferentially. He knew that there was extremely little about President Suharto that in reality resembled a kindly old uncle and that the lines around his eyes were certainly not caused by excessive smiling. Kindly old uncles don't defeat Communist coups at the age of forty-four and, thirty years later, remain in charge of the fifth most populous country in the world. There might be many excellent qualities about President Suharto – however, being a kindly old uncle was not among them. Even Dr Amin, one of the President's confidants, and someone whom the President addressed as 'son' during relaxed moments knew better than to push his luck with the old man.

Dr Amin shifted his position slightly. He was, at the end of the day, a slightly overweight fifty-four-year-old not used to standing to semi-attention for any length of time. He knew he couldn't avoid the moment any longer. He would have to start explaining the problem to the President. Dr Amin decided that reinforcing the bond of friendship between him and President was as good a way as any of launching into what was going to be a difficult subject whichever way he approached it. Dr Amin took a deep breath, cleared his throat and prepared himself for battle.

'Thank you, Pak, for agreeing to see your son at such short notice,' Dr Amin said with excess politeness while using the deferential short form for Bapak, meaning uncle. Amin paused. Something was wrong... They weren't alone. He looked across the President's office and saw two other people standing at the far corner of the massive room. One, a slim man in his early thirties, stood silently in the corner leafing nonchalantly through a magazine. Amin swore under his breath as he recognised President Suharto's second son Bambang. Bambang grinned superciliously at Dr Amin, enjoying the obvious discomfort being experienced by The Minister of Agriculture. Dr Amin cursed again quietly while nodding his head in acknowledgement in the direction of Bambang. There was no chance now of playing the old-boy card. The old boy in question would have to maintain

Bitter Discovery

great face in front of his biological son.

The most privileged dilettante offspring of the President of Republic of Indonesia and the farmer's boy from Banding made good hated each other's guts. However, they demonstrated this in an extremely Javanese and indirect way. This was particularly so when they were in the presence of the one man who called them both 'son'. This man, however, knew well their feelings for each other. He was quietly glad about this mutual dislike since it gave him another card to play should it be necessary in controlling either one or both of them. You never knew when this would be necessary. And you didn't remain in control of countries of the size and complexity of Indonesia by being unprepared.

In view of the undesirable presence of Bambang, Dr Amin decided to shift his approach to the President from a friendly one to one based on professionalism heavily laced with flattery. He took another breath and launched into his excessively respectful monologue.

'Pak, as you know, at this time of year I instruct our agronomists to focus all their attention on the prospect for the crop projections for our staple commodities. In particular, rice and sugar.'

The President remained motionless, staring hard at Amin with unfriendly, calculating eyes as he weighed up every word Amin said and evaluated each for a hidden meaning.

Dr Amin cleared his throat and continued. 'I know how important it is that the people who live throughout our thousand or so inhabited islands have sufficient food in their bellies to keep them happy. This is critical for the continued stability and prosperity of our great country.'

Dr Amin glanced up at the President, who was now staring intently at his fingernails. There was nothing for it but to press on.

'In 1969, Pak, you identified so correctly the importance of sugar in our daily diet. In your first five-year plan you set targets to increase its production. Um...'

Suharto looked up. 'Yes?'

'Er... well, as you know, ever since then my Ministry has striven to make our country self-sufficient in sugar. Despite the,

18

Bitter Discovery

er, the enormous demands placed on us by a population of almost 190 million we... um... had so far managed to achieve your goal and...'

'What the hell do you mean, "had"?' barked the kindly old uncle, standing up behind his desk and staring down at the hapless Minister of Agriculture.

Amin started to explain the delicate but deliberate use of 'had' but was cut short by Suharto.

'There can be no "had" about it. You can't have 190 million people spread over fourteen thousand islands going without sugar. It's part of their daily diet. It's a basic. It keeps them happy and gives them energy. No, no, my friend, there can be no "had" about it. That would be, as you well know, a recipe for disaster. Both for me and needless to say for you as well.'

At the back of the room, Bambang's smirk grew larger, not only because of Amin's discomfort but also because he now saw the glimmerings of a commercial activity that could make his personal net worth even greater.

Dr Amin started fighting for his life. Now that at least part of the problem was on the table he felt more relaxed and confident. The adrenaline started flowing through his tubby body.

'Pak, it is precisely because of the importance of this matter that I sought an audience with you straight away when I saw signs of a potential problem,' lied Amin, returning the stare from Suharto's unfriendly eyes.

In reality he had screamed at length at his agronomists. The haranguing resembled the President's recent outburst but delivered in much more colourful language as befits a son of the soil.

Dr Amin had ranted and raved... There was a mistake... There had to be a mistake... There was no way that a plentiful sugar crop that had been growing steadily for many years just vanished because of a period of unnaturally wet weather... The satellite crop pictures had to be wrong... That poxy, bloody, damn stupid satellite launched by the Ministry of Technology to prove it had the know-how to be in the space race had to be sending wrong information... The bloody Americans must have some devious plan to destabilise the world's largest Muslim population... They had probably chosen an extremely sensitive part of the world to take the spotlight off their own domestic difficulties regarding the recognition of Vietnam. Something had to be wrong... 'Go and find out what it is or your collective balls, if you have any, will be on the chopping block.'

In truth, however, Amin knew that as Suharto had implied, the balls that would be first to be disconnected from their rightful owner belonged to the Minister of Agriculture.

Dr Amin had sweated, cursed and sworn for three days as the information was checked and rechecked. On-site surveys were taken of the main sugar cane producing areas of Java. At the end of the day the news was not good. It seemed that three factors had combined to reduce the sugar crop to below self-sufficiency levels: floods, the change from growing sugar cane to cocoa and selling off agricultural land for real-estate development.

This much alone was sufficiently serious to threaten Amin's long-term ownership of his new ministerial Mercedes 500. But there was even worse news. The five hundred thousand tonne National Strategic Sugar Reserve had more or less disappeared into thin air at just the time when it would be needed because of the domestic shortage. The combination of these two events must surely be sufficient to ensure that a vital part of Amin's anatomy disappeared along with his flashy car.

The quiet removal of ninety per cent of Indonesia's Strategic Sugar Reserve had to be an inside job involving all sorts of well-connected people in the Indonesian hierarchy. It was just unfortunate for them that the lid had been blown off a game, which had probably been going on for years, by a totally unpredicted need for the stockpile.

In the complex way of Indonesia, the whole situation would almost certainly be hushed up by the President and some of his cronies. It had to be, in order to protect the interest of a few well-connected people whose Swiss bank accounts were almost certainly, as a result of its disappearance, millions of dollars richer than they might otherwise have been.

'Go on,' commanded the President.

Dr Amin wondered again how to present the next part of his story. He had been there when the auditor from the international

Bitter Discovery

surveying company first struck concrete. The surveyor had been plumbing the depths of what, until then, had been classified as a sugar mountain. Suddenly it became little more than an anthill. Further investigation revealed that enough concrete pyramids to make an Egyptian envious were present in warehouses spread throughout many of Indonesia's inhabited islands. Each pyramid was covered with just enough sugar to create the effect of a grubby Mont Blanc inside each of the major strategic sugar warehouses.

That was three weeks ago. Dr Amin could still recall vividly his amazement and the sickly sinking feeling as the gauge passed through one foot of sugar and then struck the top of a forty-foot pyramid of concrete blocks.

'But the fact is,' continued Dr Amin, 'the, er, fact is that... um...'

'Get on with it, Amin, you are beginning to get on my nerves,' snapped the kindly uncle.

'Well, sir,' continued Dr Amin, having abandoned Pak as the situation deteriorated, 'the fact is that, due to excessive property speculation by the Chinese, causing a reduction in land under sugar cultivation, combined with the recent floods all the signs are that we are... um... er... likely, we are likely to suffer an... a... significant sugar shortage at the end of this crop year.'

'How much is significant?'

Dr Amin drew in his breath; this was it. 'About half a million tonnes... er... sir.'

Dr Amin felt a weight lifted from his chest, having delivered half of the bad news. Not only that, but he had managed to blame the Chinese for most of it. Since the rest of the bad news concerning the disappearance of the strategic stockpile most likely implicated people close to the President, Amin felt that he would be on marginally safer ground when explaining this part of the story.

He would have loved to start his announcement with the news about the fraud. However, he had to play his cards extremely carefully. He was unsure as to what extent the disappearance of the sugar had been the beneficiary of a presidential blind eye. As it was, although Amin couldn't put his finger on why, he had

Bitter Discovery

developed a strong feeling during the course of his presidential audience that the sugar fraud had in fact been going on without the President's knowledge.

Bolstered by his renewed feeling of confidence, Amin continued.

'I regret, Pak, there is even more bad news.'

'You've got to be bloody joking!' grumbled the President.

'Sir, I wish I was. However, I'm afraid that the remainder of what I have to tell you is even worse than it would seem at face value.'

'What the hell's that supposed to mean?' demanded the President. 'For God's sake, Amin, stop talking in damn riddles and get to the point… I'm getting old and don't have time left for all this beating around the bush.'

Dr Amin paused and glanced in Bambang's direction. If the President didn't know what was going on, then did the son? He would soon find out. Having got over the worst part of the story he was going to enjoy the next bit.

'I can only conclude that what has happened involves people in positions of responsibility taking advantage of their rank to exploit our beloved country.'

Dr Amin listened to himself and was rather pleased with the way that what he was saying sounded as the words tumbled out of his podgy mouth. Further emboldened, Dr Amin continued reverting to the familiar form of address.

'Get on with it,' growled the uncle.

'It would appear, Pak, that some of these so say responsible people, have been abusing their positions and somehow selling on the world market the sugar that should have been our strategic sugar stockpile. They have done so in order to take advantage of today's high sugar prices. I believe that their intention was to replenish the stock at a later date once the world price of sugar had fallen and they could buy back at a lower price than the one they sold at, thereby making a quick speculative profit. However, unfortunately for them, and for our country, we will have need of the stock now. And it's nowhere to be found. At this stage, Pak, I'm not clear exactly who is involved or how they have operated the fraud.'

Bitter Discovery

The President grunted in disbelief. 'And how much, pray, does… or did… the disappearing stockpile amount to?'

'Um… er… about another 450 thousand tonnes, sir.'

'Holy shit,' blurted out the President, 'that makes a total shortfall of almost a million tonnes!'

Dr Amin glanced in Bambang's direction and then continued. 'Sir, I was obviously deeply shocked to find that it seems that trusted people have been abusing their positions of authority to make money out of our beloved country in this manner. I can assure you, Pak, that I will get to the bottom of this crime and bring the culprits to justice. I presume an offence of this magnitude against the state would carry with it a mandatory sentence of capital punishment?'

Dr Amin hoped that he had not gone too far overboard with the last statement.

Bambang, who until this time had said nothing, coughed politely and looked pointedly at his father whose face clouded like thunder. There was a long pause while father and son stared silently at each other. Finally, the President turned his attention to Amin and started to speak in measured tones that carried none of their earlier belligerence.

'My son, I am obviously extremely upset to hear the news you are telling me. I appreciate the customary thoroughness with which you have carried out your duties. Not only that but the promptness with which you have kept me informed of this most unfortunate state of affairs.'

As he spoke the razor-sharp mind of the kindly old uncle was turning over all the aspects of what he had just heard. He evaluated the different options available to him. Politically, the last thing he needed at any time in a country of the size and diversity of Indonesia was hungry, unhappy people. Back in the early days of his first five-year plan his only concern was to get rice in the bellies of what were then 150 million people. Amin was right, the plan had been amazingly successful. Today 200 million Indonesians had full stomachs and a much higher standard of living than in 1969.

Although the man in the street no longer worried about starvation, he still focused very much on the quantity and quality

Bitter Discovery

of everyday food he would be able to afford. The importance of sweet things, ranging from sickly, luminous gelatine and coconut milk desserts to heaped sugar in the strong local coffee, had grown immensely over the last twenty years. In addition to being an increasingly frequent part of the daily diet, they had become a sort of status symbol. An easily tasted barometer of one's wealth.

A sugar shortage would certainly not cause social unrest on the scale prevailing when Suharto defeated the Communists thirty years earlier. But nevertheless, an almost total lack of sugar would probably seriously upset a large number of Indonesians and would be particularly worrying with elections just around the corner.

Election time was traditionally a period when he made sure that abundant amounts of rice, sugar and other daily necessities were readily available. Nothing should be allowed to happen that would upset the equilibrium of the ordinary Indonesian and deter him from voting for the President.

And then there were the bloody Chinese who posed an altogether different problem. A small group but, by and large, rich as hell. Over the years they'd done a reasonable job of transforming themselves into Indonesians. Mr Tan might well have localised his name to Mr Sutanto, speak Javanese, wear a local coloured batik shirt and somehow look a bit browner than the original version. Scratch the surface, however, and the real commercial Chinese Mr Tan would be revealed lurking not far below.

The commercial success of the Chinese was resented bitterly by the average indigenous Indonesian, and was the source of continued acrimony simmering below the surface of daily life. Every now and then the situation boiled over. A relatively minor incident was often the cause. A traffic accident. A car, supposedly owned – but certainly not driven – by a Chinese that knocked an Indonesian off his motorbike and did not stop. Abuse by a Chinese employer of an Indonesian maid. Even a quite minor incident could be a sufficiently large spark to ignite the tinder-dry racial, religious and economic animosities. Animosities that always lay just below the surface in this country of a thousand islands.

What followed was inevitably not pleasant. One of the unusual

Bitter Discovery

characteristics of the normally easy going and genial indigenous Indonesian, shared with Malays as a group, is that under certain conditions he flips. It is as though life just gets too much for the poor chap and he simply loses his rag and goes berserk. There was even a word for it: amok. When going amok is combined with racial hatred, the result could well be, and indeed had been, the looting and destruction of Chinese-owned property and many hundreds of thousands of dead Chinese.

The kindly uncle knew that Amin was raising the spectre of Chinese-property speculation as being a cause of the sugar shortage to save his own skin. The analysis, however, was probably not far from the truth, or at least the popular interpretation of the truth by the Indonesian in the back street or smallholding. If news of the missing strategic stockpile ever leaked out, then surely a Chinese hand would be seen behind its disappearance and one could expect a nasty anti-Chinese backlash. Suharto could, on no grounds, risk any repeat of earlier racial troubles. He had to find out himself who was behind the missing stockpile before the zealous Amin unearthed the truth.

The President was realistic enough to know that in matters of this magnitude many powerful names within the Indonesian governing elite could be involved either directly or indirectly. These names needed to be dealt with carefully. The whole situation had to be extremely delicately weighed up. Any one of these names might be useful to him either now or in the future. There was no point of making a show in the Western way and publicly sacrificing anyone. You never knew who could be of use later on, or who might find a way of exacting his own retribution.

'Shit!' The old man swore viciously to himself at the weight and complexity of this unanticipated problem.

Finally he spoke to Amin who was still standing to semi-attention in front of the desk and beginning to feel weak at the knees.

'Let me make sure I understand this correctly: the conclusion of your rather lengthy explanation is that, for a variety of reasons, we risk running out of domestically produced sugar. Correct?'

'Er... yes, sir.' Dr Amin tensed, anticipating a sting in the tail of the logic.

Bitter Discovery

The old man nodded and then continued. 'In normal circumstances we would turn to our strategic stockpile to get us by. However, we now discover that the stockpile has mysteriously disappeared. Right? Although how the hell half a million tonnes of anything can just vanish stretches credibility to the maximum.'

'Sir.'

'Yes or no, Amin?'

'Yes, sir.'

'So the conclusion of this bloody awful mess is that we need to buy enough sugar both to feed the hungry mouths and to rebuild the stockpile. In round figures the amount needed is one million tonnes. Right?'

'I am afraid so, Pak,' said Dr Amin. Marvelling at how much simpler the situation seemed when told by the President.

'Well, I'm bloody well afraid so too,' said the President, suddenly looking tired and swaying slightly.

The third figure, who up till now had been had been sitting quietly in the far corner of the office, quickly moved up to the President and helped him to sit down at the large desk.

'Don't worry, Dukun,' said the President to his personal physician. 'I'm not about to snuff it yet despite what Amin did to me on his damn badminton court the other day!' Turning to Dr Amin he continued, 'Mind you, if he breaks any more news about potential national disasters I'm not sure if it will be any good for my health... or his!'

Dr Amin decided to remain dutifully silent as the President breathed deeply for a few moments. Finally the old man put on his glasses, sighed heavily and stared directly into Dr Amin's eyes.

'All right, Amin, this is what I want.' He lowered his voice slightly. 'Firstly, this news is to be kept strictly confidential between you and me and the others in this room. You will ensure that no one person in your Ministry has the full picture or indeed access to sufficient information to build up the complete picture of what has happened. Understood?'

Dr Amin nodded gravely, knowing that there was no way he could comply. After the tantrums he had thrown during the past few days the whole damn Ministry from the janitor to the deputy director knew about the problem. However, now was not the

Bitter Discovery

time to split hairs.

'Secondly, you will leave the investigation of the missing stockpile to my security people. I will deal with this as I see fit.'

I bet you will, thought Dr Amin.

'Thirdly,' the President paused, 'you will approach the Fangs with the utmost discretion as always and ask them to come here for an immediate meeting. Tomorrow if possible.'

Dr Amin continued nodding his acceptance of the instructions given as though by a schoolmaster to a pupil. Once the President had finished, Amin felt he ought to speak to reassert his position before beating a hasty retreat from this chamber of horrors.

'Is there anything else you would like me to do, Pak?'

Suharto growled, paused for a few seconds, and then spoke quietly yet deliberately.

'Nothing else except for you to know that I hold you personally responsible for sorting out this whole damn affair with the utmost discretion. Your job depends on it.'

Having delivered his instructions, the kindly uncle started shuffling through his papers indicating that the extraordinary meeting was over.

Dr Amin made good his escape from the President's office and collapsed once again into the back seat of his car, relieved that the ordeal of the meeting was over and that he was, at least for now, anatomically complete.

The Minister of Agriculture gave Akbar the order to move and the Presidential Guard snapped a brisk salute. 'Better send that cowboy at my Ministry for training here,' muttered Dr Amin. The outriders switched on the lights and sirens on their BMW motorbikes. Followed closely by the smiling Akbar, they launched themselves into the traffic, which dutifully moved out of the way of the VIP like fish before a shark.

If you've got it, flaunt it, thought Dr Amin as he lay back and relaxed in his favourite toy. A toy that was, for the moment at least, still his.

27

Chinatown

Singapore, Thursday, 13 April 1995

James Fang was putting the finishing touches to a reasonable round of golf at the Singapore Island Country Club. He had removed $1000 from the pocket of his opponent, and was looking forward to an ice-cold beer. The money lost and won made no material difference to either man. Both counted their wealth in millions not thousands. For James Fang, however, there was more than a little personal satisfaction. It was the third time in a row he had beaten his opponent. The latter was becoming visibly fed up with a situation that would inevitably become the subject of some discussion back at the clubhouse. Despite his Western education Fang would never forget the importance of face to the Asian way of life. There was a difference, however, between James Fang and most of his Asian contemporaries. Instead of worrying about losing face, James Fang now used the concept to manipulate people on the way to enhancing his already considerable net worth.

'Don't worry about it, old boy, just a bad run of luck. You'll see,' said Fang. He put his arm round the shoulder of his opponent and turned on his best English public school accent, an act calculated to grind salt into the wound.

Conditions for the Fang family had changed dramatically since 1936. James Fang's father, Fang Hock Joo, was then eighteen years old. He had left China, and worked his passage from Swatow in Southern China to Singapore. The original plan had been for young Fang Hock Joo to join other family members in Bangkok. This branch of the family had emigrated a few years earlier. It had managed to establish a sugar and rice trading business that drew heavily on the experience and contacts of the original family business in Swatow. The Fang clan leader, Grandfather Fang, had been happy with the reports he had

Chinatown

received from Bangkok. He had decided to build on this success. There should be a branch of the family working in the Far East trading centre of Singapore. Better to be there than allowing another family member to escape from his tyrannical rule by going to Thailand and enjoying themselves.

Young Fang Hock Joo was a bright lad. He had already shown excellent signs of knowing how to put a good deal together: one that was heavily biased in favour of the Fang family yet made the other party feel that they had also received a bargain. Grandfather Fang felt that young Fang Hock Joo had a better chance than most of making a go of it. And if he did not, well, there were plenty more junior Fangs in the pipeline.

So it was that Fang Hock Joo found himself working his passage to Singapore on a filthy tramp ship plying the South China Sea ports. In his pocket he had enough money to keep himself alive for a couple of months. He also had the names of some other pilgrims from Swatow who had made the journey a few years earlier but had not been heard of since. In his head Fang had a brain like an abacus and dreams of making his fortune.

Upon his arrival at the bustling port of Singapore, Fang Hock Joo prepared to leave the ship. Before leaving, however, he had one last task to perform in order to comply with his grandfather's instructions to leave no debt unpaid. He knocked on the door of the captain's cabin and entered carefully. The captain was sat at his desk drinking and trying to finish some paperwork to do with the cargo. Fang looked into the cruel eyes of the gap-toothed captain.

'Thank you, sir, for allowing me to sail on your ship. I hope I have managed to be of service to you.'

The captain grunted and returned to his paperwork. Relieved at having done his duty, Fang turned on his heel and escaped quickly from the smelly cabin. The young boy then picked up his pack containing all his worldly goods and jumped into one of the lighters that were already swarming around the tramper unloading its cargo of jute bags full of peas, beans, rice and sugar.

Once out of sight of the captain, Fang spat into the sea. He cursed the captain using all the foul language he could think of for the way he had been treated on the trip. He prayed that the smelly

vessel should sink in a typhoon on its next voyage and that the
disgusting captain would be eaten slowly by a shark.

All this Fang Hock Joo did under his breath so that neither the
target of the curses nor anyone who could report them to the
captain might hear. Young Fang had no intention of ending a brief
but glorious career in Singapore in a dingy back street with a knife
stuck in his back. At the time he had no idea how, at a much later
date, his curses would, in part, come true, visited not on the
captain himself but on his son.

Having dispensed with this business, Fang set his eyes on the
godowns and shop houses lining the side of the Singapore River
that he could see getting nearer in front of the lighter. He quietly
checked the presence of the coins hidden around his body.

Singapore was typical of all the major seaports of the South
China Seas, in that the bustling Chinatown started at the water's
edge. Goods were either sold from the quayside or moved into
quayside warehouses called godowns. Hundreds of shop houses
that doubled up as a mixture of business and living accommo-
dation were cluttered along the riverbank. Mixed up in this
pulsating jumble were all the ancillary services necessary for
trading or helping people with monetary surpluses or deficits:
banks, money lenders, pawnbrokers, shipping agencies, insurance
brokers, goldsmiths, and brothels...

Fang Hock Joo spent a couple of hours wandering around the
area to get his bearings. He wanted to understand as much as he
could about the business that was being conducted and to absorb
some of the atmosphere. Although he was obviously a new arrival
from China, he did not want to appear any more wet behind the
ears than was absolutely necessary when he came to start his
negotiations. By the end of the morning Fang felt that he had
orientated himself as much as he could in the limited time
available. He had also identified some traders who spoke his
dialect and who did not look as though they would throw a young
boy fresh off the boat into the river rather than talk to him.
Mustering as much confidence as he could manage, Fang
approached the first of his targets and enquired about the
whereabouts of the people on the list of names his grandfather
had given to him.

Chinatown

The initial response was not terribly heartening. The first two names on the list had died over a year ago, one of malaria and the other as the result of injuries sustained during a disagreement with the Triad. The third had definitely arrived but had not been heard of for over a year; he might have decided to move to Indonesia as a result of the Triad incident. Just as Fang Hock Joo was beginning to feel that making his fortune was going to be a little more difficult than he had originally bargained for, he struck lucky. The fourth name on the list was not only still alive, but had started a trading business that was prospering and was located in the centre of Chinatown.

The young Fang immediately hurried to the address he had been given. He found Wong Song busily clacking at an abacus. He was heavily built and in his early thirties with a short pudding-bowl haircut.

Fang Hock Joo took a deep breath and coughed to introduce himself. Wong Song looked up from the abacus and stared at the young man. As Fang started to speak, Wong Song jumped at the sound of the familiar language and accent of his hometown.

'Uncle Wong, I am sorry to disturb you at your business, however, I bring greetings from Grandfather Fang of Weiling.'

Wong remained speechless for a few seconds. Finally he regained his composure. 'You are welcome to disturb me with a message from Grandfather Fang. But who are you?'

Fang Hock Joo launched into the story of his voyage and the disgusting captain. He told Wong Song many things about developments in Weiling since Wong Song had left. By late afternoon, Fang Hock Joo had secured himself a job as a mixture of stevedore and clerk in the commodity trading business of Chop Wong Song.

Part of the deal was the use of a truckle bed located at the back of the Chop Wong Song shop house in Boat Quay. Fang was happy enough to accept this part of the agreement. He realised, however, that the location meant that he was totally at the beck and call of Ah Wong. He could start straightaway if he liked, tallying the bags of sugar that were being unloaded from the tramp steamer that had been his home on his way from China.

By five o'clock Fang Hock Joo had already completed an

31

Chinatown

hour's work for his new employer. Something was already becoming obvious to him. If he kept his ears and eyes open and his mouth shut his job would give him just the opportunity he was looking for to learn about trading in Singapore. For the first of many times, Fang Hock Joo had landed on his feet.

For two years Fang Hock Joo worked hard at understanding how the trading business in South East Asia worked. At the end of the first year he was able to write to his grandfather with a positive yet respectful report on the progress he was making. At the end of the second he made a commercial suggestion.

Perhaps his grandfather could see his way to sending a cargo of 1,000 tonnes of sugar down to Singapore on credit? If so, grandson Fang felt sure he could sell this in Indonesia and Malaya and be in a position to pay for the cargo within three months of its arrival.

In order to handle the business, Fang Hock Joo had set up a company, Fang Hock Joo Trading. It had taken all the diplomacy that Fang Hock Joo could muster to convince Ah Wong that his erstwhile employee was not stabbing him in the back. Which of course he was. The offer of a minority shareholding in the business of Fang Hock Joo Trading and an agreement from Fang not to steal Ah Wong's more lucrative contacts was sufficient to do the deal. Ah Wong finally accepted a state of affairs that he knew was inevitable. He blamed it all on the bad decision he had made two years earlier to respect home loyalty and employ the cuckoo Fang from his ancestral village in China.

Back home in Weiling, Grandfather Fang thought hard about his grandson's request. One thousand tonnes of sugar represented a sizeable amount of cash. To entrust this to the young lad was a step not to be taken lightly. With some trepidation the tough old man finally decided to ship 500 tonnes with a credit period of two months. There was no point in giving the young upstart bad habits at the outset.

The young upstart had been smart enough to anticipate his shrewd old grandfather's reaction. He had taken the precaution of doubling both the quantity and the credit period he needed in his first request. Both men were therefore happy in the feeling that they had outsmarted the other. The grandfather's happiness was

Chinatown

greater still when three months later he received a message from Fang Hock Joo. The sugar had indeed been sold and fully paid for after eight weeks (in reality four weeks). By the way, could grandfather please see his way to making a second shipment, this time of 1,500 tonnes, on similar credit terms.

The business grew steadily from this small start. By 15 February 1942, Fang Hock Joo Trading was one of the most prominent Chinese trading companies in the Lion City. This was the day on which the Japanese arrived in Singapore by bicycle down through Malaya. Their mode and direction of arrival took the inhabitants of the British Crown Colony by surprise. They had been anticipating a more traditional, sea-borne attack and had planned accordingly. Fang Hock Joo's fertile mind was, however, quick to assess the commercial possibilities of what otherwise might have been as disastrous a situation for his business as it was for the population in general.

He respectfully requested an audience with the Commanding Officer of the invading Japanese forces in order to make his services available. He was granted the meeting based on his reputation as one of the leading Chinese traders in the city. After fifteen minutes Fang was established as the main source of supply of rice, sugar and other agricultural commodities to the Emperor's invading army. At the time this seemed a much more healthy option than a bayonet in the back or a prolonged period in Changi Prisoner-of-War camp.

By the end of the war the commercial reality was that the twenty-seven-year-old Fang Hock Joo was one of the wealthiest men in town. He went to great pains to conceal this, however, and continued to live the lifestyle of a relatively poor Chinaman. Although many in Singapore had collaborated with the invading Japanese forces it certainly wasn't something to boast about.

After the war, Fang Hock Joo took advantage of being one of the few people around with ready cash. He was able to acquire many pieces of property around the Chinatown area. At all times he was careful not to be seen to be taking advantage of his fellow men, and preserved a humble facade whilst handling transactions that soon amounted to millions of dollars. In order to diversify his investments he brought together a small group of like-minded

33

men of the same dialectal group. They formed a small local bank, Chinese Overseas Bank. As a mark of respect for Wong Song, Fang Hock Joo appointed him to the largely ceremonial position of President of the bank.

Fang Hock Joo's reputation as a shrewd and extremely wealthy businessman soon spread via the Chinese grapevine throughout the South-East Asian region. Fang Hock Joo found himself spending more and more time travelling to Kuala Lumpur, Bangkok and Jakarta visiting Fang clan members and building trading linkages throughout the region.

During his visits to Jakarta he was worried to see the rise of Communism. He went out of his way to establish extremely discreet contact with those who were resisting it. By the time of the abortive Communist coup in 1965, Fang Hock Joo was already a close friend of General Suharto, who was one year his junior. Using the same flair for opportunism that served him so well as a collaborator with the Japanese, Fang Hock Joo offered his services to the new President of Republic of Indonesia. The offer was readily accepted and, as a result, the wealth Fang Hock Joo generated over the next thirty years from this liaison was sufficient to make his Japanese wartime earnings look like petty cash.

At the same time that Fang was building a business empire he also found time to take a wife. After two false starts giving birth to daughters, she finally managed to produce three sons within five years to carry on the family business. Guan Chang was the middle son, his elder brother was called Guan Lock and his younger Guan Hock. These sons, who represented the continuation of the Fang names were the jewels of Fang Hock Joo's eyes. He was determined to give them everything he had not had, starting with an education. As far as Fang senior was concerned, the best combination was English public school, followed by American business school. It was in these joint directions that the Fang boys were dispatched at an early age, complete with the respective Christian names of William, James and Henry to aid assimilation into the Western style of things.

As far as the girls were concerned, education was of far less importance to Fang. They were consigned to local schools in

Chinatown

Singapore, albeit the best schools that Fang could organise as befitted his status as a senior member of the Chinese business community.

Fang Hock Joo's plan was extremely simple. The boys would return from business school in America and live in the family home. They would immediately assume positions within the Fang Group's main areas of activity in trading, banking and property. He would ride them hard and bring them back into line after their liberating overseas experience. They would understand where their duty lay. They would work hard, taking over responsibility for these key areas of the business once they had proved themselves capable.

There was never a thought in Fang's mind that the young men would have any problems adjusting to the change of environment and lifestyle. This was what they owed to their father and a mixture of the Confucian ethics of respect, filial piety, plus family pressure and the need for cash, would ensure that it would happen. And after a fashion it did.

William and Henry adjusted quickly. They soon picked up the basics of the business, having inherited Fang Hock Joo's quick, commercial brain. Within a few years they were giving orders to faithful staff who had been running sections of the company for years but who understood fully the true implications of a Chinese family business. The business was run for the benefit of the family.

For James, the transition from free-wheeling American business school to proscribed family life under the hard thumb of Fang Hock Joo was far more difficult. Initially there were serious arguments. At one stage it looked as though James would do the unthinkable and leave the family fold. Over time, however, there was reconciliation with concessions being made on both sides. Fang Hock Joo had not lost his ability to manipulate people. James was sensible enough to realise that if he played his cards carefully he could say one thing and do another. He was, after all, his father's son.

Fang Hock Joo recognised the similarity in the characters of James and he soon after James returned to Singapore. Fang Hock Joo saw the same burning entrepreneurial spirit and the desire to

35

make a name for himself no matter what or how. William and Henry were already far more corporate and suited to the banking and property businesses. In James, Fang Hock Joo saw just the right spirit to develop the trading business. He decided to let James have his head. The combination of the right character, immense wealth, powerful clan connections around the region and the family name itself were an explosive mixture on which to capitalise. Introduced and backed up by Fang Hock Joo, James was able to take the Fang Group trading business to new heights.

Much of the business was based on the Fang family's government connections in Indonesia, Malaya, Thailand, the Philippines and China. The latter had been a specialisation of Fang Hock Joo, who had found that China was suddenly becoming more open. He could identify well with the older generation Mainland Chinese Communists who were becoming increasingly interested in structuring a deal. Particularly if it could be routed through an offshore company.

The relationship with Suharto's Indonesia had also been extremely close, albeit secretive. It would not have been politically wise for an overtly ethnically Chinese group such as the Fangs to be seen working closely with the Indonesian Government. Over the years, however, many huge transactions for rice, sugar, cloves and groundnuts had been handled. As a result, James Fang was a regular clandestine visitor to President Suharto's massive office.

It was only natural therefore, that when Dr Amin dropped his bombshell, Suharto's reflex reaction was to call once again for assistance from the trusted and discreet Fang family.

True Love of Money

Salem, Massachusetts, USA, Sunday, 17 January 1971

'I don't care, I think he's a real cutie,' snapped the slim American girl tossing her long blonde hair in annoyance.

'Mary-Jo, how could you, he's... he's... an Indian or something awful,' replied her college girlfriend.

'He isn't Indian, he's Indonesian. And he isn't awful, he's sweet. And you're a racist,' Mary-Jo added with feeling, as she stomped off to keep her rendezvous with the cutie in question.

Amin Bin Ahmed had never thought of himself as a cutie. In fact, he wouldn't have known whether being one was a compliment or an insult had he ever had to consider it. He did, however, have reciprocally warm feelings towards Mary-Jo McKennor-Smith, who was currently taking a doctorate in Law and with whom he was hoping to have dinner that evening.

It had been one year since Amin Bin Ahmed arrived at Harvard and he was well on the way towards finishing his PhD in Econometrics. After having worked hard for five years at the Ministry of Agriculture he had managed to convince his superiors that he could perform his job significantly better if he had a doctorate from an Ivy League school in the USA. In reality, the senior people at the Ministry did not believe this any more than he did. However, it did look good for the Ministry to have an American-trained PhD as a senior member of its staff. And of course there was the prestige to Indonesia as a whole... The result was a Government scholarship for a two-year doctoral programme at Harvard and an invitation to dinner from Mary-Jo McKennor-Smith.

'You know, Mary-Jo, I've never met anyone like you before.' Amin Bin Ahmed peered earnestly at Mary-Jo across the table of the fast-food restaurant.

Mary-Jo resisted her instinctive reaction to snigger at the

True Love Of Money

hackneyed line. There was something so attractive about the way this man spoke and acted. So much more genuine than the smooth rich kids that she had known for years. Instead she giggled and flashed her eyes at her dinner guest.

'How do you mean, Amin? Apart from the obvious of course.'

'Well...' Amin began fumbling for words. He was still totally unused to this American directness. 'It's just that the Indonesian girls that I know...'

'Not too many of them I hope!' said Mary-Jo, taking a bite of her burger.

Amin Bin Ahmed grinned and began to relax. 'If there were I certainly wouldn't tell you!' He continued, 'No, the very few Indonesian girls I know just don't express their own opinions in the same direct way that you do. I suppose it's just the Asian culture.'

'And I guess they don't invite men out for dinner either?'

'Oh god, no. That would be... er... completely unacceptable. Not that it is in America, I'm sure,' Amin added hurriedly, afraid he would upset the beautiful girl sitting opposite him.

From the first time he had seen Mary-Jo in the lecture hall, he was struck how this bright, vivacious girl had no reservation at all about expressing her own opinions. Indeed, she was equally quick in trying to convince anyone who disagreed with her that they were inherently wrong.

'And then, of course, there's the obvious. You do look different!'

'Well, I'm glad to hear it. I thought you just liked me for my mind.'

Amin Bin Ahmed was clever enough not to get trapped into a conversation like this. Particularly with an American girl. But it was true he was extremely attracted to Mary-Jo's blonde good looks. How different she was from the dark-haired, olive-skinned Indonesian girls he was used to seeing.

He couldn't believe his luck when it became obvious that, for some reason that he really still couldn't quite understand, Mary-Jo found him rather attractive as well. Amin had not questioned his good fortune, and had wasted no time in promoting his cause with the good-looking Mary-Jo.

38

True Love of Money

Although the two of them got along famously, the way was not so smooth with Mary-Jo's parents.

'Mummy, I know what you are thinking.' It was Sunday evening and the McKennor-Smiths were relaxing in the company of their visiting daughter.

'I'm sorry, dear?' Mary-Jo's mother looked up from her patchwork and tried to appear innocent. She patted some of her greying hair back into place and gave Mary-Jo a brittle smile. The Sunday newspaper in the corner of the room rustled as John McKennor-Smith sensed a storm brewing.

'Mother, please don't be obtuse.'

'Darling, I have no idea what you are talking about. And please don't talk to me like that. I don't like it and it doesn't become you.'

The rustling of the newspaper intensified.

'Mummy, I'm talking about Amin. You don't like him, do you?'

Caroline McKennor-Smith tensed but said nothing for a few moments. The family was old east coast money, and everyone had assumed Mary-Jo would finally settle down with some Wasp sports jock with an Ivy League background and a job with a Wall Street investment bank. However charming he might be, the dusky, short Amin Bin Ahmed was about as far away from being a waspy sports jock as one could get without falling off the other side of the earth. Which was, of course, where Caroline McKennor-Smith assumed Amin Bin Ahmed came from anyway.

'Darling, it's not that we don't like him...' Caroline McKennor-Smith tried to choose her words carefully. From her armchair she could see her husband's anguished look as he peered over the top of his glasses willing his wife to say the right thing and avoid a family row. This was, after all, Sunday evening. 'It's just that he isn't quite what we had, um, thought... I mean...'

'You mean he isn't white,' said Mary-Jo emphatically.

'Oh...' said Mrs McKennor-Smith, as though up to then she had been unaware of Amin's dusky skin.

John McKennor-Smith coughed, rustled and then thought better of saying anything and remained silent. You didn't get to be Assistant Secretary of State by intervening where you didn't need

39

True Love Of Money

to. And for the moment intervention was not necessary. And, from his perspective, certainly not desirable.

'Mary-Jo, you know that isn't true... I mean, I know it's true that he isn't... er, white. What I do mean is...' Caroline McKennor-Smith stuck her needle emphatically into her patchwork and through into her finger. 'Ouch... damn... No, what I mean is that it isn't true that his being... not being white matters. We go to church,' she added in a manner that would explain everything.

Caroline McKennor-Smith looked across at the newspaper and decided that it was time her husband came out of hiding. 'Does it, John?'

'Mmmmm?'

'John, stop trying to pretend you are reading that stupid paper and join in.'

The paper lowered. 'Must I?'

'Yes, dear daddy, you must,' said Mary-Jo going over to her father, sitting on the side of his armchair and smoothing his head. 'This is going to be a serious conversation.'

John McKennor-Smith sighed. 'Oh dear, I feared as much. I think I'll just go and get a beer to prepare myself.'

Mr and Mrs McKennor-Smith were indeed regular church-going people and Mary-Jo was the apple of their eye. Over the weeks following that Sunday evening, Mary-Jo executed her campaign with precision. A number of carefully scripted meetings were arranged for her parents to get used to the dusky little man from the other side of the earth. As a result, Mr and Mrs McKennor-Smith did not put up too much visible resistance to the formal liaison that was finally proposed between their only daughter and Mr Amin Bin Ahmed. It would be fair to say, however, that the contents of some of the prayers relayed around this time by the church-going Mrs McKennor-Smith contained aspects that were decidedly un-Christian. These, however, remained confidential to the good lady and the Almighty.

As a result of his exploits in America, when Amin Bin Ahmed returned to Jakarta, he brought with him not only his own doctorate but also another doctor, his new bride Mary-Jo McKennor-Smith, now to be known as Fadhzila when in

True Love of Money

Indonesia.

★

Settling into life in a third-world country was not easy for the girl from the east coast of America. However, she tackled the task with enthusiasm and was quite happy for the first few years.

At first she trod extremely carefully, and learnt to bite her tongue and to let conversations and relationships develop in a Javanese way. She observed closely the clever way in which her husband seemed to agree to everything and everyone. No one and nothing was ever openly accepted or rejected. 'Yes' and 'No' were words which seemed foreign to the Indonesian vocabulary and were substituted with 'should be', 'maybe', 'not quite sure' and 'tomorrow'.

She learnt to cope with Indonesian 'rubber time' which seemed to be completely divorced from what was shown on clocks and watches. At the same time, it was rude to be too late for others because it denoted arrogance. Yet one had always to be available for others no matter how late they showed up, and to continue as though nothing untoward had happened at all.

All in all, Mary-Jo was a quick learner, and accepted the fact that she was a foreigner in an Asian country married to an Asian and had to adapt herself accordingly.

At first she was also happy with their lifestyle. Although Dr Amin's salary from the Ministry of Agriculture was modest he did qualify for a large colonial house left behind by the Dutch, which enabled them to enjoy a certain style of living. Furthermore, her husband was accorded quite a significant status as the only man in Indonesia who had a doctorate from Harvard. In her heart of hearts Mary-Jo also noticed that the fact that the only man in Indonesia with a Harvard doctorate was also married to the only woman in Indonesia with the same qualification didn't seem to be too important. Being a non-Asian American female put paid to the chance of any similar recognition.

Nevertheless, Mary-Jo was happy with this state of affairs for several years and was wrapped up in daily life and caring for the two children, a boy and a girl, that had by then come along.

Little by little, however, she began to notice that their standard of living was falling behind that enjoyed by her husband's contemporaries. At first she paid little attention to this. However, when she heard that the other wives had begun to make catty comments behind her back she reacted more strongly and raised the topic with Dr Amin.

'Darling, there is something I really don't understand.' The couple were sitting on the verandah of their Dutch colonial house drinking coffee. It was a balmy tropical night of the type Mary-Jo had grown to love. This was her favourite time of day. The oppressive afternoon heat had subsided. Mary-Jo and Amin sat on padded wicker furniture. A servant poured and served their coffee. A ceiling fan lazily paddled the heavily scented evening air around the verandah to the accompaniment of the buzzing of cicadas. Amin waited for the servant to withdraw before answering his wife.

'That's funny, I thought you understood most things,' he laughed.

'No, Amin. This is serious.'

Amin's face clouded as Mary-Jo continued.

'How is it that most of the other ministers seem to earn so much more than you? I know some of them come from wealthy families. But not all of them do and they all seem to have such a high standard of living compared to us,' she finished in a rush.

'Does that really matter?' snapped Amin.

Mary-Jo was surprised at Amin Bin Ahmed's rather aggressive reaction. He was normally a remarkably easy-going man.

She looked at him reproachfully. 'You know I don't think wealth is everything. I'm much more concerned with the children and our health. But... well, you know. It's the other wives. Normally I don't care about their nasty comments. It's just that I got really pissed off with Aminah and her bloody catty comments about our old furniture the other day.'

Amin looked at Mary-Jo in surprise. Normally she didn't swear. Whatever it was that was bugging her must be serious. He looked around to make sure none of the servants was around and them moved nearer to Mary-Jo and took her hand. She burst into tears.

True Love of Money

'I'm sorry. I know I shouldn't react like this but today the bitch really got to me,' she blurted between sobs. 'That ratty little husband of hers comes from no more affluent family than yours yet they spend money like water. Where does it all come from?'

Amin took a deep breath. He considered for a few seconds whether or not to reply. At the end of the day, Mary-Jo was a woman of the world and she deserved an honest answer. He looked her in the eyes. 'Favours.'

'What do you mean... bribery?' asked Mary-Jo taken aback.

Amin took her hand. 'Sweetie, sometimes you still look at the world through those beautiful American eyes of yours.'

He went on to explain how many of his colleagues in high places had discovered the economics of the market place and the value therein of their own positions of power and authority. In the Asian way, this was not bribery. It was simply the age-old custom of ingratiating oneself with someone who could give one something one wanted through the liberal donation of something that person felt in need of. Like money, for instance.

'I see this going on around me all the time,' Amin said sadly.

'And you have never been tempted?' asked Mary-Jo softly.

'Yes, of course. Every time I see one of the others buying a new car or taking an expensive holiday with their family that I know they cannot afford from their salary, I am a little bit tempted. It would be so easy.'

His thoughts on the topic, however, were governed by the upbringing given to him by his father. What would the funny little Javanese man in clown trousers have said if he had ever found out that his son had used his education for personal enrichment? In short, Amin Bin Ahmed was as straight as a die and the staff in his department had better be also.

Mary-Jo at first understood and respected Amin Bin Ahmed for his position on the subject and found it easier to bear the catty comments of the other wives once she knew the background. As time wore on, however, and the disparity between their lifestyle and that of their friends grew greater Mary-Jo re-evaluated her position.

She did not want to encourage her husband to take financial gifts as such. However, would it not be possible to accept some of

True Love Of Money

the offers of hospitality in overseas holiday resorts, or material offers such as a new American washing machine for instance? The one they had brought with them from New England all those years ago was on its last legs. Amin Bin Ahmed resolutely resisted.

The final straw had been the badminton court. Or to be exact, the electrical power for the badminton court.

The problem started in a Ministerial meeting a few months ago. As he patted his middle-aged pot, Dr Amin Bin Ahmed had joked with the President, 'Pak, wouldn't it be a good idea if we Ministers took more exercise? When I look around the table I am beginning to wonder if some of us will be able to fit under it if we carry on the way we are.'

The President nodded. 'I hope, Amin, you don't include me in your observations!'

Amin quickly corrected himself. 'Oh no, Pak. I was really referring first to myself and then to some of my colleagues.'

'On that basis I think it would be a good idea,' chuckled the president, 'if the senior members of the Government took more exercise. Why don't you upgrade that scrappy badminton court in your back garden – make it something we could all use in privacy?' With that, the conversation had drifted onto a more serious topic and there was no more talk of exercise or badminton courts.

One afternoon shortly after this conversation took place, a troop of workman disturbed Mary-Jo sunbathing in a bikini by the birdbath-sized pool in her back garden. Without consulting with her, they walked by her, staring as they went, and started to demolish one of her favourite shrubberies. They did this as the beginning of the process of levelling the ground for what she did not know was going to be an air-conditioned badminton court.

The workmen were cut short in their activities by a torrent of invectives that would have paid tribute to someone living in the deepest Bronx rather than refined New England, hurled in their direction by Dr McKennor-Smith. The employees of the Ministry of Works were not able to understand the full meaning of the barrage of words. They were smart enough, however, to figure out that the large white lady with blonde hair and the more than ample body, who had been the sly focus of their attention

True Love of Money

since their arrival in her garden not long ago, was not too amused with their construction activities. They smiled pleasantly, stopped work and had a quick discussion among themselves. This lady was presumably the Minister's wife. If she was unhappy, then it probably followed that the Minister would be unhappy. And from this it followed that the unhappiness would trickle down until it reached them in the way that shit normally flowed downhill. Better to stop now and let someone sort out the problem before the volume of shit became too great. Having reached a consensus they trudged out of the garden smiling gently, happy to seize the opportunity to go home early. As they went they snuck a last look at the large white lady who still stood staring at them arms akimbo.

That day Dr Amin had also managed to drag himself away from the office earlier than usual, and was looking forward to spending a pleasant evening in the bosom of his family. As he walked in through the front door he was therefore totally unprepared for the barrage of abuse hurled at him by a still extremely irate Mary-Jo.

'Amin, what in hell's name's going on? I was sitting by the pool this afternoon when a bunch of bloody leering workman marched in here without a by-your-leave and started to attack my best shrubbery next to the badminton court. Did you authorise them to do that?'

Since they lived in a Government house, Mary-Jo had already decided that Amin had obviously caused to happen whatever it was that was happening.

Mary-Jo continued attacking the poor, hapless Amin Bin Ahmed, who was still clutching his briefcase and standing just inside the front door. He could see that his wife was warming to the topic and that, by the way she was getting warmed up, other older ammunition risked being introduced into the barrage if he did not mount some form of quick counter-attack.

Making a quick assessment of the situation, he reminded himself that he was a Government Minister. Drawing himself up to his full medium height, he brushed his wife aside and strode into the living room.

'For Christ's sake, Mary-Jo, shut up.' Despite many years of

45

True Love Of Money

trying he still couldn't come to address her by her Indonesian name. 'I've got absolutely no bloody idea what you're going on about. But whatever it is, it really pisses me off being laid into before I've even got into my own house.' At times like this Amin wondered whether he wouldn't have been wiser to marry a dutiful Indonesian girl. Having reached the body of the house he snapped at the servants to get lost. Remaining standing, he turned to Mary-Jo.

'Now for God's sake, get off your high horse, calm down and come and discuss whatever it is in a rational manner.'

Amin Bin Ahmed felt that this approach combined the correct degree of masterly superiority while at the same time being sufficiently conciliatory to allow him a way out if he had indeed caused some of what he was being accused of.

Mary-Jo realised that in her annoyance she had definitely overstepped the mark. She came over to Amin and tried not to look too tall.

'Amin, I'm sorry... I shouldn't have fired off like that. It was just the horrible way those men just walked in. And the way they gawped at me. I suppose it was the first time they had ever seen a white woman in a bikini. The servants didn't even try to stop them coming in. I guess they just said they were from the Ministry. Anyway, I'm sorry. Come and sit down.' She led the way over to the verandah.

As they talked it slowly dawned on Amin Bin Ahmed that the President had probably taken their conversation seriously and that he was about to become the proud owner of a renovated badminton court.

In itself this would not have been too much of a domestic problem once its proposed location had been altered to avoid the destruction of the number one shrubbery. For Mary-Jo, however, it became the manifestation of everything that was wrong with Jakarta, their lifestyle and, moreover, her husband's stubborn refusal to accept any kind of financial 'assistance' that would improve their lot.

For years they had lived in this monstrous house with its old-fashioned bathrooms and virtually non-existent kitchen in which only the servants were expected to work. Things normally

True Love of Money

reached a head when her mother visited.

'You know, Mary-Jo, I really had no idea before you met Amin that there were such grand houses in India.' Mary-Jo and her mother were taking on the verandah taking afternoon tea while Amin and John McKennor-Smith were being entertained at the Ministry of Foreign Affairs. Although John McKennor-Smith had retired from active politics some years ago, he was still treated with respect during his infrequent trips to Indonesia to see his daughter.

'Indonesia, Mother. We live in Indonesia.'

'Yes, I know you do, dear, isn't that what I just said?'

'No, Mother, you said India. And I know you know the difference! Anyway, it doesn't matter when you are talking to me. Just please do try and get the name of the country right when you are talking to other people. Some of them are quite important you know, and probably would be quite offended if the mother-in-law of one of the senior Ministers thought she was in India. Particularly when she just happens to be the wife of the ex-Secretary of State of the USA.'

Caroline McKennor-Smith giggled wickedly. 'I'm sorry dear. It's just that the two names are so confusing. Anyway, since Amin is so important, when are you going to get something new to replace that sweet little stove which must have come from the ark. When I think of the equipment we have back home it makes me so sad to think of you suffering like this.'

Mary-Jo bit her tongue for a few seconds. 'Mother, I am not suffering. You just can't look at Indonesia through American eyes all the time.' She felt that Amin would be proud of her talking like this. Then she crossed her fingers, and told a white lie. 'As it happens, Mother, the whole house is going to be renovated from top to bottom. You're right, it's far too shabby for someone as senior as Amin.' As she said this, she knew that she would have to put pressure on Amin to have something done before her parents returned to Jakarta. She had two years!

As he chatted with the Foreign Minister, Amin was totally unaware of the deadline that had been set. Had he been, however, Dr Amin would not have agreed to anything of the kind. He was quite happy to live in a house with a bathroom at all, let alone

47

True Love Of Money

four, albeit rather characterful ones. He knew his wife was not totally happy with the facilities, but this was Indonesia, not America, and she would just have to accept certain differences.

These entrenched positions regarding the house would probably have continued and become ever more polarised without leading to a major conflict had the badminton court not appeared on the scene. This tipped the balance of things heavily in Mary-Jo's favour. Not only was the damn badminton court solidly constructed with no hint of mould showing on the walls, but it was fully air-conditioned and had a shower room with modern bathroom fittings. All of this might have been acceptable had it not been wired up to a 'safe' power circuit. This combination of factors was absolute dynamite to Mary-Jo. Had President Suharto sat down and considered a way to put more pressure on the domestic life of Dr Amin Bin Ahmed he would have been hard pressed to do so.

As the lights in their bedroom flickered one evening and the air conditioner stuttered, Mary-Jo turned to her husband. 'You know, Amin, the thing that really annoys me about the damn badminton court isn't that it's there at all sitting on my best shrubbery while the house still hasn't been painted – it's that its power supply is on a bloody safe circuit!'

For years she had asked Amin Bin Ahmed to use his position as a senior Minister and have their house connected to one of the 'safe' power supplies. These mysteriously never seemed to be cut or suffer brown outs. For years, Amin Bin Ahmed had steadfastly refused to use even this privilege.

'You have no idea how embarrassing it is each time the power goes off when I am in the middle of entertaining some Minister's wife. Normally it's when that bitch Aminah is here. I just get that look that says "My husband is important enough to get us on a safe circuit while yours obviously isn't".'

Mary-Jo snorted as the lights flickered again. 'And now this damn badminton court of yours appears that not only has a proper bathroom but is connected to a safe power supply!'

There had been one notable occasion when, during an evening power cut, the master and mistress had repaired to the badminton court. They sat there in air-conditioned splendour and read the

True Love of Money

airmail edition of the *New York Times*. For Amin this had been the equivalent of sticking his head in the lion's mouth. He suffered one hour of serious complaints, during which he had tried in vain to think of any plausible excuse to escape from his air-conditioned, splendidly plumbed prison. He was saved as word finally came from the house that the power was back on. From then on, whenever the power went off, Dr Amin either sat in the garden or suddenly remembered some pressing work back at the office rather than submit himself to the air-conditioned terrors of the badminton court.

From the time of the arrival of the badminton court, Mary-Jo became increasingly verbose in her criticism of life in Jakarta in general and Dr Amin's terms of employment in particular. Even the President had been moved to ask Amin the wisdom of marrying an American girl.

After several years of pressure of this type, Dr Amin began to feel that perhaps his wife was right. The difference in standard of living between his family and that of his colleagues was becoming beyond a joke. Everyone knew what was going on and everyone seemed to accept it. Didn't he risk being more royalist than the King – or at least the President?

The evening he came back from his interview with the President regarding sugar, Amin Bin Ahmed took a major decision. After dinner, he asked his wife to join him for a swim in their birdbath. Mary-Jo was amazed at this request, the first ever of its kind, but readily agreed, aware that there must be a serious reason for making it.

As they splashed together under the Javanese moonlight, and out of earshot of the bugs which Amin knew were placed in his house, the Minister for Agriculture explained to his American wife his plan to bring them riches beyond their, or at least his, most extravagant dreams…

49

Playing Cards

Singapore to Jakarta, Friday, 14 April 1995

The early morning Singapore Airlines flight to Jakarta banked snappily into its final approach. From his window seat James Fang could see the slim batik-uniformed hostess reading mechanically from a prompt card held in her right hand while she hung onto a rail with her left. 'Ladies and gentlemen, in a short time we shall be arriving at Sukarno-Hatta International Airport in Jakarta...'

She glanced over to James and gave him a sly smile. She had been paying James more than regulatory attention during the flight. He liked that. And he was used to it. At forty-two he still looked good. And rich. James ran his eye up and down her swaying body. Too thin.

Dutifully, he brought the back of his business-class seat into the upright position, looked out of the window and involuntarily clenched his fists. However many flights he took, he still could not relax. He knew that disaster would strike the moment he stopped listening to, and worrying about, each change in the pitch of the engines.

Below them the rural Javanese landscape spread out in a mosaic of shapes and colours. Small clumps of trees sprouted out of the flat fields. Wooden huts were sprinkled around, each with a ribbon of blue-grey wood smoke drifting lazily from it in the still early morning Javanese air. James noticed with surprise the amount of water there was glimmering in the neat paddy fields. Far more than there should have been at the end of the dry season.

Ugly sprawling slums of corrugated, iron-roofed shacks replaced the lush paddy fields as they neared Sukarno-Hatta airport. The plane completed its final approach and, with engines screaming, lunged towards the shantytown. The outstretched branches of palm trees rushed up towards the aircraft as it

Playing Cards

skimmed the rusty roofs, reached the runway and landed heavily with a screech of tyres. James held his breath. He couldn't put out of his mind the story circulating at the time the new Jakarta airport was constructed – that the runways were built on badly drained marshland. The theory was that one fine day a runway would collapse under the strain of a jet landing a little too heavily. Happily, today was not going to be the day – for James at least.

James began to relax as the plane taxied towards the red-roofed terminal. The slim hostess appeared with his blazer, smiled knowingly and looked him straight in the eyes in an un-Asian way. 'Have a nice day, Mr Fang.' James winced. At the best of times he hated the Americanism he had heard so often whilst at MIT. Still, she was quite sweet and wasn't using the prompt sheet.

James returned her smile, undressed her one more time in his mind, managed a polite 'Thank you' in his upper-class English accent and then hurried to escape from the sterile cigar tube manned by robots that had terrorised him for the previous hour and a half.

He walked along several wide corridors that wound their way through grassy gardens and finally dropped down into the brightly lit main arrival hall. Queues of short-sleeved-shirted people waited to present themselves to bored-looking immigration officers seated in tall booths like overweight high priests dispensing favours.

Instead of joining one of the many queues James walked to the side of the room. He approached a portly man wearing the customary tight-fitting khaki tunic held in place by a broad, shiny, black leather belt. This uniform seemed to be worn by anyone in Jakarta carrying out a semi-official duty.

James held out his passport in the direction of the khaki uniform. 'Good morning, I'm James Fang.'

The man didn't take James' passport. Instead, he consulted a list with the annoyed air of someone being disturbed by a lower life form. He found what he was looking for on the list, grunted, took the passport without looking at James, muttered unintelligibly, 'Okay, yo... way...' and shuffled into a side room.

James waited patiently and wondered how long a system like

51

Playing Cards

this would be allowed to continue. It was all so wonderfully Indonesian. For a relatively small fee paid to a semi-official organisation in Jakarta, the services of an arrogant, fat little man dressed in khaki could be secured for fifteen minutes. During this time, he would obtain your entry visa through some mysterious process carried out in a side room, and escort you through the customs, thereby ensuring your trouble-free exit from the airport.

In James's case it saved one hour of formalities. For others it certainly meant a considerable saving of customs duties on undeclared goods, or freed the way for the importation of restricted items such as published material printed in Chinese. Indonesia was a country in which there were no problems for those who knew how to deal with the system. And the Fangs did.

Sure enough the fat khaki-clad man reappeared after a few minutes. He waddled off towards the customs for the second part of his duty, having indicated to James with a dismissive wave of the hand that he was to follow.

After organising James' quick exit from the airport, the little man would return to the arrival hall to repeat the fifteen-minute process. For each completed circuit he would be the richer for some bank notes, dutifully donated by his happy client of the moment. The value of each donation was normally greater than the average daily earnings of an Indonesian factory worker. Khaki uniforms meant money for those wearing them.

James walked out of the air-conditioned arrival hall and was hit by a blast of hot, humid-tropical air. He paused to catch his breath and then carried on walking alongside a metal barricade, which held back a crush of people eagerly looking for arriving friends, relations or business contacts. At the front of the crowd, hanging over the barrier like eager fans at a football match, was a line of hotel reps and drivers, many of whom held up scraps of cardboard announcing the names of their quarries.

James began running the gauntlet of the notice boards. Suddenly he saw who he was looking for and nodded surreptitiously in the direction of a short, squat, old Indonesian who had managed to get himself into pole position at the front of the crowd. Without any further greeting, James continued walking past the rest of the throng towards the roadside. The old

Playing Cards

Indonesian driver understood that most of the visitors to his employer, the Minister of Agriculture, wanted to keep a very low profile. None more so than old Mr Fang and his son Mr James.

James brushed away the offer made by a rabble of shifty-looking people, and waited by the roadside sweating gently while the old man hobbled slowly off towards the car park. After a few minutes he returned driving a white ministerial Mercedes, installed James in the back seat, exchanged the customary pleasantries with his charge and then lapsed into the silence that young Mr James enjoyed. Having carried out the first part of his duties, the old man crouched over the driving wheel and concentrated on delivering his important passenger in one piece to his boss.

Water-logged fields flashed by the windows as they sped down the newly constructed airport highway towards the centre of Jakarta. Coolie-hatted peasants and slick-skinned water buffalo plodded through the paddy fields together in the falling rain. Both looked equally miserable.

Enormous garish hoardings advertising Japanese and Korean consumer goods bordered the highway as they neared the centre of Jakarta. As the highway ended these were replaced by roadside shacks and stalls selling everything from noodles to second-hand shoes. Crowds of steaming-wet people jostled one another squelching in the slurry of rubbish and mud that made up the pavement.

The old driver fought his way through the dense, unruly city traffic, showing remarkable aggression for one so old. Trucks were hooted at and not given way to. Mopeds were bulldozed aside. Pedestrians interfered with his passage at their peril. The old man drove like a demon without care or courtesy for other road users, while all the time staring fixedly ahead as if daring someone or something to challenge his right of way. Side and rear-view mirrors were plainly an unnecessary optional extra for him in the execution of his daily duty.

James sat quietly behind the heavily darkened windows that seemed to be obligatory in this city of secrets and winced at every near miss. He consoled himself with the thought that if they did actually kill someone, the Ministry of Agriculture would probably

53

Playing Cards

sort things out.

The roadside scenery changed again as they approached Jakarta City proper. The narrow streets and stalls gave way to wide dual carriageways and grand buildings that were a mixture of old colonial-style administrative architecture and modern tinted glass and steel. A service road ran down the side of each boulevard giving access to the surrounding buildings. It also provided a way for motorists with luck on their side to leapfrog ahead of the slower traffic on the main road. The old driver seemed to be an expert leap-frogger, launching the Mercedes on and off the main carriageway and blasting obstructing pedestrians and motorcyclists alike out of his way.

James held on to the door handle as they careened round a roundabout, which housed the Youth Spirit Monument depicting a muscular youth carrying the 'Torch of Development'. This, along with several others, had been built during the sixties with the help of Soviet designers. James smiled silently to himself at the nickname of Pizza Man given by local residents to this wonderful example of social realist heroism.

Within a few minutes they roared up to the front gate of the Ministry of Agriculture and stopped sharply. The old driver turned round to James and smiled triumphantly, revealing a mixture of gaps and gold fillings. For a few seconds James did not respond, preferring instead to sit still to gather his thoughts after the hair-raising journey. Finally, he looked at the old driver. 'You're getting slower, Omar. We're almost late.'

James then glanced at himself in the rear-view mirror, took a deep breath and stepped out of the car, whose door was now being held by the confused-looking driver, and shook the hand of the waiting official.

'Good morning, Mr Fang,' said Osman. 'I hope you had a good journey.'

'Good morning, Osman. Good to see you again. The journey was fine except for the fact that the Minister's driver seems to be getting more and more frisky.'

The two men set off in the direction of the Minister's office. Osman laughed.

'I'm afraid he seems to be getting faster as he gets older. In

Playing Cards

fact, the minister has recently taken a new personal driver. He said that Omar was bad for his blood pressure. I think Omar must feel a bit hard done by and is trying to prove that he is still up to it. I'll have to see what I can do to slow him down, but it's not easy at his age.'

James laughed politely as they reached the top of the stairs and Osman ushered him into the Minister's office.

'James, thank you for rearranging your schedule and coming here so quickly,' said Dr Amin, getting up from his desk and walking over to shake James's hand. The Minister's mouth smiled but his eyes did not. James noticed that he had been wearing a pair of gold-rimmed spectacles, which he still held in his left hand. A sign of age. How old was he now? Must be mid fifties. Age for Dr Amin did not come alone. James noticed how much thinner the Minister's hair was since their last meeting nine months ago. It was also getting quite grey at the temples.

James and the Minister had known each other for many years. It was only in the last five years or so, however, that James had begun to take over responsibility from his father for the trading business that had been so vital on many occasions to the Indonesian economy. Dr Amin still looked down on James and considered him the lad. James resented this, but also knew that in reality it was he who was now in charge of the business and not his father. Little by little Amin would have to accept this fact.

For the moment, however, James ignored this irritant. Osman had taken the trouble to call him personally, earnestly requesting him to come to Jakarta on a highly confidential basis the next day. Something extremely urgent must be happening. And this in turn could well translate into significant profits for the trading arm of the Fang Group. On this basis, James was quite prepared to put up with a little loss of status and to give great face to the Minister.

'Minister, it was the least I could do when I received the call yesterday,' James replied, giving Amin his title and establishing their relative social positions. James knew that the more relaxed Amin felt, the easier it would be for him to negotiate something favourable to himself when the time came. And come it would.

'Something pretty important must be on the cards for you to need a meeting this urgently,' continued James, more by way of a

55

Playing Cards

statement rather than a question. It would be better for James in the long run if Amin told his story at his own speed and in his own way.

The two men sat down around a low, ornately carved ebony table. James braced himself for drinking the strong, sweet Indonesian coffee laced with condensed milk that was about to be served. Dr Amin looked at the suave, good-looking Chinese man in front of him. His eyes drifted over Fang's Armani blazer and Bally shoes. The Minister wondered, not for the first time, why a country of Indonesia's size and importance was forced to use foreigners to help them out of their agricultural difficulties. And bloody Chinese ones at that! On the one hand he remembered so well how the first deals had been struck with old man Fang. At the time Amin had been amazed at the efficiency with which the transactions had been executed. But that was nearly thirty years ago...

James fixed a pleasant smile on his face and waited reverently for Dr Amin to begin. Behind the smile, James' mind was working fast, trying to glean any clue as to why he had been summoned to appear before the Minister. He had managed to cast a sweeping glance over Amin's desk as he came in but had been unable to see anything unusual. Amin was an organised worker and the few papers arranged neatly in front of him had not revealed any secrets. Nor were there any tell-tale details left behind on the whiteboard that, as a technocrat, Amin always kept in the corner of his office. So far James could not find anything to give him a hint as to why he was here. However, from the stressed look on Amin's normally relaxed smooth brown face, something was definitely wrong.

James went back in his mind over the business that the Fang group currently had in hand for the Indonesians, to try once again to anticipate what was about to be said. He had already examined the business from several angles during the journey down but had failed to identify any aspects which might give rise to a problem serious enough to warrant an urgent request for him to come to Jakarta. However, you could never be too careful.

For years the Fangs' principal business with the Minister had been centred on rice and sugar. These were the two agricultural

Playing Cards

commodities that were of greatest strategic importance to the country. Full and satisfied bellies meant happy and contented people – which in turn meant no civil unrest and votes for Suharto.

The formula was extremely simple. Executing it was not so easy, however, given the massive size of the population spread over so many islands. Domestic logistics were always a problem. In such a big country it was inevitable that there would be surpluses in some places and shortages in others.

Moreover, the whole of Indonesia could be a country of feast and famine depending on how the crops yielded. For years, Suharto's series of five-year plans had been slowly working and both the rice and sugar crop had been growing. Unfortunately, the population had also been expanding rapidly as income levels increased. Indonesia had a long way to go before it faced the problem of the professional husband and wife wanting to pursue their own careers at the expense of producing children.

The Fang Group's job was to help the Minister balance surpluses or deficits of rice and sugar. Typically, after a meeting like this one, they would be asked to either buy or sell rice or sugar on the international market place in the most discreet way possible. The total contract values were normally so large that if the world markets got wind that Indonesia was either a buyer or seller of either commodity then the price would move sharply against them. It was the Fangs' job to make sure that news of Indonesia's shortages or deficits remained a secret for as long as possible. At the same time the Fangs would be carrying out their trading on behalf of the Minister in the international markets, quickly and quietly selling or buying what was required.

In order to carry out this deception, the Fangs had established a complex network of dummy companies incorporated in every tax haven one could think of. They had done this together with some key Indonesian contacts and international trade houses. Often these dummy companies were only used for one or two transactions. By the time the international trading community had figured out that a specific company was a front for the Indonesian Government the business had long since shifted to yet another front. By using such a web of companies, it was almost impossible

57

for the trade to get the complete picture of Indonesia's position at any one point in time.

This corporate complexity and fast-moving trading was the answer to Dr Amin's question. In his heart of heart he knew that no indigenous Indonesian group had the capacity to handle this type of trade. This was the domain of the Chinese.

Although the Indonesians were indeed extremely experienced in such transactions, the deals themselves were often so complicated that they would almost certainly not run smoothly without the intervention of the Fangs. Behind the smiling James Fang was an army of logistics people. They made sure that vessels they had chartered jumped queues, documents that were necessary for them to be paid found their way to the tops of piles, export licences were issued on a preferential basis and bad quality shipments were given to the competition. The Fangs knew what was required and the Fangs knew how to get it.

It was reckoned in the trade that over the years old man Fang had built up a mountain of obligations through granting financial favours. He had obtained files full of incriminating evidence. There were few men in Government or trading circles in Asia who would either be brave enough or foolish enough to resist a request for assistance from old man Fang – or now from his equally smiling son, James.

As far as current business was concerned, James could only think of one topic that, if discovered, would be sufficiently important to justify summoning him to Jakarta: smuggling.

Indonesia was currently importing about half a million tonnes of sugar a year. As far as Minister Amin, and for that matter the President, were aware, the Fangs were handling about 350,000 tonnes of this business through their normally discrete business channels. The remaining 150,000 tonnes was being smuggled at night, in small coastal vessels, directly into many of the larger Indonesian islands, thereby avoiding import duty. In view of the relatively small size of each shipment and the ad hoc night-time nature of this business, it was virtually impossible to put a stop to it.

James had had many conversations on this topic with Minister Amin, and together they had concluded that the smuggling was a

Playing Cards

necessary evil. It was also an extremely profitable evil for the Fangs since it was they, by hiding behind another network of small local traders, who controlled it. Old man Fang hadn't built up his empire by allowing someone else to eat into business that he considered rightfully his.

This structure of legitimate imports and smuggling had several benefits for the Fangs. Firstly it earned them even more than the already considerable amount they squirreled away from their profit on their legitimate sugar imports. It also gave them a *de facto* stranglehold on all sugar imports, and at the same time provided a convenient party to blame when the pricing on the legitimate shipments appeared to Minister Amin to be somewhat out of line with world markets.

'Ah, Minister, you know if it wasn't for the smuggling, things would be much more straightforward...'

As he smiled at the Minister, James tried to fathom whether the look on Amin's face meant that the smuggling scheme had been rumbled. If challenged, he had already prepared what he felt would be a sufficiently complicated yet plausible reason to explain the Fangs' involvement in the night-time business. However, before presenting this it was essential to find out exactly how much Amin knew.

Amin cleared his throat and started talking. 'James... it's about sugar. I'm afraid there's a small problem that will involve your group.'

James's heart sank. *Oh Christ*, he thought, *it must be the smuggling... How the hell did they find out?* James struggled to preserve half an attentive smile.

As he spoke, James' normally confident voice sounded weak and unconvincing. 'Oh... er... really, Minister?' He coughed in an attempt to give himself more authority. 'Um... What type of problem, Dr Amin? If there is anything the Fang group can do, I am sure we would want to,' James finished in a rush, hoping that he sounded interested and not guilty.

Dr Amin stared at James in surprise. What was up with the little rat? Why did he look and sound so bloody ill at ease? This wasn't like him at all. Normally he oozed the public school confidence that Amin still lacked, even as a Senior Minister.

59

Playing Cards

Dr Amin continued slowly, trying to sound as casual as possible. At the same time his mind continued working on reasons why Fang looked so out of sorts.

'For various reasons, the projections we have been working on seem to be a little... um... inaccurate,' Amin continued carefully.

James felt a warm glow spreading throughout his body. Not only was the Fangs' involvement in smuggling undiscovered, it looked like the old crocodile had a major shortage on his hands. If this turned out to be the case, it could only mean lots more money for the Fang coffers. James leant forward slightly, lowered his voice a little and tried not to look too pleased.

'I take it that the "inaccuracy" means a crop shortage, Minister?'

'Mmmmm, afraid so,' admitted Dr Amin, who had decided, on the spur of the moment, not to tell Fang yet about the disappearing stockpile. The underestimated crop figures would be bad enough. No point in giving this bloody Chinese rip-off artist more than he needed to know at this time.

As he stared at James, Amin allowed a small smile to himself. He had just had a blinding flash of inspiration. Of course, now he knew why Fang looked so guilty! The Fangs must be behind the smuggling! Judging by the look, first of guilt and then of relief, on James Fang's face when Amin had mentioned a sugar problem, the Fangs were as implicated as hell. For years Amin had been hinting as much to the President, only to be dismissed as seeing the Chinese equivalent of reds under the bed. Now he almost had proof...

James saw the hint of a smile passing across Amin's lips, and his trading antennae went onto full alert. Bloody old shark, what did he have to smile about?

'Frankly speaking...' continued Amin.

Never believe anyone who starts a sentence with that, James thought to himself. Biggest giveaway in the world. What follows is guaranteed to be an outright lie.

'Frankly speaking, the unusually wet weather we have been having has significantly lowered the sugar cane crop, particularly on Sumatra. Not only that, but the lack of sunshine has reduced the sugar yield of whatever cane we do manage to harvest. We

Playing Cards

estimate that the net result is that we will have to import an additional…'

James involuntarily leant forward and Amin hated him.

'… an additional quarter of a million tonnes this crop season,' finished Amin.

James grunted and wondered by what factor Amin was deflating the requirement. He decided to double it to half a million tonnes. If they could get a margin of $30 a tonne that would earn them $15 million.

'How sure are you on these figures,' said James, avoiding at this stage any comment on the crop shortfall itself.

'I'm afraid pretty sure,' grumbled Amin.

'Hmmm, this is going to have to be handled extremely carefully,' started James. 'The sugar market is already looking as tight as hell, we reckon China will be buying a million tonnes and Thailand looks as though it is going to have a bad crop as well…'

'I know. That's why you're here. Save me the sales pitch,' snapped Amin, deciding that of the two he really preferred dealing with old man Fang. At least he looked like a crook. The son looked like a fashion advert but was probably more bent than a corkscrew.

'I'm sorry if I offend you minister; however, the facts are the facts…'

'No, no, it's for me to apologise,' sighed Amin, having regained his composure. 'I'm afraid this whole episode is rather stressful. Anyway, let me show you some details. We have an appointment with the President at lunch time.'

James looked up sharply. An appointment with the President. Things must be really serious. Perhaps James should triple the figure Amin had given him as the shortfall!

During the next hour Dr Amin ran through the details that he had prepared for James. These had been carefully doctored to reflect the shortfall of 250,000 tonnes rather than the worst case 800,000 tonnes that Amin really feared.

After an hour it was time to go to the audience with the President. As the two men sank into the back seat of Dr Amin's Mercedes and set out for the Palace, the conversation in the car was relatively friendly. Amin had begun to appreciate the benefit of

61

Playing Cards

sharing the burden of his problem with someone who could help him even if that person didn't know the full extent of the difficulty.

★

As they made their way into the President's office, Suharto got up from his desk. He clasped James's outstretched hand in both of his as a warm greeting to the son of one of his oldest friends.

'My dear James, how are you, and how is that shark of a father of yours? I swear we have personally paid for at least fifty per cent of the real estate he owns!' continued Suharto in jovial fashion, not aware that the concept was correct but that the figure should in fact have been nearer seventy-five per cent.

'He is extremely well, sir, and asks me to pass on his best regards to his oldest friend,' responded James.

'Good, good... Now come and sit down, and let's talk business like I used to do with that rogue of a father of yours,' said the kindly old uncle as he lead the way to a heavily ornate and uncomfortable suite of furniture in the corner of his office.

'I suppose that by now the good doctor has explained the extent of our little problem?'

Amin felt faint, as he suddenly remembered that he had not had time to brief the President on his decision to withhold the stockpile information from Fang.

'Yes, sir, I am afraid Dr Amin has. And I must say how sorry I am that your sugar crop should have been affected in this way,' said James, lying through his teeth.

'And as if that wasn't bad enough, the whole damn situation is made worse by the stockpile fraud,' continued Suharto.

James' heart jumped as he heard the President's words. So this was why he was seeing the President. The situation must be really serious. And that bastard Amin hadn't told him anything like the whole picture. In his mind James doubled once again the shortage to one million tonnes, and to $50 million the profit he could make.

As he looked across the room at Amin, James saw that he wore the wistful smile of a gambler who has had one of his tricks discovered but still has several aces up his sleeve...

62

Plane, Pain, Plan

Jakarta to Singapore, Friday, 14 April 1995

The plane journey back to Singapore was a mixture of pleasure and pain for James. He calculated and recalculated how much profit Fang Trading was likely to make out of Suharto's 'little problem'. Each time he re-ran the figures in his head, a warm glow spread throughout the rest of his body. He thought about the possible colours of the new Ferrari he would try to buy if the deal came off.

He suffered greatly, however, on several counts. He could predict the resistance he would come up against from his brothers and father regarding the Ferrari. He also felt sick from the buffeting given by the early evening tropical turbulence. This not only prevented the cabin crew from providing any in-flight service but kept the same flirty airhostess that had made eyes at James on the way to Jakarta belted into her seat.

James knew that the Ferrari issue would cause yet another family argument. Over the past few years he had become increasingly bitter about the way his father and brothers shared equally in the significant profits he had generated for Fang Trading. They also prevented him from spending money on what he considered to be reasonable perks for the chief executive. There had been a heated family debate last year about an expensive golf-club membership, which would have been for the exclusive use of James and also about the acquisition of a Jaguar car. James had insisted on the club membership but conceded on the car, since he already owned, or rather the company did on his behalf, a year-old Mercedes Coupé.

All his life James had had to kowtow to his overbearing and successful father. In theory, the day-to-day responsibility for running Fang Trading had passed to James some years ago. In practice, however, James had to report on a weekly basis to his

Plane, Plain, Plan

father exactly what had happened and to seek his endorsement, which amounted to permission to carry out anything of significance. This in itself would have been annoying enough. He also had to contend with his two brothers, who were to James' thinking completely devoid of any entrepreneurial instinct. Moreover they were dipping their hands in his till without having contributed in any material way to what was in it.

As James was being bounced around inside the Airbus, considering the unfairness of life and devising plans for obtaining the Ferrari, an idea slowly came to him; an idea of such simplicity and yet audacity that he was temporarily stunned. If it came off, he could raise two fingers to his whole interfering bloody family and live a life of luxury forever-surrounded by a different coloured Ferrari for each day of the week.

For the rest of the journey, James's fertile mind was so involved with developing this idea that he was completely unaware of the continued bumpiness of the flight.

By the time they touched down in Singapore, James had determined that he needed to make two telephone calls. The second could be made on his car phone. The first, however, needed to be strictly confidential. Even old Abdullah, his Malay driver, who knew well enough when to keep both his ears and mouth closed, could not be trusted with this information.

He had also managed to slip the flirty hostess a copy of his business card with a messages asking her to ring him tonight. From the look on her face he was left in no doubt that she would.

When he had cleared immigration, James found a quiet corner in the vast airport, took out his mobile phone and made the call to London that would change his whole life. By the time he had finished talking, passed through customs and been met by Abdullah, James was convinced that the Ferrari was within his grasp. He had finally found a way to break free from the clutches of his father.

Now all he had to do was to wait for his mobile to ring again and set up a late-night dinner appointment with the flirty hostess. At forty-two, life wasn't so bad after all.

Sweet Dreams

London, Friday, 14 April 1995

'Christ, I wish it would clear up,' Robbie Smith muttered to himself as he slowly stubbed out a Marlboro and then ran a hand through his close-cropped, black hair. He looked warily at the mound of cigarette butts in the ashtray on his desk. If he didn't cut down soon his squash game would really begin to suffer. And so would his domestic life. Julia had begun to mount a serious campaign against his smoking since he turned forty-two.

Putting thoughts of impending domestic strife to the back of his mind, Robbie swung around lazily in his chair at the head of Clyde and Clyde's sugar-trading desk, twiddling a pair of reading glasses in his right hand. He had acquired them six months ago and was still not used to the idea of having to wear them. Another all too visible sign of his increasing years. Still pondering the possibility of old age without cigarettes, Robbie stopped his chair revolving and faced the floor to ceiling plate-glass window behind his desk. He looked out despondently at the dome of St. Paul's Cathedral wreathed in the April drizzle that had been falling all day. As he looked at the massive building, another squall of rain blew in and the dome melted momentarily like a phantom in the wash of a leaden sky

Behind Robbie, flickering television monitors, green computer screens and hi-tech phones hung from the ceiling and jostled for space on the desks. For the moment it was blissfully quiet. In forty-five minutes the New York sugar futures market would open. By the time this happened, the Clyde and Clyde sugar-trading desk and the typical City mix of London wide boys, Essex girls, double-barrelled pin stripers and bright, middle-class graduates working in the surrounding room the size of a football pitch would be throbbing with activity.

Sweet Dreams

Deals would be struck from as far afield as Brazil and Australia through conversations in a babble of languages. The operations desks would be equally hectic arranging freight, insurance, financing, foreign exchange and all the other backup facilities that supported the sugar trading itself.

In the midst of all this hectic activity, Robbie, who fell into the bright middle-class graduate category, would sit quietly in his position at the head of the sugar-trading desk in the heart of the football pitch listening to the trading, calculating and evaluating everything that was going on. He hardly ever picked up the phone. When he did he normally sounded offhand and remote, quoting facts and figures in a clipped but lazy way and then reverting as soon as he could to his favourite listening and calculating mode. His way of working could go on for hours. Robbie would sift through one side of conversations and look at screens. His analytical mind naturally reduced all of life into percentages and probabilities. Suddenly, but extremely quietly, he would give a curt instruction. On a good day, this might even be accompanied by a few words of explanation. 'Go long – the Cubans must be as tight as hell. The market has to go up. We'll squeeze the shit out of them.'

Based on brief commands like this, the trading might of Clyde and Clyde would run, tack and jibe through the sugar world in a way that usually left the competition way behind the finishing line – and out of the money. And being out of the money in the sugar market could have serious financial consequences.

The market was notorious for having vicious price movements. Robbie still remembered with a chill the way it had moved in the early seventies, soon after he had joined Clyde and Clyde from Edinburgh. He thought he was joining a relatively sedate blue-chip City institution. During three days of chaos, albeit acting as a 'gofer', he had became a battle-scarred member of the sugar-trading fraternity. The economics are simple and were explained to him on his first day in the company by Bill who headed operations.

'It's quite simple, laddie – not a bit like those highfalutin' economic theories you learned at that egghead institution of yours. This is the real world.'

Sweet Dreams

'Okay, Bill, try me – I'll m-m-make a b-b-big effort to come down to the r-r-real world, since it's the real world that's now p-p-paying me.'

At the time Robbie had cursed at the bloody stutter that always came out when he least wanted it to. For years he had worked at speech lessons and had all but overcome the impediment. And then suddenly, without announcement, it came back. It normally chose to do this when he was tense or under pressure – both times when it was least wanted. As the young Robbie looked earnestly at Bill he went red. The hardened Bill took pity on the lad. He didn't sound like one of those toffee-nosed types that turned up in the trading room because they were connected to Sir someone or other.

'All right, laddie, I'll explain it to you. But 'ang on tight, it's pretty complicated,' he added mockingly. 'Although the world sugar crop's large – normally more than one 'undred million tonnes – most of the stuff's consumed in the country that produced it.' He looked at Robbie to make sure he was keeping up. Robbie realised that, as far as Bill was concerned, having the ability to get into University was as much of a hindrance as a help when it came to understanding 'real things'. Robbie also began to understand that the Bills of the world, with their London accents and funny, traditional old ways, knew one hell of a lot. And if he wanted to get on quickly in Clyde and Clyde he had better start learning from them.

Bill continued, having satisfied himself that Robbie was indeed following. 'Most of the stuff that's available for export is covered by G-to-G agreements.'

Robbie raised his hand slightly as though back at school and looked quizzically at Bill.

'My God, they really don't teach you blokes anything, do they! I'm glad I left school when I was sixteen! To answer your question, Government to Government,' he added with a smile and then continued, 'this means that the amount of sugar actually left in any one year to be traded on the world market is a small percentage of total production – normally less than twenty per cent.'

'Twenty million tonnes,' muttered Robbie without thinking.

Sweet Dreams

Bill stopped his explanation. 'There you go, I knew there was a brain lurking in there somewhere!' He continued, 'The result is like doubling 'n redoubling at cards. This gearing-up business can be pretty frightenin' – the effect on the market of a small increase or decrease in the amount of sugar available for export or needed for import can be bloody amazin'.' Bill paused a little and then added for an encore, ''N as if that weren't bad enough, the commodity-fund buggers, who just love price movements, are always hovering around the sugar futures markets waiting to take a position and make a quick turn. So now you've got it.'

Robbie nodded quietly at Bill as he thought all this information through. Bill decided that he was beginning to like this new lad. He was much better than the normal snotty, arrogant ones. And the poor bastard with a stutter too. Bill decided then and there to continue his training course in 'real things' over the coming months. There was something about this lad that told him he could go places.

A few months later that year, the 'big one' came. When the sugar market really moved there wasn't a market in the world that could equal it for sheer speed and volatility. Prices rocketed up and plummeted down with breath-taking viciousness. Robbie lived thought these gyrations under the protection of Clyde and Clyde traders and Bill. He looked and learned. He saw the stress that the head trader was under as he took minute-by-minute decisions that could make or lose millions of pounds. At these times, the man was like a God. And now, twenty years later, Robbie Smith was the same God.

No one knew just how intelligent Robbie was, but it was generally agreed that he must be a genius. It was no good trying to discuss or rationalise with him when he was directing the trading desk. The man simply operated on a different, and higher, level than anyone around. He just processed facts and figures and, when he found a fit or a gap, drew a conclusion or slotted in a missing piece. To him, this was the most obvious thing in the world. Over a beer after work he would be quite happy to explain in a cryptic fashion why he had taken a particular decision, if indeed he could remember why. At the time, however, you just did what he said and assumed that the head sugar-trading director

Sweet Dreams

of Clyde and Clyde was right. Which he inevitably was.

In his own way, Robbie tried to hand on knowledge in the same way that Bill had to him. This was the least he could do. It was the promise he had made to Bill as he sat by the tough old man's bedside while he paid the ultimate penalty for chain-smoking Capstan full-strength cigarettes from the age of fourteen.

It had never really struck Robbie that he was exceptionally intelligent. He just knew that he could see things that other people missed. He had first noticed this when he had scored straight As on leaving school and had been awarded a place at Edinburgh to read Spanish and Russian. Some time later, Robbie had discovered that at the time there had been a bit of a scene and an investigation into the examination procedures at the school. The examination board had been suspicious that Robbie had obtained prior access to the papers given the almost perfect score he had achieved.

For Robert Smith, the grammar-school boy from Twickenham, Edinburgh came as quite a shock. Semi-detached life with his civil-servant father and retired-teacher mother had not really prepared him for the variety of distractions that were available to him at university. For two years he threw himself into a whirl of social and sporting activity with a minimum of work thrown in. By the start of the third year, however, Robbie had met the Physics student who was to become his wife and he settled down to a somewhat steadier lifestyle.

For those who had to work and were neither following a profession nor aiming to become an academic, a job in the City with an exclusive merchant bank or brokerage house was the most sought-after option. As Robbie did the milk round of possible employers he saw sugar broking as a rather more exciting and glamorous option than merchant banking and set his sights on Clyde and Clyde. After three interviews, Robbie received an offer based both on his squash blue and on his ability to speak Russian, since at the time the USSR was a major market for Clyde and Clyde. In the way of large organisations, Robbie had had little opportunity to use his Russian either then or since, although he had kept up a regular squash game.

Within a few months of Robbie joining, it became obvious to

Sweet Dreams

the senior members of the sugar desk, as it had to Bill, that 'the new lad' was different. He had been given the normal greenhorn job of monitoring Clyde and Clyde's European sugar trading. Unlike the others that had suffered before him, Robbie had grasped the intricacies of the pricing of EEC sugar. He mastered the complicated mixture of restitutions, levies and green currencies and devised a system to finesse the tender system. This guaranteed Clyde and Clyde a large fixed profit on each transaction that they did.

Robbie was given more and more demanding tasks. He mastered each problem in an incredibly short time. He normally also managed to modify the system in such a way that Clyde and Clyde benefited handsomely from the alteration and everyone wondered why they had not made the changes earlier.

Robbie quickly made his way up through the organisation. Following some resignations, firings and retirements, he found himself holding the position of sugar-trading director at the age of forty-one.

Along the way he had married Julia, fathered four children and bought a spacious detached house in Surrey. From the outside looking in, Robbie was a golden boy with a lifestyle that would be the envy of most.

Although he knew that this assessment was more or less true, Robbie was still impatient. He could feel the pressure from others below him who, like him, had been recruited for their raw intelligence. As Robbie sat looking over St. Paul's savouring the Dover sole he had just eaten at Wheelers, which had been washed down with a good bottle of Chablis, he contemplated the fact that he was beginning to get old for his job. What he needed was the one massively profitable transaction. Something that would inject enough cash into his offshore bonus account to allow him to retire gracefully, and yet still educate four children and enjoy the financially secure lifestyle that he had become used to.

Robbie's calculations were rudely interrupted by the ringing of his private line. As he swung round and prepared to do battle with the first call of the afternoon, Robbie recognised James Fang's voice on the end of the line.

'Hi, Robbie, how are you?' said the cultured but foreign voice.

Sweet Dreams

'What's going on in your part of the world?'

Robert Smith settled back in his chair as his brain started whirring. For Fang to call up from what was, from the sound of it, a mobile phone, something must be happening. The problem with Fang was that you never knew what. He never called to discuss the time of day. There was always an ulterior motive. It could be something as petty as wanting tickets to the latest London show. Or, more interestingly, a major sugar deal. Better to play one's cards carefully. For Robbie, the key question in his mind was the impact the earlier than normal monsoon rain was going to have on the crop in Thailand and China.

'James, great to hear from you. What's the weather like?' responded Robbie, leaving it up to Fang whether he chose to discuss crop estimates or holidays in the tropics.

'Great, if you happen to be a duck,' responded James.

It was going to be crop estimates.

'When are we going to see you here?' replied Robbie, deliberately avoiding any specifics and putting the ball back in Fang's court.

'Probably sooner than you think,' replied James.

Robbie sat back in his seat and tried to make out details on the warship's superstructure. Best to play dumb.

'That's nice. Why?' said Robbie, shifting gear.

'Hmmmm... You may well ask.'

'Yeees.'

'It's our favourite country,' said James, having been forced to make the opening move.

'You surprise me,' admitted Robbie. 'I thought the old man had it all sorted out.'

'So did he,' continued James. 'Unfortunately, God, whichever one you chose, wasn't in agreement.'

Robbie studied St. Paul's Dome through the drizzle. He fixed his mind on the crop estimates of a country on the other side of the Equator yet only a mobile phone call away. According to the latest statistics he had, the domestic crop was coming along fine and Indonesia was headed towards self-sufficiency. Any shortfall was supposed to be covered neatly by the Fangs, either through legitimate imports or smuggling. Either way the sugar was

71

Sweet Dreams

supplied by Robbie.

James's call meant something must be happening. There was no way the crop could have suddenly jumped so that they could export. It must be a shortfall that was greater than already planned. The question was how much. Or, more appropriately, how much Fang was going to admit to.

'That's the trouble with gods. They are above reading crop estimates. How much are we talking about?' replied Robbie.

There was a pause while James weighed up the pros and cons of being accurate. If James told Robbie his best guess of the real figure, then the latter would immediately ramp up the market. If James held back with the truth, then Robbie would have every right to stitch him up later in the game. Better to play the Indonesian card.

'Difficult to tell, you know; you never get the truth from our favourite country until it's too late.'

Robbie nodded in agreement but said nothing.

'Probably about 500,' finished James.

Robbie swung round in his chair and tried to keep his voice neutral, 'Above the shortfall we have already planned?'

James paused. 'Yes.'

'Christ.' An unplanned shortfall in Indonesia of over half a million tonnes would have a dramatic effect on prices.

'My sentiments entirely – even though I don't believe in him. You had better get down here. I don't want to discuss this too much over the phone. You never know.'

'Okay, I'll get the evening flight and see you tomorrow. Can you make the normal bookings?'

After a few more pleasantries Robbie hung up and swung round to look at the Dome. If that bugger Fang was admitting to a 500,000 tonne additional shortfall, the figure could probably be doubled. And if Indonesia was having a crop failure of this size then the same could probably be said of Thailand.

Robbie swung back in his chair. There was something about the look on Robbie's face that stopped the sugar desk in its tracks.

'Go long!' he barked. 'As l-l-long as you can and as quickly as you can without moving the p-p-price against us. We are going to

Sweet Dreams

squeeze the hell out of it.'

If he played it right, this could be the retirement deal he was looking for. And even if it wasn't a trip to Asia would give him a chance to escape from this bloody foul weather.

Singapore Sling

Singapore, Saturday, 15 April 1995

Robbie strode briskly past the bored customs officers and out through the green channel of Singapore's Changi Airport. It had taken him eight minutes to reach the customs since leaving his first-class seat on the Singapore Airlines flight that had departed Heathrow the previous evening. The crowd of gossiping, uniformed hotel staff carrying meeting boards were unprepared for the early arrival of the blond, curly-haired, athletic-looking businessman. They snapped to attention and then looked disappointed as Robbie walked past them without stopping. In fact, Robbie had fought hard to resist the temptation to identify himself as Mr Uguchi, thereby causing a ripple of confusion and disbelief among the bearers of name boards. Instead, Robbie carried on walking slowly towards the exit, scanning the eager faces of those waiting to greet arriving friends, relations or business contacts. Finally, Robbie found who he was looking for. His eyes met those of Abdullah, the old, unsmiling Malay driver. Abdullah nodded his head slightly, acknowledging Robbie's presence, and then set off towards the car park without further ado.

Cautious devil, thought Robbie, wondering whether Fang's legendary distrust of everyone was really necessary.

Running the gauntlet of excited relations, Robbie followed the driver, keeping a discreet distance behind the fast-moving old man.

★

The previous evening, Robbie had caught the plane with a few minutes to spare, having endured a difficult time with Julia, who had not appreciated his sudden departure.

Singapore Sling

'But, Robert,' – it was always 'Robert' when the going got difficult – 'you know we're having a dinner party tonight. I can't possibly cancel it now, it's far too late. Do you really have to go? And the boys have an exeat tomorrow. Why can't you leave to see that horrid little Chinaman tomorrow night? What's of such bloody importance that you have to disappear right now? You're a shit.'

After five minutes of trying to explain, Robbie gave up and prepared himself for a frosty reception when he arrived home – and the need to purchase an expensive gift in Singapore to make up.

He was not wrong about the temperature of the reception, which was cold bordering on arctic. Nor was he wrong about the need for an expensive gift. The required value increased, however, as Julia caught sight of Robbie's squash racquet poking out from the side pocket of his suit bag as he left for the airport without giving her a goodbye kiss.

★

The old driver was scarcely more talkative during the drive into the centre of Singapore than he had been at the airport, and Robbie passed his time looking out of the car window at the bougainvillea lining the expressway. By the time his car crunched over the gravel driveway to Raffles Hotel, Robbie's mind was moving into overdrive regarding how to play the meeting with Fang.

Robbie was still evaluating different approaches when the doorbell to his suite rang and he opened to door to find the object of his scheming standing outside, looking relaxed and cool in a double-breasted blazer, khaki slacks and brown-tasselled shoes.

'I d-don't believe it,' said Robbie, shaking James by the hand and grinning. 'You have c-come yourself rather than exercising your normal caution and sending a cardboard c-cut-out in disguise!'

James smiled back and stepped quickly into the room.

'The trouble with you, Ang Mo, is that, in addition to smelling peculiar, you are far too trustworthy,' said James in his best

75

Singapore Sling

Oxbridge accent, using the derogatory term for Europeans. 'You really should learn from the wily Oriental gentlemen!'

The two men laughed together and walked into the sumptuous sitting room. Although they had different cultural backgrounds, both felt a common bond of friendship and enjoyed working together.

'So what the hell is going on in Indonesia,' said Robbie, deciding to start with an open, direct approach.

'You may well ask. I wonder if anyone really knows what goes on in that bloody crazy country. Least of all the people who run it,' said James, adding the last bit to remind Robbie gently that the Fangs had connections in the highest places. It was only through the Fangs' intervention with those people that Robbie was sitting in Singapore discussing Indonesian business.

'They have a major problem – in fact, a series of problems which add up to one monster-sized shortfall.'

'I don't understand,' said Robbie, intent on making James Fang talk but also feeling genuinely confused as to how the situation had deteriorated so rapidly. 'I thought they were looking reasonably good this year, despite the wet weather.'

'How can they suddenly run up against an 800,000 tonne shortfall?' Robbie added, gently increasing the number that James had mentioned over the phone to see if he reacted.

'I said 500,000 tonnes,' grinned James, 'and you know it. Never trust a sneaky Ang Mo! Anyway, ignoring your little tricks since we are old friends, you are right. Up until a few weeks ago, it looked as though the domestic production was going to be about two million tonnes. That level of production, together with the imports that you and I have already planned...'

'You m-mean total imports – direct and er... indirect?'

'If you must be so specific, then yes,' said James, laughing but not meaning it.

'The total imports should have been enough to keep all our sweet-toothed Indonesian friends in fillings for the next year.' James paused briefly, then continued.

'But this is where the tricky bit comes in. Firstly, the basic statistics seem to have been off. For sure, the yield on the land that is planted to sugar cane looked okay. The problem is that

76

Singapore Sling

there isn't as much land as before actually growing the damn stuff. Our Indonesian farmer friends, as well as having sweet teeth, also have sticky fingers. They have seen that they could get more money from either growing cocoa instead of sugar or selling their land altogether for property development. Can't say I blame them. The guys in the Ministry of Agriculture were busy analysing the satellite data to see how the crop was coming on. No one bothered, however, to calculate the actual acreage being used to grow our favourite commodity.'

Robbie stroked his chin, raised his eyes heavenwards, and then looked at Fang with a sardonic smile. 'Hmmmm, go on...'

'Like the story so far? Well, the best is yet to come.'

'I thought it seemed too simple for an Indonesian story,' said Robbie, keen to keep James talking. 'What other little wrinkle has crept in?'

'Not a little wrinkle. A bloody great furrow! As you know, they have been having unusually wet weather. Had this continued for much longer, it could have had some sort of effect on the crop...'

'But I thought sugar liked plenty of water,' queried Robbie.

'You're right. But not so much that it rots the roots. Anyway, sugar cane is pretty hardy stuff and although the yield might have been slightly reduced because of the wet weather, it wouldn't have been the disaster it is.'

'Stop enjoying yourself,' groaned Robbie. 'Get to the good bit. You're going round in circles and we're all getting older!'

'Patience, my dear, is an Asian virtue which I know I cannot expect my barbarian friends to possess in abundance. However, you really seem to have been given a short supply. Anyway, as you say, we're all getting older. So how do we get an 800,000 tonnes shortfall...'

Robbie shot a glance at James and raised his eyebrows.

'Oh, come on,' said James smirking, 'you can't expect me to give you the truth and nothing but the truth so early on. You are a trader after all.'

It must be a million tonnes, thought Robbie.

'Anyway,' continued Fang, 'none of the aforementioned would have led to the current projected, additional shortfall of

77

Singapore Sling

more or less 800,000 tonnes. The next bit is truly Indonesian…'
James paused for dramatic effect and looked at Robbie who was
beginning to lose his patience.

'F-f-for Christ's sake, g-g-et on with it, James!'

'Oh, all right, if you must be so direct… Someone has
knocked off Indonesia's entire strategic stockpile.'

'W-W-WHAAAT?' Robbie almost jumped out of his seat.
You've got to be b-b-bbloody k-k-kkidding!'

'Never been more truthful in my life. Brownies honour.
Gonzo.'

'But… but… b-but, it's 500,000 tonnes. You can't just lose
half m-m-million tonnes of sugar even if you're Indonesian.'

'I'm not Indonesian, and I haven't just lost it. Its been knocked
off… borrowed – with, one suspects, little intention of returning
it to its rightful owner. Certainly not for the moment.'

'Shit. You're serious,' said Robbie as he sank back into his
chair.

'Deadly.'

'But how can someone just steal half a million tonnes of
sugar? We're talking about… at least twenty-five ships. That sugar
has to be worth about $175 million.'

'Exactly,' said James with the expression of someone who is
delighted that their message has finally been understood. 'Now
you have the motive. It would be interesting to know the identity
of the culprit, although for your continued good health I suggest
you don't try too hard to find out. As to how it was done… well, I
guess it happened over a period of time…'

Robbie looked hard at Fang. He tried to gauge how much of
the truth he was telling. And to what extent the noble house of
Fang was involved in smuggling sugar out of Indonesia as well as
in. For a moment, Robbie's mind worked around the possibility
that he had been buying back from Fang or some other
intermediary sugar he had previously sold them. God, life got
complicated. Robbie decided to be straight and ask a direct
question.

'Does this mean that some of the sugar that I have been
buying from you came from the stockpile?'

For a moment, James looked genuinely taken aback. 'Robbie, I

Singapore Sling

know you think that the Fangs are crooks, but really…'

'Does that mean the answer is "no"?' persisted Robbie.

'Of course it means "no",' said James a little too quickly. And then, 'Well, not exactly.'

James Fang was used to dealing with Robbie. Although their minds worked around problems in different ways they inevitably ended up with the same conclusion. This was probably why the two men got on so well together. It also meant that James had come to respect Robbie for his intelligence and deviousness. Fang knew that right now Robbie's fertile mind was probably analysing the role of the House of Fang, and therefore indirectly Clyde and Clyde, in the disappearance of the strategic stockpile of the Republic of Indonesia. He was almost certainly drawing some conclusions that James would prefer were left undrawn.

'The way I see it,' continued Fang, 'I don't think someone came along, shovelled up 500,000 tonnes of sugar and wheelbarrowed it away.'

I bet they didn't, thought Robbie.

'I think it was more a question of… er… substitution, or lack thereof,' continued Fang. 'I would imagine, purely conjecture you understand, that a group of powerful people might well have noticed that the value of the stockpile based on the current market price was rather high. And wouldn't it be a terrible shame to keep all that high-priced sugar languishing in warehouses throughout the length and breadth of Indonesia? Much better to sell the sugar and have the money safely tucked up in some Swiss bank accounts. The sugar itself could always be replaced when the price fell.'

Robbie nodded. 'All of which would leave the difference between the money received from the sale of sugar, and the money paid for the replacement sitting in the Swiss bank account.'

'Bingo,' said James, happy now that Robbie had grasped the full scope of the scheme. 'Not stealing, you understand… just borrowing.'

'I can see the logic,' said Robbie, 'but how about the logistics? Half a million tonnes of sugar is still a hell of a lot to move around even if it isn't carted about in wheelbarrows.'

79

Singapore Sling

'Easy,' continued James, 'er... I would imagine. As I said earlier on, the stockpile is, or was, kept in warehouses spread throughout Indonesia. There must have been 1,000 warehouses involved. Although it is called a stockpile, the sugar itself is actually constantly being replaced to keep it fresh. The stockpile administrator has ongoing sales of sugar from the stockpile to local wholesalers, while at the same time replenishing the stock with purchases on the world market. So all our friends did was to sell the local stock and pocket the money rather than using it straightaway to buy replacement supplies. They hoped that the world-market price would drop and that they could replace the sugar at a lower price and keep the difference. In the normal course of events the "borrowing" of the stockpile would not have caused a problem since the only "drawing" of the sugar was the "revolving" to keep it fresh. As we know, there should now be more than enough sugar being produced domestically to supply day-to-day requirements.'

'Topped up by the imports that we have already contracted.'

'Yes.'

'So, continued Robbie, the idea was that the "borrowing" could have remained outstanding without arousing suspicion for ages. The stockpile would have been replaced when the world price of sugar dropped. The group of friends would then have sat on their bloated Swiss bank accounts and waited for the sugar price to go up and for the whole roundabout to start once again. Only this time, the scheme came rather unstuck...?'

'Yeees,' continued James, choosing his words carefully, 'because the greedy farmers...'

'As opposed to the generous stock-pile marauders?'

'Everyone has their own interest at heart, Robbie. Because the bloody greedy farmers wanted to make a quick buck and sold their sugar-growing land for real estate development...'

'To Chinese property speculators?' laughed Robbie.

'I wouldn't know the ethnic background of the property developers... but I expect you're right. Anyway, these greedy farmers sold so much of their land that domestic production fell. In fact, it fell to the extent that there might possibly have to be a drawdown on the strategic stock.'

Singapore Sling

'Hmmmm. Inconvenient,' said James.

'You bet. Some damn smart accountant was dispatched to go and sniff around 1,000 warehouses to check the amount of sugar there. Imagine his surprise when the little rat stuck his pole into the mound of sugar in the first warehouse. And rather than a mountain of sugar, he discovers instead a sprinkling of sugar over a mountain of concrete blocks. And a lot of red faces. A scenario that was repeated many times.'

Fang gave a little snigger when he arrived at the end of his story. He sat quietly waiting for Robbie to make the next move.

'Imagine also,' mused Robbie, 'the level and extent of the corruption involved in executing this little "borrowing" scheme. And how unlikely it is that anyone would want this to blow out of proportion. Or even to become public knowledge.'

'Exactly,' said Fang quietly. 'You always were an Ang Mo who appreciated the subtleties of situations like this.'

'And also the possibility of using them to make money,' snapped Robbie, his razor-sharp mind having evaluated the situation and decided a course of action.

'My dear boy, what do you mean,' said James, with mock concern.

'I mean that if these people in high places want to keep their little scheme quiet and to replace the sugar without pushing up the market to the extent that it kills them, they will need to use the best people around who will handle the situation with the utmost discretion. And that becomes expensive. Very expensive.'

'Good heavens, Robbie, are you finally coming over to the side of the enlightened and asking for a kickback?' said Fang, genuinely surprised.

'No, of course not,' replied Robbie quickly. 'I leave that sort of thing to others.'

James smiled.

'What I mean is that Clyde and Clyde is the only company with the international contacts to put a deal like this together. And that they will want to make a bucket load of money doing it. For my part, I would hope that I would be amply rewarded by the company – but legitimately, not through some kind of backhander.'

81

Singapore Sling

'That's my good Englishman,' said James. 'As long as what was the Empire still has people like you in it, people like me can make a living!'

'That as maybe,' said Robbie, 'but you still need to know how to put the deal together. Why don't you ask me?'

'Oh Lord,' said James, 'I thought we Asians were the only ones who liked to be given face. Very well, how would the Honourable English Gentleman propose to the Wily Oriental Gentleman to resolve this little problem?'

'Not very simple,' said Robbie. 'A scheme that would make your... sorry, the sugar-borrowing scheme of the people in high places look like something from a kids' story book. But it will cost you. First, you can order a bottle of Roederer Crystale on room service since I have just decided you are going to pick up the tab for the hotel. Then I'll begin.'

Robbie continued as James groaned with mock grief and picked up the phone.

'The small problem we face is how to purchase a hell of a large chunk of the sugar freely traded on the world market without causing a ripple. Or to put it more correctly, a tidal wave. A tidal wave of nasty rapacious people trying to get in there first and make a buck as we are forced to pay more and more for less and less. You know, it's not just Indonesian farmers, property speculators and well-connected people who want to make a fast buck.'

As he spoke, Robbie looked quizzically at James and wondered to what extent the Wily Oriental Gentleman would himself be part of that tidal wave taking a safe bet on a one-way ticket up. For his part, Robbie had already decided to involve a discreetly located shelf company owned extremely indirectly by the house of Clyde and Clyde. It would purchase significant quantities of what would turn out to be white gold on the futures market. They would then sit quietly by, waiting to cash up as the price rose, as it inevitably would.

'Robbie, I think we know the problem. It is the solution we are after,' said James, not altogether kindly, as he tried to work out what was going through the mind of this devious Ang Mo who was staring at him so intently.

82

Singapore Sling

'Relax, the kingdom of heaven belongs to those who have the grace to be quiet while world-class sugar traders explain what they are about,' said Robbie, sensing the uncharacteristic tenseness beneath James's normally suave exterior. He must really be in this up to the top of his oriental eyeballs.

'My dear chap, I don't think that the kingdom of heaven was ever high on my list of priorities despite the efforts you lot made to convert the heathen. Anyway, get on with it, for Christ's sake.'

'Okay, okay, calm down, I have given this rather a lot of thought over the past fifteen hours and I reckon if we play our cards right we could pull it off,' continued Robbie.

'The only hope in hell we have of disguising the enormous quantity involved is to lay false trails all along the way. We can't hope that they will remain undiscovered forever. However, they have to remain secret until we have managed to buy enough sugar so that it doesn't matter what people do.'

James nodded, waiting for Robbie to get to the nitty-gritty. One thing he had learnt during his years at Cranborough was that Englishmen take time.

'I have already started building up cover on the futures market on your behalf, through a network of companies newly created in various tax havens around the world.' *And also a little bit for Clyde and Clyde*, thought Robbie. 'If we can make enough quiet purchases on the futures market then we won't have to worry so much about buying the physical sugar. The futures contracts will act as a price insurance. Once we have the futures contracts in place then we can start buying the physical sugar.'

'You mean a classic hedge – if the price of physical sugar goes up then it doesn't matter since I already have a futures supply contract. The futures market will go up in sympathy with the physical market and I will be able to offset any big increase in the price of physical sugar by selling my futures contract?'

'Exactly,' said Robbie. 'You have actually been paying attention during the trading that we have been doing over the years!'

'Oh, you know what we Chinese are like. It doesn't matter whether we are property speculators on Indonesia or Chinamen sugar traders!'

Robbie laughed and continued. 'The plan seems to be

83

Singapore Sling

working. Although the futures markets started to get a bit firmer yesterday in both London and New York, I don't think anyone has really twigged what is going on. We will carry on buying futures as and when the market dips so as not to get things overheated. I reckon that as long as we keep our mouths shut and use as many smoke-screens as we have at our disposal we shan't cause too many problems to begin with.'

'Go on,' mumbled James.

'The next bit of the jigsaw will be to actually make the physical purchases. This is where you come in.'

'Me?' said James with mock surprise. 'What, pray, am I supposed to be able to contribute to such a well thought out master plan?'

'Easy,' continued Robbie. 'Origin contacts.'

'Oh? How?'

'Well, I am sure it hasn't escaped you that the less distance you transport commodities, the less it costs.'

'Robbie, you never cease to amaze me.'

'Well, in the case of our little challenge, we need to find a country that has surplus sugar to export and is located near to China.'

'Er, China?' said James, beginning to feel that he was about to lose track of this devious Englishman.

'Sure, where else do you send sugar when you don't want it to be seen going to Indonesia?'

'Don't stop, I'm beginning to enjoy myself.'

'Well, it's like this. The answer is Thailand. Which brings us to the next question.'

'The answer to which is me?' asked James.

'Exactly,' grinned Robbie. 'Who else in this room is related to some of the biggest crooks in the Royal Kingdom, who to a man own sugar mills.'

'I have to admit guilt, but where does China come in? The little problem exists in Indonesia.'

'Sure, so the last thing you want is to advertise hundreds of thousands of tonnes of sugar destined to go there. Much better to lose the sugar in China, which is already a major buyer, and then quietly reroute it south.'

Singapore Sling

'You are a crafty chap,' said James, not altogether joking.

'Oh, it gets better,' continued Robbie. 'What I want to do is a bit of magic to confuse matters even further. We buy a mixture of raw and refined sugar. All of it gets shipped to China. The refined sugar is delivered to the Chinese and then swapped for an equal quantity of white sugar available from a range of Chinese ports. The raw sugar gets delivered to a number of Chinese refineries, which process it into white sugar, which is then also swapped for export cargoes. Hey presto, the whole world gets totally confused and your friends slowly get out of a hole. All you have to do is to arrange with a few of your crooked relatives in Thailand to supply the mix of raw and refined sugar in the first place. I will arrange the rest.'

'Consider it done,' said James, relaxing in his leather armchair.

All conversation stopped as the two men sipped the ice-cold champagne. James felt a warm feeling of admiration sweeping over his body. He looked towards Robbie and smiled slowly. Perhaps his Swiss bank account would not be too badly damaged after all by the unfortunate events in Indonesia. If he was quick enough to start building up a personal sugar position of his own, he might even turn them to his advantage.

★

A little later in the evening, after James had departed, Robbie stood on his balcony under the stars, clutching his mobile phone. He drew a deep breath and rang Julia. To his relief, last night's storm had blown over. The boys were at home on exeat and Julia was not only enjoying being a mother but also beginning to feel guilty about dispatching her husband half way round the world without saying goodbye. Robbie lowered his voice and spoke softly to Julia.

'Look, something has come up...'

'Robbie, I can't hear you...'

'Wait a minute.'

Robbie walked back into his room, shut the balcony door and looked nervously around the room. 'Can you hear me n-n-ow?'

Julia reacted quickly to the telltale stutter. 'Robbie... are you

Singapore Sling

all right?'

'Yes, yes… I guess I'm just t-t-tired,' he lied. 'Sweetie, I need you to do something for me… us.'

Julia sensed Robbie's unease. 'What do you mean?'

'I think the market is going to go up like hell. I want us to buy sugar futures contracts before the market moves.'

'But Robbie, you know you can't do that… it's… it's against company policy.'

Robbie sighed heavily. He knew Julia was right, but this was their big chance. The chance he had been waiting for to get his drop-dead money.

'I know I can't do it. But you could.'

'Oh no, I couldn't,' said Julia quickly, her scientist's mind snapping into action. 'It'd be just as illegal and you know it.'

'Shhh, I know, I know. But if we do it right, no one will find out and we will make enough to r-r-retire on. I'm not pretending it's legal.'

Julia said nothing as she digested what her husband was saying. He was asking her to be an accomplice in a blatant case of insider trading. She began to feel sick. 'Robbie, do you know what you are saying?'

'Yes. And I reckon we can do it in a foolproof way and make at least £5 million. People are doing it all the time. Why the hell shouldn't I? I know exactly how the market works and how to take advantage of it. I've thought it through. I w-w-ant to go for it.'

Julia remained silent for a few seconds and then said quietly, 'All right, Robbie. I trust you. What should I do…?'

★

By the time Robbie had finished giving Julia detailed instructions he was exhausted and almost fell into bed. As he drifted into sleep, Robbie dreamed of making enough money out of James's little problem to retire forever from this madness. No more travelling at the drop of a hat to see little Chinamen. He would be permanently at home for the boys' exeats and Julia's dinner parties…

Armless and Legless

Bangkok, Sunday, 16 April 1995

Robbie looked through the window of the white Mercedes at the carpet of stationary cars stretching as far as he could see along the highway. The unseasonably early afternoon thunderstorm had swept away from Bangkok more than an hour ago. The traffic jam it had caused would last a few hours longer.

The highway sliced through central Bangkok. On the steamy street below, Robbie could see the neon lights of restaurants, bars and shops that were preparing to satisfy the anticipated evening trade. Hawkers set up their barrows selling a brightly coloured mix of fake designer-brand clothing, leather goods, watches and videotapes. The touts outside the girlie bars were on the look out for early tourist clients to whom they showed printed menus of acts that the girls would perform during the course of the evening. Conveniently positioned clinics offering to treat all variety of venereal diseases were dotted along the street in between the bars.

Oblivious to the scene below, James was talking in Toechew dialect on the car phone to his cousin, the owner of the Mercedes. As he finished and hung up, Robbie turned to him.

'So what have you arranged with your crooked cousin while you were yakking away in that foreign lingo?'

'Aha, foreign to you but a useful mother tongue to me. I can say all sorts of devious or insulting things and you wouldn't have the faintest idea what was going on.'

'That, my friend, is exactly why I am asking you.'

'Well, to put you out of your misery, most of the conversation was concerned with boring family matters. In between I did manage to persuade him to arrange an extremely private dinner tonight in an interesting restaurant. While we are there we can try and encourage him to sell us thousands of tonnes of sugar at a

87

Armless and Legless

below market price. Mind you, the way this traffic isn't moving we might have to remake it as a breakfast meeting.'

It was eight o'clock by the time the two men arrived at the Oriental Hotel. They were immediately surrounded by a swarm of uniformed bellboys who whisked them away to the suites obligingly reserved for them by cousin Somboon.

Somboon's father, Fang Hock Chong, the elder brother of James' father, Fang Hock Joo, had been sent from Fukien to Bangkok in 1930 by Grandfather Fang to establish the Fang Empire outside China. Drawing on the experience of the family business in Fukien, Hock Chong had started a sugar and rice trading company based in Bangkok's bustling Chinatown sprawled along the banks of the Chao Phraya river around which Bangkok grew. As Hock Chong's business prospered he kept in touch with his younger brother in Singapore. The overseas Chinese were well aware of the potential advantage available to them of using the network of family and clan members spread throughout South-East Asia. These were linked through a common bond of family and dialect.

There was another factor that was always at the back of the minds of the overseas Chinese. They were an obvious racial minority in most of the countries in South-East Asia in which they settled. Obvious in most instances not only through the shape and colour of their faces and their hair, but also because of their seeming ability to make money wherever they put their hands. This combination meant that they were always at risk of attack from an indigenous population jealous of the commercial success and clannishness of the Chinese. It was not for nothing that the Chinese were known as the Jews of Asia. It was only in Hong Kong and Singapore that the Chinese not only drove the economies but, were also racial majorities. Elsewhere in the region they were economically important but a racial minority, so it was vital that they melted into the local population as much as possible.

A prerequisite of the melting process was to change the family name from a Chinese to a local one. At the same time they needed to preserve some essence of the original. This would uphold the family lineage and give a discreet indication of their origin to

Armless and Legless

other Chinese with whom they were dealing. In the case of Fang Hock Chong, he searched long and hard for a Thai name that would meet these dual requirements. Finally, he settled for Hockchong Kanifangsak. This was a typical Thai mouthful but seemed to Fang Hock Chong to do the trick.

Somboon Kanifangsak was forty-four, two years older than both James Fang and Robbie. The two cousins had more in common than just their age. Both had sharp commercial minds and playboy personalities. Both suffered from being second sons who were innately more intelligent than the first sons, who were destined to inherit the bulk of the family empire and on whom their respective fathers doted.

The Kanifangsak Empire still had its roots in sugar and rice but had quietly purchased and built sugar and rice mills to complement their trading activities. Over the years, warehousing and lighterage had also been added, together with sugar refining. Today the group was one of the largest, if not *the* largest, processors and exporters of sugar and rice in Thailand. And since Thailand was one of the world's largest exporters of both commodities, the Kanifangsak family's international position was undoubted. As was its wealth.

Somboon had taken full advantage of the latter and had so far managed to spend most of his forty-four years on earth living the life of a little rich kid. Ostensibly his job was to run the sugar-export side of the business. In reality, however, most of the world's sugar-trading houses were beating a path to Somboon's door. Each one was offering him all sorts of incentives to favour them at the expense of the others. As a result, his job was not too demanding. All he had to do was to play the buyers off against each other and to enjoy life to the full. Which he did.

Robbie recognised clearly the similarity between James Fang and Somboon. Like all the other international traders, Robbie worked hard at developing his relationship with Somboon. He worked even harder, however, on his relationship with James. As a result, the house of Clyde and Clyde had pulled off some of the most audacious Thai sugar transactions in recent history. Somboon and James had added considerably to the wealth of their families and Robbie had become Clyde and Clyde's head trader.

89

Armless and Legless

By quarter to nine, Robbie and James had showered and were waiting in the lobby of the Oriental when Somboon arrived with a flourish. The bellboys were well aware of who he was and of his ability to tip heavily – especially when he wanted them to keep their eyes closed. Tonight, however, he was unaccompanied and obviously wanted to be seen. Somboon exchanged a brief greeting in Chinese with James and then turned to Robbie.

'Hello, Robbie, how's things going in the big city?'

Robbie smiled at Somboon's handsome, golden-brown face with strong Chinese features and wondered as always at the Oxbridge accent that came out of it.

'Hello, Somboon. You know the city, tough as always.'

'Hmm, if I believed that I would also have to believe that all Westerners didn't look alike! Anyway, I'm hungry, let's get going to the restaurant I have booked before the dishes get fed up and go home.'

Within fifteen minutes their white Mercedes draw up outside a gaudily lit building. A showroom of luxury cars was parked outside. Their drivers stood around in gaggles laughing and joking, while their employers ate inside the restaurant.

'Here we are,' said Somboon enthusiastically. 'Robbie, I don't believe I have brought you here before? Let's get in.' Somboon was enjoying his role of host and general coordinator of all that he surveyed.

As they walked into the restaurant, Robbie was amazed to see a glass wall to his left, behind which sat at least one hundred girls staring nonchalantly at a video. Each had a number pinned to the front of her dress. Robbie looked in slightly embarrassed amazement. He suddenly realised that the glass was one way. None of the girls could see the gaggle of men who were leaning up against the glass arguing about the girls' relative merits.

Somboon looked at Robbie and laughed. 'Don't worry, my prudish English friend, you won't have to do anything you couldn't tell your mummy about. And what's more I have chosen the dishes for you. Come on, stop ogling and get into the room.'

Somboon followed the smartly dressed girl who led the way up a narrow staircase that opened out into a red-carpeted landing. On the way up she bantered in Thai to Somboon and continued a

Armless and Legless

barrage of fluent laughing, screeching noises as she threw open the door to one of the rooms that led off the landing.

Two of the girls from the goldfish tank stood up, looked at the new arrivals and beckoned them to come in. Robbie hesitated.

'Go on, Robbie,' laughed Somboon, 'they won't eat you, even if you don't eat them!'

Robbie walked into the small room and sat down at one side of the table. One of the girls sat down next to him and smiled.

'Me Jeem... you?'

'Fred,' said Robbie, who made a point of never using his real name in situations like this.

'Eh?'

'Fred.'

'Flet?'

'Yes. Near enough.'

'Well, now that the social niceties have been dealt with, let's have a drink,' said Somboon, waving at the girl in the smart red suit and commanding imperiously, 'Bring a bottle of Chivas Regal.'

Robbie groaned to himself. It was going to be one of those hard evenings. Whatever happened he would have to keep his wits about him while at the same time not losing face to Somboon by failing to match him in the drinking.

While Robbie was considering the likely developments during the evening, he was caught by surprise as the girl called Jeem suddenly popped something into his mouth. He looked in amazement at her while both Somboon and James burst out laughing.

'What the hell is she doing?' demanded Robbie, looking affronted.

'Feeding you.'

'Well, I wish she wouldn't,' said Robbie. 'I know where she's been!' he continued, trying to regain his composure and to become lighter on his feet.

'That's a bit difficult,' laughed Somboon, 'it's what she's paid to do. This is a no hands restaurant. You have to do nothing throughout the whole meal except open your mouth. That leaves your mind totally free to negotiate with me!' He laughed in a not

91

altogether friendly way.

And that's exactly your game, thought Robbie. Try to put me on the wrong foot, fill me up with expensive whisky, distract me with a hostess and then try to get the better of me on a sugar deal. Well, no bloody way, Jose. We'll see who wins at this game.

'Okay, now I see. Very thoughtful of you, Somboon. Let me show my gratitude by ordering something. Miss, please bring a bottle of Dom Perignon and three glasses and open a bill for me.' Robbie smiled at Somboon. 'In the meantime, bottoms up.'

Robbie threw the Chivas down his throat and looked Somboon in the eye to ensure he did the same. Almost immediately, Somboon's face started to flush as evidence of the inability of the Asian metabolism to process alcohol at the same speed at the Western one. Robbie knew that if he could speed up the rate of alcohol intake he could get Somboon at a disadvantage. Furthermore, he knew from an earlier New Year's Eve party that Somboon handled champagne extremely badly.

There was a knock at the door and the party was momentarily disturbed by the arrival of a young, gorgeous-looking Thai-Chinese girl. Somboon looked up at her, made no move to greet her but instead spoke roughly to her as befitted a Thai-Chinese tycoon showing off his current mistress to his business contacts.

'You're late. Sit here.' And then, as if by an afterthought, 'This is Lee Lee.'

Lee Lee smiled shyly around the room and then sat next to Somboon, who ignored her. The two hostesses gave her cold stares, while continuing to split open sunflower seeds and thrust the kernels into the waiting mouths of James and Robbie. Once he knew what was going on, Robbie began to feel far more relaxed and smiled at the sunflower seed-splitting Jeem who seemed engrossed yet at the same time disinterested in her work.

Somboon, or to be more accurate Somboon's secretary, had ordered the food in advance and the table was soon covered with a mixture of Thai dishes. The Dom Perignon arrived and Robbie took control of the bottle lest Jeem and her companion, who were splashing out Chivas Regal into tumblers, got hold of it. He popped the cork and poured a generous measure into another tumbler that he handed to Somboon.

Armless and Legless

'Somboon, this is a great idea for a restaurant – bottoms up!'

As the champagne ran down his throat, Robbie tried to gauge the effect it was having on Somboon. Little as yet.

'I agree, absolutely great, cheers...' gushed James.

Oh God, thought Robbie, remembering that James would have an equally difficult time digesting the alcohol and that he was more or less on his side. Robbie shot James a severe glance, which he totally ignored, seeming more interested in getting to know his food server. *Nothing for it but to start the negotiations*, thought Robbie, something he would normally have let James kick off.

'So, Somboon, how's the crop looking?' said Robbie.

James raised his eyes sharply recognising instantly a deviation from the set play that he and Robbie normally followed with Somboon.

'That's a change,' said Somboon. 'Normally James opens the batting. I shall really have to be on my guard tonight. Anyway, since you have to be a buyer, I suppose I should say that things are looking distinctly dodgy and the price can only go up!'

'Somboon, you don't...' Robbie spluttered as Jeem popped something soft, meaty and round into his mouth. James and Somboon laughed.

'For heaven's sake, can you tell this woman not to feed me unless I ask her to?' snapped Robbie.

Somboon muttered something to Jeem in Thai and she pouted at Robbie.

'What on earth did you tell her?'

'Just that you thought she had no manners and that she needed better training.'

'Thanks a bunch. Now I suppose I shall go hungry for the whole evening.'

'Quite possibly, as far as she is concerned. Don't worry, there are plenty of others where she came from. What was it you were about to say before you were so... er, so foodly interrupted?' Somboon hooted with laughter at his own joke and threw down some more Chivas.

'Something like it wouldn't take a genius to figure out that we were probably buyers and that as a seller you wouldn't tell us the truth. Anyway, you old rogue, what you don't know is the type of

93

deal that we want to propose to you over the course of this delicious dinner. At the end of which I am sure we will come away with an agreement that will make everyone feel he has achieved what he wanted. For the moment, cheers. It's good to see you!'

More champagne was swallowed, followed by Chivas chasers. Jeem, still smarting from the earlier rebuke, was slumped against her chair morosely splitting sunflower seeds and gobbling them up herself. Robbie nudged her to ask for some food. Lee Lee, who up to then had remained silent, said something in Thai and Jeem reluctantly gave Robbie something to eat. Robbie smiled at Lee Lee, who returned a shy but warm smile.

Hmmm, Somboon sure knows how to pick them, thought Robbie. *Still I suppose it helps if you are stinking rich and everyone knows it.*

As they worked their way through the first few courses, Robbie and James explained to Somboon the outline of what they wanted. On the plane from Singapore they had worked out a plan of attack. This would ensure that Somboon could make enough money to keep him interested while not revealing too much of their hand too early. As far as Somboon was concerned, he was to believe that he was supplying sugar to China. The country had a short-term requirement that the joint service of Clyde and Clyde and the house of Fang was satisfying. He was to know nothing initially of the Indonesian background to the deal. James would sort this out with Somboon later on and would doubtlessly blame the nasty devious Englishman for not being totally straight with Somboon in the first place.

Slowly, under the influence of pressure from Robbie and James and copious quantities of alcohol, Somboon began to see the logic of the deal he was being offered. By the time the group was halfway through the meal he was becoming positively enthusiastic and the earlier commercial aggression had been exchanged for a growing feeling of bonhomie.

As the evening relaxed, Robbie began to pay more attention to Jeem, who was still showing little to no interest in feeding him. Finally she stood up unannounced and stomped out of the room. Robbie decided to seize on the opportunity to find a replacement for the bad-tempered hostess. He too left the room and picked his

Armless and Legless

way carefully down the steep stairs until he reached ground level and the goldfish tank. Peering through the glass he surveyed the remains of the team of hostesses. None of them would have passed a beauty parade; however, beauty was not too high on Robbie's agenda. At this stage he just wanted to be fed by someone with an even temper. Finally he chose a girl sitting at the back who had what he hoped would be the homely qualities. He gave her number to the goldfish-bowl attendant. He leered at Robbie in a most unpleasant way as he barked the number into a microphone. The girl woke up with a start and smiled blindly from her side of the one-way glass.

When she appeared, Robbie quickly found out that she spoke no more English than Jeem. However, she did appear to be better tempered. Robbie pointed up the stairs and she skipped up ahead of Robbie, who by this time was beginning to feel the effects of the vast quantities of alcohol he had been drinking. As they reached the top of the stairs, he was greeted by a screech.

'Who she...?'

The bad-tempered Jeem was waiting by the door of their room glowering at the homely girl, who grabbed Robbie by the arm and began to square up to Jeem. With a sinking heart Robbie realised the error of his ways. The bad-tempered Jeem had not downed tools but simply taken a loo break.

'Why you want this bitch? You no like me?'

Robbie decided attack was the only form of defence. 'No, as a matter of fact, I don't like you. You are bad-tempered and rude. And not very pretty.' As Robbie added the last bit he knew this was a mistake.

'She ugly. Like cow. Ugh!'

At this point, 'Like cow' sprang into action, and lunged at Jeem with an ear-piercing screech and the two girls started scratching at each other's faces. One by one, the doors of the dining rooms around the red-carpeted floor opened up and no-hands hostesses appeared to see what was happening. Within seconds they had split into sides favouring either Jeem or Like Cow and were screeching at each other in Thai.

Finally Somboon and James appeared, ruddy-faced, at the door of their dining room. Somboon bawled what sounded like

Armless and Legless

some extremely rude words in Thai and slowly the girls stopped screaming at each other. Jeem and Like Cow were left on the floor glaring at each other.

'Christ, Robbie, what did you do?' asked Somboon. 'I thought you Englishmen were supposed to be diplomatic. You almost started World War Three!'

Somboon then pulled some cash out of his pocket, thrust a wad of notes at each of Jeem and Like Cow and told them to get lost. He then guided Robbie back into their dining room. The other diners also returned to their own rooms seeing that the fun was over.

As the three men sat down again, Somboon started laughing. 'And I thought this was going to be a bit of a boring evening negotiating a sugar deal. Robbie, I don't think you should be trusted with any more goldfish. Let Lee Lee help you, but don't do anything to her that I would.'

Lee Lee came and sat down next to Robbie, who was still shaking slightly from the earlier experience. She smiled gently at him, put her hand on his knee and started feeding him.

'A toast to the Rebel Rouser,' said Somboon, filling up their glasses with Chivas Regal. 'Cheers.'

The drinking and eating continued for another two hours. By the end of the evening, all three men were decidedly the worse for wear. However, a deal had been struck which Robbie and James were happy with.

Outside the restaurant Somboon slumped into the back seat of a Mercedes 500 with Lee Lee. Robbie and James fell only slightly less drunkenly into the back of another of Somboon's fleet of Mercedes.

'Do you think he will remember the deal?' asked Robbie as the two men were driven through the brash night-time Bangkok streets.

'Sure. You know he has a mind like a razor. Anyway, he thinks he has a good deal so he will remember. The point is, do you think we'll remember! Anyway, I'll stay behind here for a day to remind him while you go and see your friends in Hong Kong. We can meet the following day in Beijing.'

Robbie grunted but said nothing.

Armless and Legless

Robbie fell onto the bed in his hotel room, felt the swirling pits welling over him and made it to the bathroom marginally before throwing up. As he lay draped over the toilet bowl two thoughts kept swirling through his head. Why did James want to stay back in Bangkok without him, and why had Lee Lee kept squeezing his knee when she was feeding him?

Robbie still hadn't answered either question when he woke next morning still slumped on the bathroom floor and nursing the mother and father of all hangovers.

Thai Dreams

Bangkok to Chiang Mai, Monday, 17 April 1995

Somboon's Cessna Citation VII jet banked lazily to the left and set course for Chiang Mai. The scream of the jet's engines died down a little and Somboon relaxed slightly. He still dreaded flying despite the fact that he, or at least his family, owned the plane. The problem was not helped by the fact that he was still nursing a stinking hangover that refused to go away despite being bombarded with painkillers plus a little hair of the dog.

James, who was still wearing the sunglasses he had needed to put on at the beginning of the day, leant over towards Somboon and began talking in Teochew lest the South African crew of the plane understood what he was saying to the hung-over Somboon.

'I had an interesting conversation in Kiev the other day.'

Somboon groaned, shifted his position and spoke without moving his head.

'Guan Chang, I wish you'd stop talking in bloody riddles. Firstly you ask me to take a joyride with you in this infernal contraption, which you know I hate at the best of times, let alone when I've a shitty hangover. Then you start rambling on about conversations in places I've never heard of. What, upon the soul of our beloved mutual grandfather, are you cooking up in that devious mind of yours?'

'Joo Chiang,' replied James, using Somboon's Chinese name, which, between them, they considered his real name, 'it's hardly my fault if you drank more than was good for you last night and are lousy at geography. What I'm trying to propose is something that will solve our joint mutual problems.'

'The only mutual problem I can think about at the moment is a bloody hangover,' said Somboon grumpily. 'Anyway, go on, but please don't talk in riddles. My brain can't cope with it.'

'Okay, okay,' continued James, 'the main mutual problem,

Thai Dreams

which will last longer than our hangovers, is the fact that we're not first sons. Although we make tons of money for our families we still have to put up with being ordered around by our fathers and elder brothers. True or not?'

Somboon sighed deeply. 'Most true, my dear cousin.'

'I'm sorry to mention it, cousin, but you also have another problem, which thankfully I've managed to avoid.'

Somboon shot a sharp look at James. 'Wha'd'ya mean?'

'Somboon, heroin addiction is something that is difficult to keep quiet from a concerned cousin.'

'How the fucking hell...'

'Calm down, calm down. It doesn't matter a bugger to me. It's just that it does mean that you have certain expenses that are difficult to reconcile with an interfering father.'

'So what the hell are you driving at?' demanded Somboon, sitting up, his hangover now forgotten.

'As I said,' continued James, confident that he had Somboon where he wanted him, 'I had an interesting conversation the other day with a nice man in Kiev, which for your education is the capital of Ukraine.'

'Thanks for the geography lesson, what did he say that warrants dragging me up here?'

'Papaver Somniferum.'

'Eh?'

'A poppy. But not just any poppy. In fact, the only one of the dear little plants that is worth bothering about.'

'Ah,' said Somboon, relaxing slightly as he began to understand what James was saying, 'you mean the type of gardening that our cousin is engaged in up north.'

'Precisely.'

'Which is presumably why we're sitting in this horrid contraption on our way to his home town.'

'Got it in one. I can see that your hangover is clearing up.'

'So what's all this got to do with your friend in... in... Kia... Kee...'

'Kiev. I know you are the country member of the family, content with sitting in Thailand growing sugar. However, it can't have escaped your notice that the Soviet Union is no more.'

99

Thai Dreams

'Shut up and get on with it.'

'Well, as the old Soviet Empire broke up, new trade routes developed for all sorts of things. Armaments, oil, commodities and…'

'Poppies?' added Somboon.

'And in particular the refined product of Papaver Somniferum, heroin.'

'Apart from my own personal interest, which I would ask you to keep quiet about…'

James nodded assent, with a far from pleasant smile.

Somboon continued, 'Apart from that, I still can't understand where I'm supposed to fit into this conversation.'

'Okay, let me make it clear,' said James. 'My friend Kroll in the Ukraine controls the major distribution network for heroin in Europe – both West and what was Eastern. This makes him one of the biggest drugs barons in the world, South American cartels included. A major part of his supply comes from the Laos, Burma, Thailand golden triangle, produced in part by Khun Sa in Burma in conjunction with our gardening uncle. Between them they do a grand job of collecting the opium from the poppy-seed pods and pressing it into morphine base. Our uncle does the hi-tech bit of treating the morphine with chemicals and producing heroin. The trouble is that, since Khun Sa hung up his insurgent boots and stopped fighting the Burmese government, the source of supply is becoming disrupted. My friend is prepared to pay good money to re-establish that supply. And he has asked me to help him.'

'All that makes good sense, but where do I come in?' asked Somboon.

'You, my dear cousin, are to be the shipper.'

'Eh, what do you mean? I don't know the first thing about shipping drugs. And what's more, I don't think I want to bloody well learn!'

'Isn't that rather selfish? Being prepared to use the stuff without being prepared to move it?'

'I thought we had agreed to let that drop. Anyway, it's rubbish. I use the telephone without having to shin up telegraph poles. I really don't think I want to get involved with drug running whether or not I use the stuff.'

100

Thai Dreams

'Why don't you listen to what is involved before you decide? Let me continue.'

'All right, but I don't like the sound of it.'

'For the record, I'm not too keen on drug running either. Not for any moral reason, simply the danger. So rather than set up a regular supply line with all the risks of discovery, my plan is to arrange one big shipment and then quit.'

'So how big is big?'

'One tonne.'

There was a long pause during which Somboon gulped.

'You have to be out of your devious little mind. I've just been reading in the Bangkok Post about some Singaporeans caught in Osaka smuggling the largest amount of opium ever discovered in passenger luggage. Do you, know how much it weighed?' asked Somboon.

'Er… no.'

'Six point oh four kilos of opium. Which as you have pointed out is the crudest form of the stuff. And you are talking about one tonne of heroin!'

'Yes.'

'You *are* out of your mind.'

'I don't think so.'

'Madmen never do!'

'No, Somboon, listen. Firstly, we're not part of a chain as such, we're the originators; or at least the origination is all in the family. We don't have to rely on a lot of middlemen, any one of whom would shop us for an extra dollar. Secondly, we're not carting the stuff around in passenger luggage.'

'So how are we going to move one tonne of it?'

'Simple. Disguised as sugar.'

'You're joking.'

'Never been more serious. Look, we've already worked out that this Chinese contract will involve about one million tonnes of sugar. Assuming an average vessel size of, say, 15,000 tonnes that means about seventy ships. If the sugar is packed in the normal fifty-kilo bags used for sugar, then each vessel will carry 300,000 bags of sugar. If our special cargo is also packed in the same type of fifty-kilo bags, then all it will

101

Thai Dreams

take is twenty bags to package the whole drug shipment. Twenty bags could very easily get lost among 300,000. If we take the whole sugar contract we're only talking about twenty fifty-kilo bags of heroin hidden among twenty million identical bags of sugar. Now do you see the difference between what I'm talking about and the poxy six kilos in your stupid newspaper article?'

There was a long pause as Somboon thought about the figures. Finally he mumbled a reluctant 'Yes'.

The Citation banked and James looked out of the window.

'That's interesting. Right over the top of it.'

'What?' asked Somboon, his knuckles white.

'The golden triangle. You see down there – that little sand bank in the Mekong River. That's where the borders of Thailand, Laos and Burma join.'

'I'll take your word for it,' said Somboon, staring straight ahead.

'How much did you say we were talking about?' he asked, preferring to stick to the business rather than geography.

'I didn't, but I can give you an idea. One tonne of heroin has a wholesale value of just over $11 million. The retail mark-up is 900 times that, giving it a street value of about a billion US dollars. My friend will pass back a quarter of this value to us. That makes about $250 million. To be split fifty-fifty between us.'

Somboon groaned.

'So are you interested or not?'

Somboon groaned again. 'Interested,' he mumbled.

'Good,' said James with a self-satisfied little sigh. 'Now all we need is for our horticultural uncle to show up at the airport as I asked him to and everything will be roses.'

'You mean poppies,' grumbled Somboon.

'I can see you're getting better!' said James. 'By the way, do you know where morphine gets its name from?'

Somboon groaned again as the plane made a final turn before landing, and shook his head slowly.

James looked at his cousin, and then smiled slowly. 'From Morpheus, the Greek god of dreams.'

Golf Balls

Jakarta, Monday, 17 April 1995

It was just turning five thirty in the morning as Dr Amin's car left his house and set off in the direction of the golf course. The tropical dawn had just started breaking and already the streets were beginning to fill up with people going about their daily jobs. Hawkers were pushing their carts to their normal daytime plots. Swarms of small Honda motorbikes buzzed noisily along the side streets and flowed out onto the cool boulevards, which were as yet free of the grinding hot traffic jams that would clog them up like unwanted pond weed later in the day. Daily life for many Indonesians living in Jakarta was still governed by the sun, just as it been for Amin Bin Ahmed when he was a boy in Banding. These days Dr Amin's work-day routine normally followed a more sedate timing of breakfast at eight-thirty on the verandah with Mary-Jo. However, today Dr Amin's life was also governed by sunlight. As his driver swung the big car into the driveway of the exclusive Jakarta Golf Club, dawn had broken and shy rays of sunlight were beginning to dapple the first tee.

*

The overweight, balding, late-middle-age Indonesian looked cautiously at Dr Amin, who smiled kindly back at him.

'That's a bit of a leading question,' said the man. 'I realise that there had to be a reason for you asking me to play golf for the first time in twenty years, but even so…'

When he had asked Hartono to play golf, Dr Amin had realised that the invitation would seem slightly odd. However, he needed somewhere safe to talk to the aging Indonesian and the golf course seemed less unusual than his birdbath, which was the only other option he could think of.

Golf Balls

'The trouble is, uncle,' Dr Amin started to say while lining up a put, 'that it's difficult to have the type of conversation that I need to have with you,' – Dr Amin paused to steady himself for his put – 'without asking unusual questions.'

The ball missed the hole by six inches.

'Shit!'

Hartono felt that he was still not on the same wavelength as Dr Amin. The well-preserved sixty-year-old, who sported immaculate designer golf kit, squatted down slowly to look at the lie of the green. As he did so, he felt a twinge of indigestion and the mild thump of a hangover. Both the result of last night's heavy dinner with two of his three lazy sons and a long-time business contact. He turned slowly to Dr Amin.

'But I would have thought that after all these years of... er... working together you would understand how the business went.'

'It may surprise you but I have deliberately not taken too much interest in what goes on between my Ministry, you, the crook Fang and whichever unfortunate trader is supplying the goods. As long as I get the goods I require – whether wheat, rice, sugar or whatever – when I want them and am therefore able to keep 180 million people happy, I feel I have done my job.'

Hartono gave a little grunt. 'Most commendable if a little short-sighted.'

Dr Amin laughed hollowly. 'Well, I have to admit not totally short-sighted or commendable. Over the years I have noticed certain pieces of paper passing over my desk. When I combine these with other bits of paper they give a rather interesting picture of your involvement in a number of transactions. And the money you made as a result.'

Hartono stared at Dr Amin in amazement. 'You're trying to blackmail me, aren't you! And I always thought you were such a nice boy.'

Dr Amin let his mind drift back to his student days when he had first met Hartono. At the time Hartono was a young, ambitious entrepreneur providing vital supplies to Suharto. In reality, he was the Indonesian face of Fang Hock Joo. Hartono's support of Suharto in those early troubled years had been repaid many times over to the extent that he was now rumoured to be

Golf Balls

running a fleet of twenty-five Rolls Royces located worldwide in various resorts for the rich and famous. Dr Amin could certainly vouch for having seen two of them.

'I am a nice boy, more or less. But today, a little less than more,' said Amin preparing his third put. 'And blackmail is such… such an emotive word. Let's just say that I'm trying to establish a different way of working together.'

Dr Amin, crouched over the ball, carried on talking. 'You see, uncle, I have you and your cronies by the balls. And after many years of making you incredibly rich I'm going to squeeze them.'

Dr Amin's ball dropped into the hole with a clunk and Hartono winced involuntarily.

'There's no need to put it so dramatically. You only ever had to ask instead of looking at me so po faced. I quite understand the position, and would love to help you.'

'I was sure you would,' said Amin. 'I just didn't want there to be any confusion.'

'There isn't. What would you like me to do for you?'

'It's quite simple. Cut me in on the next sugar purchase. I want half of your normal skim which I believe on average is $50 a tonne.'

Hartono coughed, thought hard but said nothing. The hangover, which had previously not bothered him, started to thud painfully in the back of his head in tune with his heart beats.

'Christ, I'm getting high blood pressure,' Hartono worried to himself. 'This little shit is beginning to get to me.'

'I have the evidence…' said Dr Amin quietly.

'Yes, yes of course. But my skim, as you call it, is gross. There are plenty of people I have to keep happy who have been far more willing to ask for a donation over the years than you have.'

'What percentage does that take up?'

'Oh… er… about thirty per cent,' said Hartono, trying to sound convincing.

'I don't believe you; I don't think the others take any more than ten per cent of your total earnings.'

'I should know,' protested Hartono, 'it's a minimum of twenty-five per cent, often more.'

'Look,' said Amin, feeling that the conversation was becoming

105

Golf Balls

degrading. 'I'll accept that you have to pay away twenty per cent of you earnings. That makes $10 out of your fifty leaving forty to be split half-half.'

Hartono grunted.

'And what's more,' continued Dr Amin, taking Hartono's grunt as agreement, 'I don't want any trouble from your fat, slobby, layabout, good-for-nothing sons.'

'Neither do I.'

'Good. Then we are agreed. Where will you pay me?'

Hartono sighed but recognised that he had little option but to agree to the reformed Amin.

'We use an extremely discreet Swiss bank based in Geneva. Banque du Rhône. I'm sure they would be delighted to make the acquaintance of another Minister.'

As he spoke, Hartono was calculating how much Amin was really going to cost him. His normal rake off was in fact nearer $75 a tonne. His other contribution normally amounted to no more than $5 a tonne. After he had paid out the rat Amin he would still have $50. Assuming the contract was for the normal 200,000 tonnes he would still net $10 million. He spoke slowly to Amin.

'I guess you hope to get about $4 million for the normal 200,000 contract?'

'No, twenty million.'

'No way,' spluttered Hartono. 'I told you, I have a lot of hungry mouths to shut up. Cronies, as you call them, don't come cheap.'

'Don't worry, it's not the rake off you have wrong, it's the tonnage. The next contract will be for a million tonnes.'

'Holy shit, you have turned nasty.'

'I told you, I have been planning and waiting. Don't forget that,' said Dr Amin staring hard at Hartono and squeezing a golf ball in front of his face until his knuckles turned white.

There was a long period of silence during which the two men looked at each other with hatred-filled eyes. Finally, Amin spoke slowly and deliberately.

'Just don't forget.'

Amin tossed the ball to Hartono and walked back towards the clubhouse.

Golf Balls

★

For the second time in a week Mary-Jo found herself in the birdbath with her husband. She leant over towards him. 'Well, don't keep me in suspense any longer. Have you done it?'

Dr Amin had his back to the side of the pool and was splashing his legs about. A cool breeze rustled the leaves of the travellers' palms, which bordered the garden. Tropical insects buzzed around lazily in search of naked flesh to bite. He stopped splashing, smiled quietly and spoke softly. 'Yes, it will come to twenty million.'

'Oooh,' said Mary-Jo putting her arms around Dr Amin and winding her legs around him, 'you are a clever man. I always knew you had it in you.'

As she started to gyrate slowly against him, Amin began wondering why he had bothered being commendable for so long.

All the Fee in China

Beijing, Wednesday, 19 April 1995

Robbie looked across with a startled expression on his face at the full-sized orchestra playing a Strauss waltz in the hotel's lounge area. He had just eaten an introvert and tranquil breakfast in his room in the China World hotel and come down in the lift to have his senses assailed with the sights and sounds of this bustling and noisy hotel. He stared first at the grandly ostentatious columns, which were painted a lucky Chinese red colour, and then at the thirty-foot high murals of Chinese emperors and gods carved in ebony. Everything about the hotel was over the top; the orchestra was the crowning glory.

Robbie walked towards the lobby area feeling rather jet-lagged and at risk from the world in general. He looked around for James and finally saw him with a quizzical look on his face, waving silently from the far corner of the large room.

'Sorry,' said Robbie when he finally stood opposite James, 'couldn't see you for looking.'

James laughed. 'Don't worry, we all look alike. And there are a billion of us.'

'I reckon most of you are in here! Shall we go?'

'Sure, I guess we have to.'

The Beijing weather was still cool, and as they walked out of the hotel into the hazy sunshine both men shivered involuntarily in the crisp air before getting into the overheated car.

The car pulled out from the hotel onto one of Beijing's dual-carriageway ring roads. Within five minutes they were grinding along slowly in the middle of the normal morning traffic jam. 'Your bloody traffic gets worse and worse,' muttered Robbie.

'Excuse me,' protested James, 'I'm a Singaporean from that clean and green land where traffic jams aren't allowed.'

'I meant Asia, you fool,' laughed Robbie. 'Although, as you

All the Fee in China

say, all Chinese look the same.'

'I think this particular one might have something to do with our ballerina friend up there,' said James pointing ahead.

About fifty feet ahead, at a junction of two boulevards lined with as yet leafless plane trees, a traffic policeman stood on a large, gaily-painted drum of the type elephants balance on in circuses. He was still dressed in his winter Cossack-style uniform and wore a long, heavy, green overcoat garnished liberally with stars. He directed the traffic through a series of staccato arm movements, delivered while pirouetting like a dancer on a child's clockwork musical box. As he twirled around like a dervish, his overcoat ballooned out revealing shiny black shoes with bulging clown toes. Two shiny red blotches like cheeks on a marionette glowed on his otherwise expressionless wooden face.

'Pretty impressive. Do you think he's shining like that because he is hot or cold?' asked Robbie.

'Probably suffering from carbon monoxide poisoning,' chuckled James. 'Either way, if he fell off his silly little podium and stopped delaying the traffic I would be eternally grateful to him!'

Finally they made it across the intersection and arrived in front of the imposing, heavy Russian-style building at five to ten, just in time for their meeting.

★

James and Robbie sat together with their interpreter on one side of the large, oval, wooden table. The lacquer covering its rounded edge was marbled with cracks and had been peeled off in many places, presumably by idle fingers keen to relieve the tedium of long negotiating sessions. Opposite them sat Jiang Yong Ruen, chief sugar trader for the Chinese State Agricultural Corporation, normally referred to as SAC, which Robbie always thought an extremely apt acronym for an agricultural company. Two assistants sat alongside Jiang, one of whom acted as an interpreter. Jiang always used an interpreter despite the fact that he spoke excellent English, perfected during his five year posting to London – a secondment given to Jiang as a result of his political connections.

109

The other function of the assistants was to record verbatim what was said by both sides during the meeting and to pour tea. They had to report to a 'higher authority' everything that was discussed at meetings with foreigners. The higher authority was specifically interested in anything said which could damage the interest of SAC in particular, or the People's Republic Of China in general.

The tea pouring was carried out in a ceremonial but sloppy manner. Each person was allocated a grubby mug patterned with a tastelessly garish Chinese scene and with a lid. Some supposedly special tea leaves were emptied into each mug, and hot water was added from a large metal-bodied Thermos flask with a dark-stained cork stopper. The guests were offered tea in order of importance, followed by Jiang and finally the tea makers themselves. It was difficult, if not impossible, to drink the tea for some time since the large leaves floated on top, making drinking a messy and unpleasant business. The final part of the ritual would come later in the meeting when Jiang would suddenly feign embarrassment that he had been an inattentive host and invite his guests to drink the tea. At this time the top of the mug would be used to push any remaining floating tea leaves to one side and the tea consumed. The trick, of course, was to hope that visitors would be unfamiliar with both the knack of dealing with the tea leaves and also the etiquette of waiting to be invited to partake and would themselves be embarrassed on both counts and put at a social and hopefully negotiating disadvantage.

Robbie left his tea isolated on the table in front of him, looked across the table at Jiang and smiled thinly as they shook hands. He thought how much he hated the revolting man with bad teeth, with whom he had had frequent dealings in London and who had established himself as a compulsive gambler on the sugar futures market. Jiang looked back at Robbie without establishing eye contact. His round Chinese face wore the blank expression of a true Chinese communist. One who neither liked Western exhibitions of overt emotion nor needed to indulge in them. He was a senior representative of one of China's most powerful corporations and therefore by implication, of the People's Republic itself.

All the Fee in China

James in turn stretched across the table to shake hands with the despicable Jiang and muttered a few words of greeting in Mandarin. Robbie noticed that although Jiang's response towards James was still formal he reacted more positively towards James than he had towards himself. Robbie knew that without James sitting beside him at the negotiating table this next stage of the plan would never go ahead. He also knew that whatever was discussed over the next four hours was for the formal consumption of the two minders and that the real deal would be struck later in the evening over dinner. Robbie stifled a yawn, brought on by both the prospect of the negotiations and the overheated office, as he started the long process of talking officially to Jiang.

Protocol directed that as a senior director of the most powerful sugar-trading house in the world, Robbie should give Jiang face by leading the discussion for their side. He would deliver a set-piece monologue in English. This would be translated into Mandarin for Jiang who would pretend that he had not understood a word. He would, from time to time and for greater effect, ask for clarification about various aspects of the translation. In return Jiang would make his own set-piece speech in Mandarin that would be translated into English by the translator provided by the hotel. Although James spoke fluent Mandarin it would have been unthinkable for him to lower himself to the level of translator in this formal meeting. That would come later if necessary.

The advantage of this rather ponderous system was that it allowed time to mull over what one was going to say next. In Robbie's case, however, he not only knew what he was going to say next but also during the course of the whole meeting. He and James had run over the plan in detail over late-night drinks at the hotel.

'Mr Jiang, may I start by thanking you for agreeing to see us at such short notice, since I realise that someone in your position always has an extremely full diary. However, as always, it is a pleasure to see you.'

There were a few seconds silence as the two minders scribbled in their notebooks. Robbie looked at them and wondered what really happened to the miles and miles of notes taken during the course of a year. Did anyone really refer to them? He also

All the Fee in China

wondered why people in China invariably seemed to make notes in last year's diaries.

The older of the two minders cleared his throat and translated for Jiang who nodded, thought for a moment and responded in Mandarin while the minder scribbled. There was another pause.

'Mr Jiang say he honoured that you visit Beijing again and ask to see him. He also say he indeed very busy and like to hear what proposal you have that could be interested to the State Agricultural Corporation.'

'Mr Jiang, we believe that what we have to propose will be of interest not only to the State Agricultural Corporation but also to the People's Republic of China as a whole. Furthermore, it will offer a chance for the People's Republic of China to help one of the other countries in Asia to overcome a temporary problem...'

As the translator went to work, Robbie's mind drifted to the previous day he had spent in Hong Kong. He had enjoyed catching up with old friends. However, he was still suspicious as to why James had wanted him out of the way for the day. He had raised the issue obliquely with James when they had met up in Beijing for drinks yesterday night. His only response was to say that he needed time on his own with Somboon to ensure that his dear cousin really understood what was required of him and would indeed perform. James was now convinced that Somboon was firmly on the right track.

'Mr Jiang say that, although it is important to help our Asian neighbour, his most important interest is in... promo... promoted business of the SAC. He hope you understand and can propose him somethin' very interestin'.'

Bastard, thought Robbie.

'Please tell Mr Jiang that of course we understand that he has to work for the best interest of SAC and that we believe our proposal will be extremely attractive to SAC.'

Almost without realising it Robbie had slipped into his well-worn path of negotiating in China. This started by prevaricating so much that the opposition was finally forced to ask what the proposal was. Better this way round than to try to sell a deal to an audience that was unwilling to listen.

'Mr Jiang say he would be pleased to hear your proposal if you

All the Fee in China

could make it now…'

Good, thought Robbie, and began to run through the plan, presented in a way that he and James had decided would be most attractive to Jiang. For his part, Jiang remained expressionless while the two minders scribbled notes in their out of date diaries.

Beside him, James changed position in his chair but remained silent. He knew that the combination of himself and Robbie was pretty unbeatable and that by the end of the day Jiang would be dead meat.

'Mr Jiang say that although he see some… er… logic for your proposal, he is not sure that it is enough attractive to SAC to make it worth… er… pursuing. He ask time to think about it.'

Robbie smiled to himself. Jiang was hooked.

'We quite understand Mr Jiang's position. It is important that he only agrees to a proposal that he knows will be to the undoubted benefit of SAC and the country as a whole. Perhaps Mr Jiang would like to think about the proposal for the rest of the afternoon and do us the honour of joining us for dinner this evening?'

The minder looked at Jiang, who nodded his head gravely.

'Mr Jiang thank you and accept your invitation.'

This signified the end of the meeting. Jiang got up, shook hands curtly without smiling and walked out of the room escorted by his two henchmen, leaving Robbie and James to find their own way out of the dingy building.

Seated together in the back of the hotel car, James and Robbie carried on a stilted conversation. This was intended to reinforce the merits of the proposed scheme for the benefit of the driver, who they knew was a spy, and whatever bugs were switched on in the car. It wasn't until they were walking through the Beijing lunchtime air, having asked the concerned driver to drop them off a few hundred yards from the hotel, that they dared to have a proper conversation.

'So what do you think?' asked James.

'Hooked,' replied Robbie. 'The only question is how much he wants and we will discover that this evening. Let's go eat; I'm floating in bloody Chinese tea.'

113

All the Fee in China

★

The restaurant for the meal that evening had been chosen by James on the basis of security and quality of food – not for the decor. The tables were covered with pink tablecloths peppered with small holes through which could be seen parts of the bright-green laminated top of the wooden table. A chipped-glass lazy Suzy that allowed food to be revolved in front of the diners was in the centre on the table. Each place setting was denoted by grubby mismatching pink napkins folded into a fan shape. A single, plastic red rose leant drunkenly in a vase on top of the lazy Suzy. The table was surrounded by metal framed stacking chairs covered in gold flowery material.

The floor was covered with a stained red carpet, while red loops of material hung inexplicably from the low ceiling. The walls were covered with faded pastel-coloured wallpaper decorated with a faded bird pattern and hung with a mixture of Chinese brush paintings, a mirror with Budweiser written on it and a poster advertising live fresh-water crabs.

A sound system produced a distorted version of Mantovani playing such favourites as 'Stranger in Paradise' and 'Somewhere Over the Rainbow'.

Robbie had used the small private room in this restaurant many times despite the revolting interior decor and so far the business concluded in it had been successful and they hadn't contracted food poisoning.

Robbie and James had arrived early and were enjoying a beer, eating peanuts and chatting when the door was flung open by a tubby waitress with a ruddy face. Jiang entered with the junior minder.

He walked over, shook James and Robbie by the hand and smiled an evil smile that revealed a mouth full of teeth blackened through a combination of chain smoking and lack of cleaning.

Jiang was the first to speak. 'Goo' evenin' gen'men, sorry we're late. The traffic in Beijing gets worse every day.'

'It's a pleasure to see you, Jiang,' said Robbie calling him by his family name as he had been asked to do when talking to the man in London. 'You are right, the traffic gets worse each time I come

114

All the Fee in China

here. I sometimes wonder where all the money comes from,' Robbie continued, starting the conversation off on a topic that he knew would be continued later in the evening.

James over-ordered the food, carefully selecting a number of expensive dishes to flatter Jiang, and opened a bottle of XO brandy. He splashed a large quantity into everyone's glass without asking. Jiang turned to the waitress and ordered a Seven-Up – which, in true Chinese style, he added to the vintage cognac.

They worked through the meal talking in English about many topics but making no mention of the sugar proposal. James and Robbie kept on glancing at the minder, who paid no attention to the conversation but ate and drank voraciously.

Finally the food was finished, and Jiang sat back in his chair belching with satisfaction and picking his teeth with a wooden tooth pick. He looked sharply at the minder, who said something in Mandarin to Jiang and then spoke for the first time in over one hour.

'Please excuse but I have to go now. Long way home. Sorry. Thank you for food. Goodbye.'

He stood up, his face the colour of a beacon, swayed slightly, shook Robbie and James by the hand while bowing slightly and stumbled out of the room.

Robbie waited a few seconds and then asked quietly, 'So what do you think of our proposal, Jiang?'

'I think I would like hear more about detail. Precise detail.'

Both Robbie and James knew that the next part of the conversation had to be dealt with extremely diplomatically. Jiang was only interested in how much he could make, and how the amount could be hidden from prying eyes on the mainland. If the business went wrong, Jiang could easily end up behind bars. That was the easy option. He needed to know the details of the transaction, however, and these had to be discussed in a clinical manner so that the whole arrangement was made to seem matter of fact and he did not feel uneasy.

'We thought it might be interesting if the transaction took place through a company in Hong Kong,' said James, and then, lowering his voice, 'Ever Rich Limited, I believe.'

Jiang looked nervously around the room at the mention of the

115

All the Fee in China

shell company he had set up in Hong Kong while working in London, and through which several transactions had already passed, giving him a healthy balance at Banque du Rhône in Geneva. He nodded without speaking.

'We could arrange this along with the relevant banking services if it would help? This would be done in the same manner as we organised previously.'

Another nod.

'The service fee earned by Ever Rich would be one per cent.'

'Two,' snapped Jiang, looking wild.

'No,' said James firmly. 'I'm sorry, Jiang, but the nature of this transaction doesn't allow such a large fee, although I know this is what Ever Rich has earned in the past. Ever Rich could possibly earn up to one and a half per cent for its services. If you consider the total amount that the company would earn of over $4 million given the size of the contract base, we hope you will find the business attractive.'

Jiang thought and calculated. This money, plus what was already in Switzerland, came to nearly $8 million. Enough to make the investment in the London hotel he was considering along with some other Chinese cronies. 'Okay.'

'A deal?'

'Yes.'

'Good.'

The men all shook hands, and gulped the remainder of the brandy. Jiang then left hurriedly without any more comment.

Robbie and James smiled at each other and waited until Jiang was well out of earshot. 'I thought we'd agreed to offer him two and settle at two and a half per cent,' said Robbie.

'I know, but I really don't like the bastard, and the feeling got worse during the meal,' said James.

'Quite understandable,' laughed Robbie. 'Whatever it is, a large chunk is going to have to go back to Clyde and Clyde anyway. He still owes a bundle on sugar futures deals that he did in his personal capacity and lost on when he was in London. Shitty little rat.'

'A little rat with a big appetite,' said James. 'Come on. Let's get out of this horrible place and go and have a nightcap to celebrate. I need to look at some people with clean teeth.'

116

Swiss Roll

Geneva, Thursday, 20 April 1995

All seemed right in Robbie's world as he walked over the Pont du Mont-Blanc and mulled over the status of the deal. He ran and re-ran through his mind how things were progressing from both a professional and a personal viewpoint. The supply from Thailand seemed secure. Cousin Somboon had dollar signs in his eyes and there was no reason why he shouldn't perform. Similar dollar signs flashed in the head of the revolting black-toothed Jiang. By including the Chinese State Agricultural Corporation in the loop of the transaction, Robbie could mislead the market for a few critical days into believing that the purchases Clyde and Clyde were making were part of their ongoing business of supplying China. The whole market already knew about this, and therefore wouldn't react by pushing up the price. By the time the market realised that China was just a dummy and that the sugar was in fact destined for Indonesia, which had a previously unknown and massive shortage, it would be too late. Clyde and Clyde would have locked in all the supplies they needed to supply Indonesia, and James Fang, Dr Amin and the President would all be extremely happy. Clyde and Clyde would make a killing on the transaction and Robbie would hopefully receive the biggest bonus of his life of over a million pounds and would slip gracefully into retirement. So far so good.

But it would get better. If Julia's clandestine purchases of sugar futures were still going to plan, they would have a piggy bank full of the things by the end of the week. Once the market found out about Indonesia and the price took off they would sell the futures and rake in a profit of at least £5 million on the whole quick exercise. They would have to be extremely careful about concealing the funds. However, retirement could certainly be incredibly graceful with that much in the bank. Robbie looked

Swiss Roll

around him as he strode along through the cool spring air. He was certainly in the right place to organise someone to look after his money.

Robbie's feeling of contentment was enhanced by the mid-morning glass of whisky pressed on him by the gracious Monsieur Gerard as Robbie vacillated over his choice of cigar from M Gerard's extensive stock. During the past ten years Robbie had developed a taste for the expensive pastime of smoking Cuban cigars and a relationship with Gerard et Fils. The latter had grown in direct correlation with the increasingly large amounts that Robbie spent on cigars chez Gerard during his frequent trips to Geneva. Robbie had finally chosen a box of his favourite Flor de Rafael Gonzalez. These had been chosen with great assistance from the attentive Monsieur Gerard following much discussion about the size, strength, condition and colour of the final selection.

Having made his choice, Robbie downed the remainder of the whisky and puffed contentedly on the mid-morning cigar made especially for M Gerard and handed out reverentially by him to 'preferred' clients. He strode out happily into the crisp April sunshine and started out along the bank of Lake Geneva in the direction of Banque du Rhône.

Geneva worked around him with the quiet precision of the Swiss watches for which it was famous. Immaculate BMWs, Porsches and Mercedes drove snappily through the neat streets lined with carefully pruned trees that were just beginning to come into bud. The traffic dutifully respected the traffic lights and endangered the life of any pedestrian that did not. Beautifully dressed fur-clad women walked neatly clipped lap dogs past enticing doggie smells on the walls of watch shops, jewellers and chocolatiers.

The whole city had a feeling of money. Quiet, efficient, discreet money. The type of money that was dealt with in a surgical way with the minimum of embarrassing questions being asked. Everyone, whether depositor or borrower, who used banks in Geneva had a specific reason for doing so. They were the first-class graduates of the University of Money. Business was serious, efficient, extremely secretive and involved values the length of

Swiss Roll

telephone numbers.

The first time he had met the bankers who handled Clyde and Clyde's more 'imaginative' sugar deals, Robbie had been amazed at the type of banking they would do. His previous exposure to bankers had been his regular grovelling petition for a larger overdraft, delivered to the manager of his local National Westminster branch in Edinburgh student days. In reality, he had never qualified to see the manager and was usually fobbed off with a short-back-and-sided manager's assistant with a nasal twang who had delighted in making Robbie squirm. There was no more similarity between this type of banking and that practised by Banque du Rhône than there was between a crossbreed mutt and a racing greyhound. Both were dogs with a leg at each corner and a tail at the end but there the similarity finished.

Over the past twenty years Robbie had developed a close working relationship with Banque du Rhône. The bank had financed Clyde and Clyde's transactions involving many parts of the world: Cuba, USSR, China, Brazil, South Africa and various Middle Eastern Countries.

The bankers who worked for Banque du Rhône all seemed to come from the same mould. Aristocratic, suave, multilingual, cultured, intelligent, totally amoral and ruthless. Although the bank had an extremely small network consisting of luxurious offices in London, New York and Hong Kong, in addition to its Geneva headquarters, the bankers themselves had no geographic limitations. They thrived on 'difficult risks'. This translated as countries with political, economic or social problems that had to resort to 'innovative' ways of obtaining basic commodities such as sugar, grains or petroleum. The way in which these transactions worked inevitably involved structures that were complex from both a commodity and a personal perspective.

The difficulty of financing the commodity side of the operation meant that those needing the services of Banque du Rhône had to agree to demanding terms. Terms that added significantly to the already considerable wealth of the partners of the bank.

From the personal angle, the extraordinarily discreet private banking department of Banque du Rhône was ideally positioned

119

Swiss Roll

to help the promoters of the transactions financed by the bank. Such people, be they generals, politicians, presidents or just extraordinarily well-connected businessmen like the Fangs, were either already unreasonably rich or were about to become so.

Robbie had worked with Victor de Gruchy at Banque du Rhône on many of his more complicated transactions. They had grown to trust each other so Victor was now Robbie's natural choice of banker when, having put the transaction in place in Bangkok and Beijing, he needed to talk to the money men. From both a business and a personal perspective.

Still enjoying his morning cigar, Robbie turned left over the Pont du Mont-Blanc, which spanned the Rhône as it flowed from Lake Geneva. A clock struck in the clear air that enveloped this orderly Swiss lunch hour. Robbie looked down at the rocks, visible through the blue grey waters of the Rhône and at the swans and ducks that were congregated at the shoreline of the lake; presumably also hopeful of food. Robbie quickened his pace lest he should be late arriving at the elegant doors of the Banque du Rhône building that he could see in front of him. He was in Switzerland after all.

The elegantly tailored male receptionist looked at Robbie and smiled thinly yet deferentially. 'Good morning, sir. Shall I tell Mister de Gruchy that you are here?'

In the private banking tradition the discreet Swiss receptionist announced Robbie's arrival without checking his name. In Swiss banks there were those whose identities were to remain a strict secret, known only to those to whom knowledge was essential and certainly not to be announced at the reception of the bank. Robbie was whisked away into an anonymous, tastefully furnished waiting room. It had window blinds that made it impossible for passers-by to see in but permitted those lucky ones inside an uninterrupted view of the lake. Within seconds the door opened and Victor appeared. He wore an expensive, dark-grey suit and an elegant smile to match. He stretched out a soft, manicured hand.

'Robbie, good to see you. Sorry to keep you waiting,' he said, knowing full well that Robbie had only been in the waiting room for thirty seconds.

'Victor, good to see you too, even though you do tell lies; you

120

Swiss Roll

know bloody well I've only been waiting here for a few seconds.'

Both men laughed with the easy reassurance that came of having worked together for many years.

'Well, you are a client after all,' said Victor. 'Come on, let me continue the charade by buying you lunch at our favourite restaurant.'

Victor de Gruchy ushered James out through the imposing but discreet doorway of Banque to Rhône towards his waiting Jaguar that had magically appeared on the kerb side.

Robbie looked at Victor during the short journey around the lake to the expensive but low-key Italian restaurant that had become their favourite lunch place. He noticed for the first time that Victor was going quite grey around the temples. The greyness made him look distinguished, but also much older than his forty-two years. Robbie also noticed stress marks under Victor's dark eyes. Despite his carefully calculated aura of carefree self-assuredness, Robbie felt something was not going well for Victor.

'How's Agnes,' asked Robbie, thinking, as he always did when talking of Victor's elegant French wife, how much more attractive her name sounded when pronounced as a French 'Aness' rather than an English tea lady Agnes.

'Oh, she's fine, complaining about the Swiss as always but otherwise quite happy. She always maintained that the best thing about Geneva is that it is near France.'

'Is she managing to work?'

'Here? You have to be kidding. The Swiss have things tied up far too tight. Anyway, the kids are taking up a lot of her time. You know the sort of thing, bus driver, nursemaid, homework helper, piano teacher…'

Robbie nodded quietly in agreement as he thought of Julia coping with their four children while at the same time holding down a job as a Physicist. Things had become easier for her now that the boys, now fourteen and sixteen, were both boarding at Radley. At the thought of them he had another pang of guilt about being away for their exeat weekend. It wouldn't be long now before the twins were both boarding at the Cheltenham Ladies' College. God, he was going to need this deal to be successful just to pay for the school fees alone!

121

Swiss Roll

As he listened to Victor talking, Robbie was happy to think that the well-connected offspring of a rich Jersey family married to a svelte Frenchwoman had some of the same family problems, as did he, a bright Twickenham Grammar School product married to an English scientist.

'And how are Julia and the children?' asked Victor, forever polished and avoiding having the conversation focused on himself for too long.

'Oh, fine. Much the same sort of story. The only difference is that Julia is managing to keep her hand in as a boffin, although the combination of home and work is beginning to send both of us crazy.'

'That's the problem with educating women,' joked Victor as he pulled up outside the restaurant. 'Here we are. Let's see what they can do for us today.'

The restaurant owner greeted them with friendly, but not too friendly, efficiency and showed them to a table which would have looked equally at home in a Swiss bank. It had a panoramic view of Lake Geneva, which shimmered in the crisp late-April sunshine. Outside on a small balcony was a window box that would bloom with mountain flowers in a month's time. The balcony also prevented those who were walking down the narrow footpath outside M Antonio's restaurant from seeing who was eating with whom. The same privacy could not, however, be secured from those dining inside the restaurant although they paid little attention to the arrival of the two boring businessmen.

Having dealt with the most important business of ordering the meal Victor opened the business conversation.

'So what new devious scheme has the house of Clyde and Clyde come up with now? Nothing too illegal I hope. We are getting stricter and stricter about things these days. When I think of some of the earlier deals you and put together I cringe.'

Victor dropped his voice as he delivered the last sentence. He fixed Robbie with a serious look, as if to secure a confirmation that Robbie would also cringe and would not for a minute dream of revealing secrets of done deals.

'Hmm, I know what you mean. I've just seen one of my friends from Edinburgh sent down for three years for using

122

Swiss Roll

cleverly some preferential information he was smart enough to acquire. Something that I honestly believe would have earned him a partnership not a prison sentence ten years ago. Anyway, Swiss secrecy is one of the few reasons we agree to pay your exorbitant fees!'

'One of the many reasons I hope! So what brings you to our little restaurant today?'

'Something that doesn't have the complexity of the earlier Cuban and Russian deals, but makes up for this in terms of size. In fact, I'm honestly a bit concerned whether you'll be able to swallow the whole thing.'

Victor pulled a face that was at the same time attentive, concerned and smug. 'Try me.'

'How about $350 million?'

'US?'

'US.'

'Hmmm,' said Victor. 'Are you sure there will be any sugar left for my kids to have in their cocoa? That must be about…'

'A million tonnes, give or take a few bags and some for your kids.'

'You can't be serious?' said Victor, beginning to look concerned.

'Want to bet? It would appear that our Indonesian friends have been doing naughty things and have been caught with their proverbials down.'

'Not the Chinaman?'

'Well, no and, I suspect, yes. You know how difficult it is to figure out what the hell he is up to.'

'Do I ever,' said Victor with a degree of feeling that surprised Robbie.

'Well, the official version is that the Fangs have been brought in by the Indonesians to help them out of a hole. And that is the version I'm sticking with. Between you and me and M Antonio's window box, however, I've a strong suspicion that the hole they are in could have been dug in great part by the Fangs themselves. I don't really want to know.'

'Except that it always helps to try and find out what or who is motivating our little Chinese friend. Greed I know. It is the other

123

Swiss Roll

bits of his stories I want to find out about. It is always good for my relationship with my fellow directors if the deals I finance get repaid,' Victor smiled rather thinly.

'Let me fill you in on the details and you can make up your own mind. Only before I start, do be an accommodating host and fill up my glass with some more of that rather expensive red wine…'

Singing for Supper

London, Friday, 21 April 1995

'Robert, are you sure you know what you're doing? We are building a hell of a big futures position. The futures funds are all sniffing around like crazy trying to work out what's going on. It's beginning to worry me. Robbie, what the bloody hell *is* going on?'

Robbie looked across the boardroom table at the Chairman whose chiselled features looked unusually severe. The rest of the Executive Committee members shuffled through the computer printout of Clyde and Clyde's futures position, which had been circulated minutes before the daily meeting had started.

'Charles, I know what you mean but there's no need to worry. I haven't wanted to say too much outside these four walls in case the story got out. As you know, I just got in from Geneva this morning so now I can give all of you the whole picture.'

Robbie hoped he sounded confident and reassuring despite the jet lag that was beginning to catch up with him. It was just one week since he had received James's call from Singapore. Since then he had bounced around Asia like a dud cheque and put together what he believed would turn out to be the sugar deal of the century. As he had looked at the haggard face staring at him while shaving in the Metropole hotel in Geneva before catching the early morning flight to London Robbie had decided that he was getting too old for this lifestyle. That was before he had called Julia.

'Robert, what are we doing? I placed the orders to buy sugar futures contracts in my name as you said. The broker said he needed deposits so I paid these by using the money in our savings account. Robbie, it's come to over £200,000! That's all of our savings plus a bit of overdraft. That idiot Jones at the NatWest is beginning to ask questions and I can't tell him anything because I don't know anything! And all you can do is to call me from all

Singing For Supper

over Asia telling me to buy, buy, buy bloody futures, which I never have understood anyway, and to make sure that I spread the business over several brokers and keep it dead secret.'

'Look, sweetie, you're the mathematician! Just go to Jones and tell him that you want an increased overdraft to invest in the futures market. No need to tell a lie. He won't understand any more than you do. All he has to do is to look at the value of our damn house, which they already have as collateral for the mortgage loan. It's worth at least 300,000 quid more than the mortgage so he shouldn't have any problem. Anyway, you could always pledge those gilts that we bought with my last bonus if you needed to; that should keep the little twit happy.'

'But Robbie, what's going on? We haven't had a sensible conversation since you took off like a scalded cat for Singapore a week ago to see that horrid little Chinaman. It's all to do with him isn't it? You know I hate him. He's just too shifty. Robbie, I'm worried. When are you coming back home?'

Robbie had promised that he would be home early that day and would explain everything. But in the meantime would she please go and do what he asked without making life too difficult. Julia had reluctantly agreed. Robbie hoped the Exco would be as easy to convince.

★

Robbie looked around the boardroom at the worried faces of his fellow directors and then at the Chairman. 'Charles, it's basically quite simple. I reckon Indonesia has a need for over one million tonnes of refined sugar. Fang called up.'

'Which one?' Charles cut in.

'The son, James.'

'He's even worse than the father,' grumbled Charles, 'and the old man's a sodding crook.'

'I don't disagree, Charles. However, the father has more or less handed over the business to the sons so we have to deal with the next generation if we are to keep the business. And the Fang connections in Indonesia are still impeccable. They've got their hands in everyone's pockets; or rather they put contributions into

126

Singing For Supper

the pockets of all the right people. Either way, if we're going to do business in Indonesia we'd better keep on working with the Fangs.'

'I know, I know,' sighed Charles. 'That's the trouble with our business, it's full of bloody crooks.'

And none of them is more crooked than you, thought Robbie as he looked at Charles. With his iron-grey hair, and Savile Row suit he could be mistaken for a merchant banker. However, Robbie knew better. The sixty-year-old Chairman was the biggest buccaneer of the lot. Charles was cast in the mould of the head of Jardines or any of the other Hong Kong trading houses that had once controlled China's trade with much of the Empire. He had a track record of transactions that would make any Taipan green with envy.

'I'm afraid so. It's just a case of making sure that the ones that win are on our side. And in Indonesia the Fangs have a consistent track record of winning.'

'Okay, so what's happening and why do you consider it appropriate to build up a futures position that is the largest I have seen since we squeezed the former Soviet Union? This could kill us stone dead if it went wrong.'

Robbie summarised the Indonesian situation and the events of the past week. At the end of Robbie's explanation, Charles lent back in his seat at the head of the boardroom table.

'Okay, Robert. My vote is that we back you. As usual you seem to have worked things out pretty well. But be aware that you are gambling with the future of this company. If you screw up we are all dead meat.'

This was the old pirate talking. He smelt a good gamble a mile off and was prepared to run with it. His was the flair that had struck the most audacious sugar deals seen this century. Any one of which could have sunk the company. But none did. And as a result, Charles sat on a fortune that could keep his family out of work for generations.

'Gentlemen, what do you think?'

The question was largely academic. It would be a brave man who questioned the combined resources of both Charles Clyde and Robert Smith, his head sugar-trading director. There was a

Singing For Supper

mumble of assent from around the table.

'Good. Then I propose we let Robbie get on with it. I would ask everyone to concentrate on this project. I need hardly remind you that the flip side of disaster is extraordinary profit. Gentlemen, if we pull this one off then I think none of us will need to work again. Ever. I would like all of us to have this option. And not just me.'

Here, here, thought Robbie as the meeting broke up.

★

Although he was dog-tired, Robbie couldn't allow himself to relax just yet. Having designed the master plan, organised the supply of sugar and the banking, and placated his fellow directors, he just needed to put the insurance cover in place. And for a deal of this size and complexity he would have to do that himself.

'That's the problem with this job,' he mumbled to himself as he set off for the coffee house where he had arranged to meet his long-standing Lloyds Broker friend. As he had walked through Leadenhall Market on the way to the meeting, Robbie had wondered for how many years merchants like him had been making the same journey to Lloyds. He had joked with the fishmonger gutting a catch that would end up later in the day either on the table of one of the expensive, old City eating houses or in the shopping bag of an Essex secretary. Fred's family had been running the fishmonger business from the same premises in Leadenhall for well over one hundred years and for the past twenty Robbie had walked past Fred's shop at least once a week.

'You have to be joking,' said Alastair Pemberton as he stirred sugar into his cappuccino. 'One million tonnes of sugar would blow the socks off the market. That has to be worth... er...'

'$350 million and rising.'

'I just can't wait to see the reaction on the underwriters' faces.'

'And don't forget we will need cover for the vessels as well as the sugar. And what's more, to make life easy, the ships will all be old rust buckets owned and operated by the Chinese.'

'You sure know how to pick 'em. Anything else you need to tell me to help me sell the deal? How about under a thin coating

128

Singing For Supper

of sugar the real cargo is Chinese nuclear weapons being smuggled to mad Middle Eastern Mullahs via Indonesian Muslim fundamentalists?'

Robbie smiled at Pemberton. The two men had worked together for years even though they made an odd couple. Pemberton the Lloyds broker; Harrow, Sandhurst; Army and old family money; a typical rugger bugger. Robbie Smith; grammar school, Edinburgh; no family money but now in the driving seat of the business.

'Sugar rots the guidance systems of modern weapons of mass destruction. Plays havoc with the rubber bands. You reckon you can propose my deal?'

'Oh, sure. It's just a question of how to prevent people from having heart attacks long enough to back it.'

Pemberton looked thoughtful for a few seconds. 'I'll tell you what,' he said with the confidence of someone who knew his way around every corner of Lloyds. 'Remember what we did when you wanted to get cover for that shady Cuban business?'

'It wasn't shady!' exclaimed Robbie in mock horror. 'It was a highly structured, slightly innovative transaction. The fact that you guys couldn't understand it was hardly my fault.'

'I think the problem was that we understood it too well! Anyway, if you recall the solution to getting the cover was a guest appearance on the floor of Lloyds by one Robert Smith. Slightly unusual but it seemed to do the trick. Are you game to do this again?'

'Well, I survived the last ordeal. When should we do it?'

'How about now?' said Alastair looking at his watch. 'If we get our skates on we could do the rounds before the end of the session and invite whoever makes the most positive noises out to lunch.'

As Pemberton led the way into Lloyds, Robbie couldn't resist having a jibe at the odd design of the building that still sent shivers down his spine.

'You know the latest story about this building?'

'No,' said Pemberton looking warily at the security guard who was in the process of issuing Robbie with a pass to the floor, 'but do you think now is a good time to share it with everyone?'

Singing For Supper

Robbie grinned at Pemberton. 'It's nothing really. Just that there is an oil rig in the North Sea that looks just like an office block.'

The security guard looked at Robbie as he slid the pass across the counter.

'That isn't the latest story, sir. In fact, it's rather old.'

'Don't worry, Sid, he is a bit slow on the uptake,' said Alastair, smiling as he picked up the pass and pushed Robbie into the building before Sid could have second thoughts.

Robbie looked around the inside of the glass and steel building. It looked little better from the inside. Escalators moved people between the floors that were divided by the type of risk being covered: shipping, aviation, sovereign. Each floor was itself divided into groups of underwriters, some busily talking to dark-suited City types, others reading newspapers or gossiping. In front of some underwriters there was a short queue of brokers. Each carried a notebook and waited patiently for his turn. This could come in minutes or hours depending on the complication of the business being proposed to the underwriter by those in front of him. The queue formed a discreet distance from the underwriter.

'Mmmm. Let's go and talk to Jonathan, he doesn't seem to be too preoccupied. From memory he should have some availability for your type of shady business.'

As the pair walked up to Jonathan he looked up from his computer screen and groaned.

'Oh God. Last time you two made a guest appearance, I had two months of sleepless nights!'

'And one year of good profits!' retorted Alastair.

'You don't know. It's all a deadly secret. How are you, Robbie,' he drawled in his easy-going patrician style. 'Do I need to count my fingers after I shake hands with you this time?'

The two City types shook hands with the sort of professional bonhomie that was the basis on which Lloyds operated; both aware that they possessed all the expertise that their professions had to offer, and neither would let the other get away with anything.

For the next hour and a half Alastair sold the business to a selection of chief underwriters while Robbie did his job of

130

Singing For Supper

explaining the more technical sides of the operation. By the time Robbie, Alastair and two of the more friendly underwriters were sitting down to devour some of Fred's Dover sole, the business had been done. On a series of handshakes, insurance cover for $350 million worth of sugar and related shipping had been arranged. As it had been for hundreds of years.

★

Back at the office Robbie had a quick look at the pile of messages on his desk and dialled the message recall on his mobile phone.

'Robert, that little burk Jones is getting stroppy. He says we have to fill out a load more documentation in order to use the house as cover for the overdraft. Can you have a word with him? I know he doesn't like me. I don't think he likes dealing with women. Male chauvinist, small-minded pig from East Croydon. I hate the little bastard. Please talk to him. I'm getting fed up with all this. Please hurry up and come home and explain what is going on! I'll cut out of the research committee meeting early and be home by seven thirty. We can go to the Italian restaurant after you have spoken to the girls and you can tell me what's going on.' There was a pause during which Julia had regained her composure and softened her voice. 'Love you.' The message went dead.

Robbie groaned. If there was one thing he didn't feel like doing right now it was spending the evening at Paulo's restaurant eating yet another damn meal and being interrogated by Julia in logical scientist mode. He looked down ruefully at the unused squash racket still jutting from his flight bag. At least he now had a wife who wanted to talk to him even if he didn't particularly want to talk to her. Opening up his briefcase he double-checked that he still had the box containing the freshwater pearls he had bought on Monday in Hong Kong.

As he walked out of the building and got into the company car Robbie felt a wave of jet lag sweeping over him.

'Home, James,' he sighed, still managing the chuckle that he felt obliged to give to the unfortunately named chauffeur.

James had long since learned to accept his lot and to put up

Singing For Supper

with the young traders who all at once became directors of the company and therefore clients of his. In any event this Robert Smith seemed a nice enough bloke. Not like some of the arrogant ones. Bill had been right.

'Home it is, sir,' said James as he swept the XJ6 out of the City in the direction of Julia, Paulo's and the third degree.

Rats

London, Saturday, 22 April 1995

Robbie held the rugby ball in his hands ready to give it a punt. His sport-mad teenage sons tensed in 'get set' position, waiting to scamper off after it; Jeremy, the fourteen-year-old, pushing six foot but still quite thin; Toby, beginning to live up to his name – although still only twelve he was five foot eight and filling out like a prop forward.

Robbie lowered the ball. 'Do you know why Parliament Hill Fields are called that?'

The boys groaned and gave each other the knowing looks that siblings reserve for those frequent occasions when parents become insufferably boring.

'Yes, Dad!'

'Oh... Why then?'

'You know... because it was from here that that bloke Guy Fawkes looked down on the Houses of Parliament and plotted to blow 'em up.'

Robbie looked perplexed. 'Have I told you that before?'

'Yes Dad, tons of times... In fact, most times we come up here! Can't you just hurry up and kick the ball?'

'Cheeky sods,' muttered Robbie as he booted the ball in an arc. The two boys laughed gaily as they ran off chasing it.

Not for the first time recently, Robbie began to wonder whether he was beginning to lose his edge. He consoled himself with the thought that he had just been overdoing it and that he was still jet lagged. Still...

As he jogged off through the damp, late afternoon, London spring air to catch up with the boys, his mobile phone started ringing.

'Damn!' Robbie rummaged though the rubbish in the deep pocket of his dark green barbour. 'Bugger!' The shrill warble of

133

Rats

the mobile became more insistent. Finally he found it.

'Hello?'

'At last,' said the Ivy League American voice. 'I'm the one who is supposed to be asleep not you. Hope I didn't disturb anything. I know you're not at home – I just spoke to Julia. Getting ready for one of your fancy British dinner parties?'

'Only a ramble with the kids.'

'A what?'

'Never mind. What's up?'

'To be honest, I'm not sure, Robbie. It's just that I think my buddy at the Department of Agriculture was trying to tell me something last night. He looked really worried. I reckon there could be some big news about to break. If it is really that big then they might leak it over the weekend to give the markets time to think about it. I heard you were in the middle of a big deal so I thought you should know.'

Robbie took a breath. He thought once again how glad he was that eight years ago he had hired Charles, alias Chip, Brown, the well-connected Yale preppie, to join Clyde and Clyde's New York office. 'You bet I should. Do you have any idea what it's about?'

'No. Although my guy was bursting to tell he said it would be more than his job was worth. What's your expression... tighter than... than... something to do with geese...'

'It's a duck. And you're too young to learn naughty expressions.'

'Well, anyway, he wouldn't let a thing slip. I tried to fill him up with booze. No good. Just said that since I was a good buddy he would advise us to have a perfectly balanced trading book. For which information he expected a hell of an expensive dinner..., which I bought him. You'll be getting the bill...'

'If the information is good then you're forgiven. In fact, looked at overall, our books are pretty well balanced. The normal mix of futures and physicals. That's as long as everyone who is supposed to supply or buy performs and the futures markets don't go crazy. We still need to unwind our futures cover when we want to.'

'From the way my guy was talking, it sounded that whatever it was he was hiding under his hat would be big enough to send a

134

Rats

tidal wave through the market.'

Robbie drew in his breath. 'That's what bothers me. You never know how people will react if something really big hits the market and moves the price. Honest people suddenly become less honest when they start looking at how much cheaper they could buy for or how much more they could make on their sales. It only needs one big default from only a supplier or a buyer who wants to rat on their contract to completely unbalance the whole thing and screw us up.'

'I guess that's the problem with always being in the middle...'

'You bet. The role of the honest broker,' said Robbie, trying to sound relaxed and failing.

'Anyway, Chip, thanks for calling. Give me a buzz as soon as anything happens. I'll be home in about an hour.'

'Don't worry, old boy, I'll give you a jolly old buzz, what.' Chip was obviously in weekend mood.

'Go away and let me finish my ramble – which, by the way, is English for a walk. Complete with ducks.'

As he cut the call, Robbie stood staring thoughtfully at the view over London. Clyde and Clyde's books might be balanced but Robert and Julia Smith's certainly weren't. Like a good soldier Julia had continued buying futures contracts like crazy. They now had futures purchases of over 10,000 tonnes of sugar at a purchase price of more than $3.5 million. Peanuts in terms of Clyde and Clyde's books but extremely big nuts for the Smith domestic economy. As long as the price kept going up they would be fine. All they had to do was to hold onto the contracts and watch them increasing in value. Any day now, news of the Indonesian shortage would leak out and the market would rocket. Robbie and Julia would then quietly sell their futures contracts, pocket a million dollars profit and retire. Easy. As long as Chip's news kept the market moving up they were in clover. If it went the other way... Robbie didn't even want to think about it.

Robbie's ruminations were interrupted by Toby.

'Come on, dad. You're not Guy Fawkes! Let's go and look at the ponds.'

Ducks, thought Robbie, trying to put thoughts of the sugar market behind him as he ran after his stocky son.

Rats

★

Robbie rose from the table. 'Excuse me. Shouldn't be a minute.'

'Note the use of "shouldn't"!' said Julia, to the laughter of the other guests, as Robbie walked swiftly out of the room to take the phone call. It was Chip.

'I hope you're right about being balanced...'

'Cut it out, Chip. What's up?' snapped Robbie.

Chip Brown wondered about the tenseness in Robbie's voice. Normally the boss was the master of coolness.

'The dinner was worth it. I just heard from my friend who told me that the USDA will be announcing in a few minutes that laboratory tests conducted over a ten-year period have proved conclusively that excessive consumption of sugar causes cancer in rats.'

'And?' demanded Robbie.

Chip drew in his breath. The boss didn't sound in a good mood to hear really bad news. But there was nothing for it. The 'buddy' at the USDA was his brother and there was no way the news leak was wrong.

'The USDA will be issuing an official Government health warning regarding excessive sugar consumption. It will refer specifically to the risk of cancer. Every food item containing sugar will be obliged to carry it.'

'Whaat? That's bloody crazy!'

'Robbie, you and I know that, but the great American public won't. From now on, consuming natural sugar will be seen as the equivalent of committing suicide.'

'I know, I know,' said Robbie regaining his composure but beginning to feel sick. 'The drinks companies will dump sugar wholesale in favour of artificial sweeteners – no matter how unnatural and bad for you they may be. Has there been any reaction yet?'

'There hasn't been an announcement yet! This is strictly advance notice. The balance of the payment for last night's dinner. Wait a minute... not any more it isn't... it's coming up on Reuters.'

'Don't go. Let me have a look at the screen.' Robbie took the

Rats

portable phone into his study and flicked the switch on his Reuters monitor. The screen flashed and then lit up properly.

'I've got it… reads exactly like you said… Shit!' Robbie's mind started racing. 'Try and get hold of your contacts in the drinks companies to see what they say. I'll talk to Charles. Call me as soon as you've got anything.'

Before Robbie could put the phone down, the other line rang. It was Charles.

'Robbie, I just got an extremely nasty call.'

'I know. Have you read Reuters?'

'No. But I take it it's the same. Cancer in rats.'

'Yes. The soft drinks guys will go nuts. I guess all the big food companies will. Don't even mention the brewers.'

'I won't. The market is going to drop like a bloody stone. What's our position.'

Robbie began to go hot and feel sick. He stammered. Charles was in no mood for delays.

'Robbie, what's our damn position?'

'N-n-nothing to worry about.'

'I didn't ask you for an opinion, Robbie. I asked for facts.' The old buccaneer was beginning to show steel.

'Calm down, Charles.' Only Robbie dared cross swords with the Chairman. 'I can quote you the exact t-t-tonnages in a few seconds once I have our position up on the screen. But what you really want to know is that we are more or less square.'

Robbie could almost hear Charles grinding his teeth.

'How much less?'

'If anything, we could be sitting pretty in the event that the market collapses. We have agreed our sales to the Indonesians on a fixed-price basis. We are buying from the Thais on a floating-price basis. At the moment our exposure between the fixed and floating price is protected by purchases on the futures market. We don't care whether the price goes up or down. But that also means that we can't take advantage of a drop in price to lower our purchase cost.'

Robbie began to feel sick as he thought of the impact a drop in price would have on their own personal position. He tried to pull himself together… Must think about the company… Talking to

137

Rats

the Chairman…

'And the Chinese?' asked Charles.

'They are purely in the picture to mislead people and to stop the market seeing the direct link between Thailand and Indonesia. The market already knows we have plenty of Chinese business going on. As far as this additional Indonesian business is concerned, the Chinese are just acting as middlemen. Whatever happens to the price, whether it goes up or down, they don't care. They simply receive a fixed price per tonne.'

Charles mumbled his understanding but said no more.

Robbie continued. 'The point is, Charles, if we are quick when the market opens we can get rid of the purchase hedge and then try to pick up some cheaper sugar as the market falls. This means that we could increase a hell of a lot the profit we are making on supplying the Indonesians. If it goes right we could make a killing.'

Charles thought for a moment, and then spoke slowly. 'I don't mind killing. It's being killed I don't like… bad for the health.' The old buccaneer was indeed beginning to calm down.

'Do you still want the exact tonnages?'

'No thanks, Robbie – as you say, that's your job. But for Christ's sake, don't screw it up. If you do, we'll be dead. Bad for the health.' The phone clicked as Charles hung up.

Robbie staggered slightly and leant against the wall. He put his hand to his head. God, this was turning into a nightmare… he had to think…

Julia's slightly impatient voice rang out from the hallway. 'Robbie, hurry up, we're missing you!' Then, 'My God, what's the matter?'

Robbie turned, ashen-faced, towards her. 'Nothing, love, I j-j-just need a few minutes to sort myself out.'

'Robbie, you don't look like this when it's nothing. Please tell me, you know we don't have secrets. I may be able to help.'

'But what about the dinner party?'

'Don't worry, it can run without us for a few minutes. In fact, the way John was spouting it could be a few hours.'

Robbie handed Julia the Reuters report he had printed from the screen while talking to Charles.

138

Rats

'Look at this. It's saying that the USDA has announced tests that prove sugar causes cancer.'

' No it doesn't!'

'Darling, that isn't the damn point!'

'Well, what is then?' said Julia, remaining calm and reading the report carefully with scientist's eyes. 'If I was a rat I'd be pretty worried. That little Chinaman of yours might be. He fits the right category!'

Robbie managed a thin smile. Julia had never understood what he did, and now wasn't the time to teach her.

'The point is, love, that the market will drop like shit.'

'So…? Wait a minute, it's those damn futures things, isn't it!'

'Yes… we're sat on the wrong end of a bloody enormous position. We've bought a hell of a lot.'

'But I thought you said that the price would go up when the market got to know about the Indonesian thingamabob?'

'Well, that was true before this…'

'I know, I know… this ratty thing will try and make it go down. But won't the two bits of news sort of balance each other out and the market float around in the middle?'

Robbie's face began to light up. He put his arm around Julia. 'You know, sometimes you're brilliant.'

'Most of the time I am. Just because I don't understand what you do doesn't mean I'm a congenital idiot. It just means I don't understand what you do. Anyway, to me it all seems extremely simple. You just have to play with the information to get what you want. A bit like a car salesman.'

'I'll ignore that… but in a way you are right. All I have to do is to make sure that the impact of the ratty thing is neutralised by the Indonesian thingamabob. If I play my cards extremely carefully on Monday, giving you time to do what you will have to do with our futures, then we could be back in the money. In fact we could make even more.'

'There you are. I told you your business was simple. It's much more complicated being a boffin. We'd better get back to the other complicated people. John may be drying up.'

Robbie laughed.

'It would be the first time.'

Rats

'I agree, but we shouldn't take the risk.' Julia smiled quietly as she slipped her hand into Robbie's. 'We wouldn't want to take risks, would we?'

Roller Coaster

London, Monday, 24 April 1995

Robbie looked at Julia across the breakfast table. She ran her hand through her slightly greying dark hair, drank her coffee and skimmed the *Times*. He was always amazed how she managed to get the family going in the morning, deposit the little ones on the school bus and yet still leave the house looking like a professor. It was all he could do to shave and find his cigarettes. He coughed as he dragged on the first Marlboro of the day.

'Are you sure you remember what you have to do?'

Julia looked up, feeling grumpy at being disturbed during one of the few pools of serenity available to her during her day.

'Robbie, I'm not an idiot. We've run through it ten times already. And you shouldn't smoke so much.'

Robbie ignored the smoke warning – today would definitely not be a day on which to give up.

'I never said you were. Just tell me again what you have to do. It's good for me too.'

Julia sighed, folded the paper, looked straight at Robbie, held up her left hand and started checking off points on her fingers.

'Shortly after nine o'clock, I ring the six brokers we…' – Robbie shot her a glance – '…er… I mean, I am using.'

Robbie nodded, 'That's better.'

'And I ask them…'

'You don't ask, you instruct.'

'Oh, for Christ's sake, stop being such a bloody pompous idiot. I *instruct* them to sell a total – split *between* them, of course, not each,' Julia glared at Robbie and continued, 'a total of 10,000 tonnes of sugar. I tell them that I feel I've made enough out of my little speculation and I would be extremely happy if they would sell our futures contracts at a price of not less than two hundred and fifty. Which, given we paid an average of two hundred,

Roller Coaster

should give us... I mean me... a tidy little profit. Strangely enough, I do *not* tell them I have heard anything about cancerous rats. How am I doing?'

Robbie looked seriously at Julia. 'Fine. In the meantime, the market will start off falling like a stone on the ratty news, so it's very unlikely that our brokers will be able to sell anything, let alone at the price we want.'

Julia looked worried. 'Robbie, you keep on saying that. Do you really believe it? We could lose a fortune!'

'We could, but we won't. As soon as I get into the office, I'll feed information into the market through Reuters about the Indonesian shortfall. I'll also start buying like hell to create the impression that Clyde and Clyde is caught on the wrong foot and has to cover for the Indonesians whatever the price.'

'So this should be enough positive news to stop the market falling and give us a chance to get out. Once the orders have been executed I call you on your private private line, as opposed to the one that all your hundreds of best friends use, to confirm. Do I pass?'

'Great, yes, but it won't stop there.'

'Robbie, what do you mean? All we need to do is to cash up our futures-market profits and then run for cover!'

'Not exactly love. I've got a business to run. If I can play it right, this is a day when I screw the market both ways and make enough money for both the company and us so that we never have to work again. Fingers crossed.'

'Plus anything else handy,' muttered Julia as she picked up the newspaper and shoved it in her briefcase. 'I like living in this house, even if you do disturb me in the mornings.'

★

'The next hour could make or break this company. It is my job to make sure it is the former. But I need 150 per cent of your efforts to make it happen.'

Ten pairs of eyes were fixed on Robbie who was sat in his large leather chair at the head of Clyde and Clyde's trading desk with the other traders gathered around him. It was the first time

Roller Coaster

most of them could remember such a briefing.

Robbie leant forward and spoke earnestly. 'My thinking goes this way...'

My God, he has never explained anything before, it must really be serious, thought ten brains.

'The USDA report is just that. A report. So far there has been no follow-up reaction from any of the beverage or food companies. Of course, there will be a reaction from them. But don't forget that they all have massive forward buying positions for sugar too – just like us at the moment – so they have to play their cards dead carefully.' Robbie looked around the room for effect and then continued, 'It is a safe bet that by the end of a week the price of sugar is going to be half of current levels. Our own Thai/ Indonesian position is based on fixed price sales to the Indonesians covered by hedged floating price purchases from the Thais. I want to dump the futures cover on the purchases so that we can pick up the full advantage of the anticipated price drop. On one million tonnes of sugar, this could mean millions of dollars of extra profit.'

There was stunned silence as the trading team took on board the magnitude of the gamble.

'But what if the price doesn't come off?'

Robbie looked at the junior trader who had dared to ask the question that was on everyone's lips.

'It will. But not straightaway. First of all, it has to go sharply up so that we can dump our positions into a strong market. This should turn it with such force that it goes through the boards before we buy it back again.'

'You wouldn't be thinking of a private call to Reuters would you?'

Robbie smiled at Gordon, his long-time number two, who had, over the years, learnt a lot about Robbie's trading methods.

'Let's just say that I think it is about time that the market got to hear about not only the Indonesian short position but also that of the Chinese. They are, coincidentally, buying a million tonnes of refined and raw sugar from Thailand. We happen to know it's all the same contract, but there's no need for the market to know that so soon.'

143

Roller Coaster

Gordon looked worried. 'But Robbie, the USDA rat report is going to have a hell of a bearish impact on the market. It's going to drop like a stone.'

'Of course, you're right, Gordon. The bet has to be that, based on the USDA report, all the major sugar traders have a strategy to sell the hell out of the market as soon as it opens. They will be betting that they will be able to buy back their sales once prices have dropped. On the other hand, they are all going to be looking like hawks at each other to see if anyone is going the other way.

'Our strategy will be to drop news of the Indonesian or Chinese short position into the market just before it opens. We then have to make enough people believe that this will outweigh the short-term impact of the USDA announcement. If we are successful – and we bloody well have to be – then the market will stop falling and take off upwards. We have to make that happen. And when it does we'll quietly reverse our strategy and start selling our position. If there is enough upwards momentum then we should be able to get shot of at least three quarters of a million tonnes before the market realises what is happening and starts falling again. Simple.'

And by that time Julia's little bit of business will also have been done, thought Robbie.

'Shit, Robbie, that's one hell of a gamble,' said the normally supportive Gordon. 'If it goes wrong we could be paying for our mistake for years.'

'No, Gordon. If it goes wrong, by the end of today Clyde and Clyde won't exist. There's no question of years…'

There were nods of solemn appreciation from around the table.

Robbie noted that the seriousness of the task ahead had sunk in. Unless these guys did their job right, there was no way Julia's position could be unwound. He needed the might of Clyde and Clyde to help them escape. *This is exactly what insider trading is about,* he thought to himself, before continuing.

'Don't look so glum. We can do it. We're the biggest and best in the world. I'll drop our little gems of information into an already confused market. With the help of a chunk of opening-purchase orders from us, the market will ignite. Then all we have

Roller Coaster

to do is to ride the roller coaster. The trick will all be in the timing. And that's my problem. All you lot have to do is to execute the orders. And at the same time create the strong message that Clyde and Clyde are caught short of two million tonnes. This will push the market where we want it to go. But first of all I have to make Gordon's anticipated phone call.'

★

Robbie swung back in his chair, looked at St. Paul's and waited for Philip Drew, his old university friend, now chief editor of Reuters' sugar desk, to pick up his phone.

'I don't believe it. The great man himself phoning a poor old reporter. How am I going to stop myself from being cynical?'

'By believing that this will be the last time I ever talk to you if you don't,' snapped Robbie, not altogether kindly.

'Hmmm. Serious stuff. What do you have to tell me?'

'In the interest of market disclosure, I think it is important for you to know that the Indonesians have a massive crop shortfall. They will be importing at least one million tonnes in the near months. Not only that but the Chinese will be needing to buy a similar amount – again they are having crop problems. We have been handling this position on behalf of both buyers.'

'Am I supposed to link the two?'

'I shouldn't recommend it – they hate each other's guts. Communists are still an endangered species in Indonesia.'

'So what you are telling me is that there will be at least two million tonnes of hitherto unreported purchases having to be made in the immediate future. And that Clyde and Clyde is stuck in the middle.'

'I believe you could interpret it that way, you silly bugger. Of course, that's what I am telling you.'

'And what, pray, do you expect me to do with the information?'

'Since you are a news agency, how about reporting it?'

'Can I trust you?'

'Philip, I know we have both grown up, but I don't think we should forget where we came from.' Robbie laughed. 'Anyway, I

145

still have the photos!'

'Hmmm. I am not daft enough to believe you are an angel and that you are telling me this as a Christmas present. But I am daft enough to trust you to be telling the truth. With or without the threat of the photos. And, by the way, the girl is now my wife!'

Robbie chuckled. 'I know, and the other one with me is now my wife. God, it seems a long time ago. Anyway, hurry up and get the information on the screen, there's a good chap. I'll give you a call later – it's about time that lady in the photo and you came round for dinner again.'

Robbie hung up. 'It should be on the screen a few minutes before the market opens. I want you to hit the market with purchases of 100,000 tonnes. Don't use any of our tame friends to disguise our purchases. I want the whole world to know that Clyde and Clyde is caught short and buying like hell. If the two events don't get things moving upwards we shall have to think of something else.'

The room went silent and tension rose as the seconds ticked away before the market opened.

Gordon was the first to speak. 'It's coming up on the screen. Word for word. Two million tonnes... Clyde short... brilliant timing, the market's just opening.'

As if started by a gun,Clyde's traders burst into action, barking purchase orders over phone and intercom with the market floor. The previously inactive screens began flickering price changes. All the phone lines lit up at once as the trade pounced on the Reuters news and tried to find out what was going on. Heart rates and the noise level in the trading area shot up in tandem.

Robbie sat back in his chair. 'What's the opening sentiment?'

'Man, Dreyfus, Phibro, Czarnikow, the whole damn lot have all opened as sellers. Every dentist and drinks manufacturer in the world must be selling.'

'Gordon, any idea how much is being offered?'

'Anything up to a quarter of a million tonnes and rising...'

Robbie clenched his hands.

'We're being filled in... people are rushing to sell... the price is off... five... no ten...'

'Don't panic, guys, it will take at least ten minutes to work,'

Roller Coaster

said Robbie trying hard to convince himself.

After five of those ten minutes the market was still falling without touching the sides when Robbie's private private line rang.

'Robbie, it isn't working. The brokers can't sell anything. The price is falling like a stone… We have already lost our profit and are a quarter of a million dollars down on paper… Haven't you told Reuters about Indonesia? Robbie… do something!'

Robbie cupped the phone against his chest and spoke quietly yet clearly towards the trading desk. 'Put bids out for another hundred thousand.'

Ten pairs of eyes flickered up towards Robbie. They noticed that for the first time ever Robbie's knuckles were white. Something was seriously wrong with him.

Robbie returned to his private line. 'It's b-b-bound to take a little time, love. The information about Indonesia is on Reuters… It's just a matter of letting it s-s-sink in… Just hang on. The loss is only on p-p-paper.'

Robbie wondered who he was trying more to convince, Julia or himself. It was never like this when he wasn't involved personally.

'Robbie, I'm scared to death.' Julia rang off.

The noise level on the desk had increased several more decibels. Each trader was holding two phones and talking into a microphone at the same time while staring at the moving numbers on the screens.

Robbie's normal private line rang. Robbie answered and heard James's agitated voice.

'Robbie, I know you guys are mad but what the fucking hell's going on? I just saw the announcement on Reuters. Who let the cat out of the bag?'

'I did.'

'You *are* mad.'

'Look, James, your job is to handle the Asian end of the business. I do the trading. Let's just leave it like t-t-that.'

'Okay, okay, but I feel completely out of it over here.'

'You are, that's why you've got me here,' said Robbie seizing the opportunity to ram home his position. 'Look, James we are a

147

Roller Coaster

bit b-b-busy right now, I'll call you in half an hour.'

Robbie turned towards Gordon. 'How's it looking?'

Gordon cupped his hands over the two phones he was speaking into and held them against his chest. 'It's a bit early to tell but I reckon Man's backing out. They're beginning to go quiet.'

Robbie imagined the similar chaos that must be reigning in the trading room of Man, the second largest sugar-trading house in the world, a quarter of a mile away in the City.

'Phibro and Dreyfus too. I reckon only Czarnikow is still offering in any quantity. Looks as though it's beginning to work.'

'Keep pumping the orders,' barked Robbie.

'But Robbie,' said Gordon, 'we are getting right royally stuffed.'

'Just d-d-do what I say Gordon.'

'Wait a minute, Man are bidding – Jesus, they must be in for a hundred... it's beginning to pick up – up five... ten...'

'Right,' said Robbie, 'bid another hundred.'

Ten jaws dropped.

'Robbie, we don't need to buy any more... We're already overloaded and the market is beginning to go the way we want...'

'Just b-b-b-bloody shut up, Gordon, and do what I say. Buy!'

Gordon didn't have time to feel hurt for more than a few seconds. 'Shit, someone's coming in with a hell of a lot of bids...'

'Probably the funds,' said Robbie. 'We must have hit a trigger point.'

Robbie's private private phone rang.

'Done it!' said Julia. 'The market picked up and we've sold the lot. Do you realise, we just made a half a million dollars?'

'Great, keep on.'

'Whaaat? Are you mad?'

'I hope not.' Robbie turned towards the Thames and mumbled urgently into the mouthpiece, 'Sell the same again but don't go below two hundred if the market turns.'

'Are you sure?'

'Yes. Just you see.'

Robbie hung up, closed his eyes and heaved a sigh of relief. The house was safe.

148

Roller Coaster

'It's up another ten. There must be bids for three hundred thousand coming in…'

All eyes were fixed on Robbie, who suddenly put his hands behind his head, swung back in his chair and said nothing. Whatever was bugging the boss was gone. This was classic Robbie. For a few seconds that hung like years Clyde and Clyde's trading desk was silent.

Robbie's chair rebounded as he brought his fists down on his desk.

'Right, gentlemen, I think we have it by the balls. It will take a train to turn this one around and make it fall. Let's get on with the business of the day. It would be impolite not to let all our nice friends have the sugar they are asking for. We have to get rid of whatever chips we have thrown into the game this morning in order to get the thing moving up, plus the best part of our million tonnes before the market realises we're shafting it and the bottom falls out. Just start nice and easy… It would be a shame to upset the market…'

★

Robbie's private line rang again.

'Robbie, I've got one very confused cousin sitting in Bangkok to say nothing about me. What the hell's going on? Somboon doesn't know whether to take out his revolver or a champagne bottle. First he sees the price he will get for his sugar dropping like lead. Then half an hour later, after the market has shot up, it looks as though he will be several million dollars better off than he ever thought he was going to be, and then it starts falling again…'

'Based on track record in the no-hands restaurant, I think the revolver would be less dangerous than the champagne. Anyway, it's his fault. We offered him a fixed price and he refused. So now he can have the fun of riding the roller coaster.'

'To be honest, Robbie, it isn't Somboon who worries me, it's the others. I wouldn't want them to get too confused with what's going on. I think a visit from the sugar Bwana to explain the mysteries of the sugar market and calm their nerves would help.

Roller Coaster

Can you make it?'

'Hell, James. I've only just come back.'

'I know that, I was with you, if you remember. It's just the Asian way. Personal contact and all that. I'm serious. Can you get on a plane this evening?'

'If you really think I have to, I will.'

'I do.'

'Okay, I'll go straight to Bangkok. See you tomorrow.'

★

'For Christ's sake, Robert, what's the matter with you? Why do you need to go and see that horrid little Chinaman again. You've only just got back. Are you two having an affair? Since the last time you went you've almost lost the house, made half a million dollars and heaven knows where we are now. I've just sold 10,000 tonnes of sugar we don't have, and as far as I can see the price is going up like a rocket, which I do believe is the wrong way.'

Robbie sighed. 'No, I'm not having an affair with James. He isn't my type. And the market will drop without touching the walls once it realises we have conned it. And when it does we buy the 10,000 tonnes of sugar that we don't have for less than we sold it for and make some more money. It's also the reason I've got to go back to explain to your favourite little Chinaman and his friends what's going on.'

'All I can say is good luck to them. I hope they end up understanding more than I do.'

'Would you like to come with me?'

'Don't be stupid. I have a normal job to do even if you don't. Now please get off the line and make this horrid market go down.'

Robbie laughed quietly. 'Don't worry, it will.'

'Robbie, we sold 500,000 tonnes before the market figured out what was happening and another five hundred on the way down before it got too low for us. Right now it's heading for Australia. Valued against our fixed price sales to Indonesia we are already picking up an extra $100 million and the figure is going up every minute.'

150

Roller Coaster

Gordon relaxed for the first time in two hours and smiled at Robbie. 'You've done it again. By the way, while you were on the line, the Chairman of Man called. He wished you good day and that your balls would drop off.'

Robbie groaned while getting out of his chair. For the first time he noticed that his back was wet with sweat. As he walked stiffly towards the door he turned to Gordon.

'If you happen to be talking to him, please return the greeting and tell him that I think they already have.' Robbie paused and then turned towards the desk, grinning. 'But we took a lot of money off him in the process. Thanks lads.'

Hot Stuff

Bangkok, Tuesday, 25 April 1995

Robbie walked briskly out of Don Maung airport arrival hall and almost jumped into the back of Somboon's waiting car. The market had been open for one hour in London while he had been stuck in the plane. He grabbed the car phone and dialled Clyde and Clyde's sugar-trading desk and was delighted to hear Gordon's reassuring voice answering the phone.

'Gordon, I've just arrived. What's it doing?'

'Still going down without touching the sides. The trouble is it's all one way... Since some madman conned the market yesterday into believing it should go the other way and the trade in general lost their shirts, there haven't been too many buyers around. Other than that it's been quite quiet.'

'Any announcement from the food industry?'

'Yeah, Coke and Pepsi have announced new brands containing only artificial sweeteners. Nothing yet from any cake or sweetie people but the buzz is they will go the same way. So far the plan is paying off – we're making out like bandits. What's happening with you and our little Thai friends. Can you talk?'

'No problem, it's just me and the driver. Anyway, nothing yet – I've only been out of the plane fifteen minutes. I've got dinner with Somboon and James in a couple of hours. That's when I've got to do my act. It's going to be tough. At this rate Somboon is going to get millions less for his sales than if he had fixed the price last week. I hope he doesn't get any funny ideas about trying not to deliver for the moment and hoping the price picks up.'

'That would certainly screw things up a bit.'

'More than a bit. Can you give me a call in about an hour to give me the latest? Earlier if anything interesting happens.'

'Okay, will do. By the way, I wouldn't hurry back. I don't know what your life insurance is like but after yesterday there are

152

Hot Stuff

a few people who wouldn't mind finding out. And by the way, despite the normal multiple bookings you were spotted at Heathrow so the trade knows where you are.'

'It all sounds pretty cloak and dagger. Anyway, thanks for the warning. Speak to you later.'

★

Robbie looked Somboon straight in the eye.

'Look, Somboon, it's hardly my fault if the bloody Yanks make a completely unanticipated announcement. It's caused us a lot of problems too. Obviously we're concerned about your position otherwise I wouldn't be here. To be honest, I should be at home minding the shop.'

They were seated around the dining table of a private room in the Oriental Hotel's Thai restaurant. Somboon looked sullenly across the table at Robbie, seemingly unimpressed with Robbie's explanation. Lee Lee sat next to Somboon staring down at her plate.

James cleared his throat. 'Er... I think my cousin feels that a company with Clyde and Clyde's connections must have had an idea what was going on and that he is being... er, how can I put it...'

'Stitched up?' suggested Robbie.

'Yes,' said Somboon. 'Bloody well stitched up by your fancy company with its smart traders.'

Robbie paused for thought. 'Somboon, look at it this way. Why would we need to stitch you up? We are relying on you to be the supply for a contract on which we will make a reasonable profit doing what we are supposed to do, i.e. putting buyers and sellers together.'

'To make more money,' answered Somboon, who in his heart of hearts had never been comfortable selling to Western trading companies who did fancy things on the futures market. Why couldn't he just sell to the Chinese himself without these damn foreign pirates getting in the way?

'Perhaps Somboon might feel better if he knew that Clyde and Clyde had also lost money due to the latest market changes,'

153

Hot Stuff

suggested James, wondering why Robbie was taking so long to play the 'loss-of-face card' that they had discussed earlier. James was always amazed that these western trade houses seemed to have no idea that, in Asia, face could be almost as important as profit.

Robbie let out a long pre-rehearsed sigh. 'James, you know I am not supposed to discuss my company's position with anyone, let alone clients. As a director, I receive a lot of privileged information and if anyone found out I was releasing this I could be slung out.' Somboon looked unmoved by this show of western ethics.

Robbie coughed and continued. 'Anyway, given the circumstances, I am prepared to bend the rules a bit. I can tell you quite truthfully that the American information caught us completely by surprise and that as a result we have lost a hell of a lot of money.'

In saying this Robbie felt he was telling at least a form of truth. As far as he was concerned if he had *had* any inkling of the impending USDA announcement he would have taken a massive position and made millions. As it was, an opportunity had been passed up. A state of affairs known in Asia as a Chinese profit.

Somboon looked sullenly at Robbie. 'How much?'

'Somboon, don't push me too far. I've had a rough couple of days and a long flight. I'm sorry that on paper you're losing money. Let's just leave it that; I am too.'

James said something quickly in Teochew to Somboon, who grunted in assent. James spoke carefully to Robbie.

'Given the current uncertainty in the market, I think it might be attractive to Somboon to fix the price of at least half of the contracted tonnage. Am I right, Somboon?' James turned to his cousin.

'No. Not half. Fix the lot. And at last week's price. I still don't—'

James cut in. 'Somboon, it's no good crying over spilt milk. You know as well as I do that the price of sugar moves both up and down. Why don't we just agree to fix fifty per cent at today's price and be done with it?' He fixed Somboon with a look that made it clear he was to argue no further and then added

Hot Stuff

something in Chinese. Lee Lee looked up sharply, her eyes wide open, but said nothing.

'No. Fix the price for the whole contract at the best price we can get now. And I want letters of credit opened by Clyde and Clyde to guarantee payment. If I am to believe Robbie that Clyde and Clyde has lost so much, then I don't particularly want to take the risk of them being unable to pay me in a few weeks time.'

'Aren't you both assuming rather a lot,' cut in Robbie. 'It might not be possible to fix the price of that much sugar the way the price is moving at the moment. And as for the letters of credit, I have to say that I'm bloody insulted.' Having made his point Robbie continued quickly to avoid losing the momentum of the conversation. 'Anyway, let me call London to see if the pricing can be arranged. I'll go up to my room right now.'

The waiter who had been hovering around took the opportunity to ask for orders.

'Shall we get on with ordering the meal,' said James. 'Perhaps we will all feel a bit better once we have eaten.'

'Fine by me,' said Robbie. 'Choose whatever you want. I'll only be away a few minutes.' As he got up to leave, he glanced apologetically across the table at Lee Lee, who gave him a shy but warm smile.

★

Robbie stood in his hotel room, phone in hand, looking out of his window over the glinting Chao Phraya river and waiting for Gordon to answer his direct line. Finally…

'Gordon, he's hooked! The crafty bastard wants to fix the price on the whole contract. He's still bloody pissed off about not selling at last week's price…'

'But that's his damn fault, he could have fixed the price any time he wanted… Just because the greedy little bastard wanted to hang out for an even bigger profit and got his balls cut off in the process…'

'Gordon, that's a wonderfully intellectual, Western view on life. Try telling that to a Thai miller who has just lost – according to his view – $150 million of profit. You wouldn't get very far.

Hot Stuff

You might not even leave the country alive – it costs twenty quid to have someone knocked off here!'

'I guess that's why you're sitting there, not me! But, honestly Robbie, I couldn't put up with all that funny Asian face crap... Anyway, how do you want to play it?'

'The way I see it is like this. Somboon is still convinced in his heart of hearts that we should have seen the American announcement and the price drop coming...'

'But that's craz—'

'Gordon, shut up and listen! Your puritanical Scot's view on trading ethics isn't going to help us out of this hole!'

'Okay, boss. Sorry.'

'Somboon's convinced that he is being ripped off in one way or another. We have to make some sort of gesture to him to give him face and to make sure that he doesn't just walk away from the contract and sell to someone else just to spite us.'

'Do you think he would?'

'Sure as hell... What would he have to lose? If we just fix the price at today's level of about $200 a tonne and he could get the same price from any other trader then he could well walk away just to stuff us up. He loses nothing financially and gains a lot facewise.'

'Shit.'

'Exactly. So we've got to give him a deal that keeps him happy but doesn't cost us too much.'

'So how much are you thinking of giving the little bastard as a present?'

'$50 million.'

'Whaaat!' Robbie could almost feel the line go cold as Gordon tried to come to grips with giving $50 million to someone just to stop them feeling hard done by.'

'Robbie, you're talking to someone whose canny Scottish mother was horrified when she discovered I had taken a mortgage of £30,000 to buy a flat. I don't think I can quite handle this!'

'Look, Gordon, none of us are angels in this deal. By getting rid of the futures that were protecting our price exposure on the Thai purchase price we can take advantage of the drop in the market, right?'

Hot Stuff

'Right.'

'The way we engineered the market the other day in order to dump the futures wouldn't have pleased your mother, right?'

'*Absolutely* bloody right. Although I reckon she would have been pretty good at it!'

'I bet! Anyway, we're selling to the Indonesians at $350 a tonne. If we agree to buy from Somboon at two hundred and fifty instead of the current market of two hundred we still make an extra hundred dollars a tonne and give him a birthday present of $50 million. On one million tonnes we make an additional hundred million dollars. Think of that, Gordon, an *extra* one hundred million dollars. So what if we give the little shit $50 million into the bargain even though we don't think he deserves it!'

'My, my, boss, you have been busy. And I thought you were just sitting in the tropics drinking gin and tonics.'

'Some of that too. I've had to spin Somboon a real hard-luck story about how much we've been losing because of the price moves. We can't make fixing the price of his sugar look too easy. Why don't you call me at the Chao Phraya restaurant over the next hour or so letting me know how you are getting on and how much you have been able to fix. It would probably help if Somboon talked to you direct to hear how tough it is. You know the sort of thing.'

'You bet. Life *is* tough.'

'My heart bleeds. One other thing, I was so bloody convincing in my story about how much we were losing that our friend now wants us to open letters of credit to guarantee the payment.'

'But we would never do that for someone like him... What about our face?'

'You're right. I made out I was deeply offended – which in fact I was. Anyway, I suppose it adds to the authenticity of our story. And for an extra hundred million dollars I'm prepared to lose face as well as give it to Somboon!'

'I think you're selling your soul to the devil.'

'Look, mate, if I can play these guys at their own silly games and make lots of money out of it, I don't give a shit! The only concern I have is persuading de Gruchy to overstep his bank line

Hot Stuff

for us. Can you get him on the other line so that I can set things up while you listen in. Let's see what Banque du Rhône can really do.'

★

De Gruchy rolled down his shirtsleeve, put the syringe in his desk, closed the drawer and locked it. He sat back and relaxed as his body sucked up the heroin. He smiled to himself as he thought of the simplicity of his secretary, who believed he suffered from diabetes.

After a few minutes, he turned towards his laptop and tapped in a code word. He scrolled through his list of private clients. If the introduction made yesterday by Hartono came off he would have almost a billion dollars of client money sitting on deposit.

His direct line rang softly. He heard Gordon's voice on the other end.

'Hello, Victor. I have a hard-working boss currently in Asia on the line for you.'

Victor closed his eyes briefly. He fought to concentrate his mind on Robbie's end of the Clyde and Clyde sugar deal that overall was bringing him so much business to Banque du Rhône. It was imperative that he compartmentalised the different aspects of the transaction that he was handling. For a few seconds his mind swam and Victor thought he would have to hang up and pretend they had been cut off. Finally the pieces fell into place.

'Hi… Gordon. Can you put the great man on?'

The line clicked and Victor could hear Robbie's hollow voice being patched through.

'Hello, Victor. Can you hear me?'

'Sure. Clear as a cracked bell.'

'I guess that's the best we can hope for. Gordon, can you hear too?'

'Aye, boss.'

Robbie took a breath before starting the conversation. 'Victor, we're going to need your help.'

'Given what's happening in the market I thought you might,' replied Victor in a non-committal way, preferring to wait until

Hot Stuff

Robbie had had time to explain what he wanted.

'To cut a long story short, our deal still stands and given the way things have developed we shall be making more out of it than we originally anticipated.'

Victor said nothing. He was beginning to wonder what sort of deal this was. One that seemed to make everyone from China to Indonesia enough money to require the private banking services of Banque du Rhône, while at the same time making a fortune for the traders as well.

There was a pause on the line.

'Victor, can you hear me?'

'Sure. So far I have heard the good news. I'm waiting for the bad reason you are phoning me up!'

'Cynical bugger.'

'Cynical, probably. Realistic, certainly. Not many people from Asia call their banker in the middle of their night for a social chat or to spread good tidings.'

'True as always. But it's not really bad news... just a change in the way the deal will have to be structured.'

'Let me have it.'

'Well, it goes like this. It seems I did such a good job in convincing the supplier...'

'Somboon?'

'Yes, Somboon... in convincing Somboon that Clyde and Clyde were not ripping him off... and that indeed we had ourselves suffered losses due to the gyrations of the market... that he wants all our purchases covered by letters of credit from now!'

'And did you?'

'What?'

'Make socking great losses.'

'Oh. Only Chinese ones.'

'Eh?'

'You know. A missed opportunity to make a profit. However, between you, me, Gordon and the rest of the board we are making out like bandits. But it wouldn't improve the prospects for the deal if Somboon found out.'

'Mmmm. Now I understand why you've called. You want Banque du Rhône to issue letters of credit now for the total value

159

Hot Stuff

of the deal. Say about $200 million. Something that would blow your line of credit of $50 million out of the water and over the equator.'

'If you put it that way, yes. Only the amount will be two hundred and fifty million – we have to build in a few Swiss chocolates for our Thai friend.'

'Typical. And if you don't build in the chocolates and we don't issue the letters of credit, the deal's off.'

'Yes.' Not for the first time, Robbie was amazed at how quickly de Gruchy understood the complexities of a deal. 'But if you do, you'll make a bomb in letter of credit fees.'

And private banking deposits, thought Victor as he sat back in his chair and planned how he could sell the idea to his board.

'Robbie, I'll have a go, but it will be essential that I have cast-iron evidence to work on as far as your sale is concerned. There's no way in hell I can persuade the board to commit to such a large amount of exposure, even for Clyde and Clyde, without cover.'

Robbie replied quickly – he had been working with de Gruchy long enough to know how his mind worked and had already prepared the structure.

'I don't think that'll be a problem, Victor. As you, and only you, know, the final buyer is the Indonesian Government through Hartono – the agent that they've always used. We've got a contract from Hartono and it looks okay. We are flipping the deal through the Chinese just to disguise it. As normal, the individuals concerned want to use their Hong Kong pet company Ever Rich. We'll have the usual contract. All normal stuff that you've seen before.'

'I agree,' said Victor. 'Horrible but normal.'

'Gordon can have our operations guys fax you a copy of all the contracts. But for Christ's sake, keep them confidential. They're dynamite.'

There was a pause. Then Victor spoke coldly. 'Robbie, you're talking to a bank. I hardly think...'

'Okay, Victor, sorry; I overstepped the line. Things are a bit stressed out here...'

'All right. I guess things must be tough for you right now. If Gordon can get me the paperwork I'll give it a shot with the

Hot Stuff

board. There's a credit committee meeting in about an hour. I'll bounce it off them then. No promises.'

'I understand. Can you give me a call on my mobile with the verdict? I'll be trying to keep the Thais happy over dinner.'

Robbie signed off with Victor and Gordon and returned to the dining room. James and Somboon were having an animated conversation in Chinese, with Lee Lee looking on wide-eyed but silent. When they saw Robbie enter the room they fell silent and then switched to English.

'How did it go?' asked James 'You were away more then a few minutes. I'm afraid we started – Thai food isn't good cold. Has the great house of Clyde and Clyde been able to accommodate the request of my honourable cousin? I hope so. He's becoming more than a bit enervated.'

Robbie did his best to put on a confident but concerned smile. He turned towards Somboon.

'Somboon, it'll be tough but I hope we can fix a price that will be better for you that the current market of about two hundred. Gordon will call back over dinner with progress reports. As for the letters of credit, I've spoken to the bank and these are being arranged. Even when Clyde and Clyde have lost a bucket of money it appears that our credit rating is still good! Why don't we all just relax and enjoy dinner while the people in Europe do the work?'

Somboon frowned and agreed grumpily.

Robbie looked at the Thai food spread out over the large table. He was beginning to feel quite hungry. He took a spoonful of the Thom Yum Kung soup and stopped dead in his tracks. The chilli hot but tepid liquid burnt his tongue and the back of his throat before it cut into his stomach. Robbie felt beads of sweat bursting out of his forehead. He looked across at Somboon who for the first time this evening was smiling faintly.

'Have some green curry to go with your soup,' said Somboon, pushing the small bowl of curry in Robbie's direction.

Bastard, thought Robbie. *He never gives up. But he won't win this one.*

'Great stuff, Somboon,' said Robbie taking a gulp of cold Singha beer to douse the fire already raging inside his body. 'You

161

Hot Stuff

know I love Thai food.'

Gordon called up twice during the following hour giving the agreed tales of grief and woe regarding the progress he was making on pricing the sugar. During the second of these calls Somboon spoke to Gordon, who made all the right noises in response to Somboon's bad-tempered questions.

During the course of this conversation Lee Lee caught Robbie's eye and smiled demurely. As Robbie stared at her he was struck not only by her beauty but by the fact that her lips were curling slightly at the corners and her eyes had a knowing look. He quickly looked away, in Somboon's direction.

Robbie's phone rang again. It was Gordon. Robbie spoke to him briefly and then turned to Somboon.

'Okay, so you have fixed the whole million tonnes at an average price of $250 compared to the current price of two hundred. That's $50 a tonne better than you would have got if you were dealing with any of the others. Don't ask me how we did it but, I can tell you for nothing, you should be happy.'

Somboon grunted but said nothing.

As they were drinking their second espresso the phone rang for the fourth time. It was Victor.

'Okay, my sugar trading friend, you've got everything you want. I've probably used up several of my nine lives and stretched the credibility of the board beyond normal Swiss breaking point in the whole process. Anyway, you can sleep easy. Your deal is safe as far as the banking is concerned.'

Robbie tried to suppress as well as he could his feeling of elation so as to keep his response to Victor as flat as possible.

'Thanks. So the letters of credit will be opened later today?'

'It deserved more than a "thanks" but I guess you must be up to your ears with nice Thai people listening in. Please tell them to expect the letters of credit to be advised by their bank tomorrow morning their time. That should make life for you a bit less stressful.'

'I hope so. Thanks again.'

As Robbie rang off he turned to Somboon.

'The letters of credit will be on your desk tomorrow morning. Now you know why you are dealing with Clyde and Clyde and

Hot Stuff

not some tin-pot broker.'

Robbie suddenly felt extremely tired. He stood up abruptly. It was time to make a gesture.

'I hope you lot are now all happy now. You're getting a better price than you deserve and Clyde and Clyde are opening letters of credit – something that we would never normally agree to do. I hope you understand what we are doing for you and how much we want to preserve our good relationship in these difficult times.'

Robbie looked at Somboon who was still unmoved. *Bastard*, he thought. *Perhaps Gordon was right and I've sold my soul.*

'Anyway, whatever your feelings, I'm going to bed.'

★

As Robbie came out of the shower there was a knock on his door. Pulling the thick towelling bathrobe around him, he answered the door to find Lee Lee standing outside. Robbie stared at her in surprise.

'Lee Lee, what on earth are you doing here?'

She smiled the same knowing smile that she had given him earlier in the evening.

'Ask me come in, 'n I tell.'

'You must be crazy,' Robbie blurted. 'Somboon will kill me and probably you too into the bargain.'

'Let me in quick, he don't know. Keep me waiting ou'side 'n you prob'ly right.'

Robbie looked nervously up and down the empty corridor, and then opened the door fully. Lee Lee smiled foxily and walked in.

'Lee Lee, I don't want to seem r-r-rude but what the hell are you doing here?' asked Robbie feeling distinctly ill at ease.

Lee Lee draped herself over an armchair, shook her long ebony hair and lit a cigarette. 'I think I got something int'restin' for you.'

Robbie laughed nervously, lit a Marlboro and looked at Lee Lee's slender legs, which were scarcely covered by her short figure hugging black dress.

163

Hot Stuff

'Does Somboon know you're here?'

Lee Lee looked upwards in exasperation and blew out a stream of smoke. 'You crazy? Course not. He late drinks with cousin James. No need me for three hours maybe.' She paused and giggled. 'Then he can't do much!'

Robbie relaxed slightly. 'Why do you stay with him? He treats you horribly.'

Lee Lee smiled thinly. 'Easy say... money. He very rich... give me nice things,' she paused, ''n drugs.'

Robbie looked startled. 'You m-m-mean you're... er...'

'Junkie. Yes.'

Robbie stared at her in amazement. 'But you don't... er...'

'Look like druggie?' she said, staring straight at him and leaning forward. Her dress rode even higher up her thighs. She made no attempt to pull it down. Robbie felt himself starting to sweat. He took a deep drag on the Marlboro.

'Well... yes... I suppose so. No you d-d-don't look like an addict.'

Lee Lee laughed sharply. 'Same Somboon.'

Robbie looked startled. 'Somboon!'

Lee Lee smiled her knowing smile, happy to have dropped the first of her bombshells. This nice kind Englishman was so innocent. Not like the horrible Somboon who treated her like shit and made her do horrible things. Now she would get her own back. This nice Englishman would help her even if he didn't know what he was doing.

'Yes. Big junkie. Many year. That how we met.'

'Fuck,' said Robbie sitting down.

'There much you don' know,' said Lee Lee flatly. Then she turned to him and smiled. 'That why I like you.'

She came and sat down next to Robbie, put her hand on his knees and then slid it between his thighs. Robbie tensed.

'If you nice to me... very nice, I can tell you many things... big, interestin'. Don' forget, I Thai but Chinese. Understand ever'thin Somboon and others say. And some things v-e-r-y interesting. But first, you be nice to me. Then promise to pay me part of sugar-deal profit.' She slid her hand up to Robbie's crotch and started massaging him gently. 'What you think?'

164

Hot Stuff

Robbie's head started to spin. First the no-hands restaurant and now this. He looked at Lee Lee and tried to think. His heart was pounding. He put his hand on her hip. God, she was a hooker and a junkie with almost certainly a dose of everything nasty known to mankind. But... perhaps... if he was just a little bit nice... he could find out what she was talking about.

Back Trap

Jakarta, Wednesday, 26 April 1995

Dr Amin stood uncomfortably in front of the kindly old uncle shifting his weight slightly from one foot to the other like a naughty schoolboy waiting nervously in front of the headmaster. The uncle looked up from his papers, smiled one of his cold smiles and started to talk. Amin's mind whirred as he tried to pay attention to every nuance of what the President was saying and to detect with as much advance warning as possible the attack that he knew was bound to come. It had to be connected with this damn sugar thing. But what angle was the President going to pick on?

Ever since the price had started to gyrate like crazy, Amin had been trying to get hold of that shark Fang, who was never available. And when he finally did manage to get hold of the rat, all he heard from him were platitudes and soothing words Hartono was no better. But then he was only a post box anyway, and couldn't be expected to do anything more than sign contracts with one pudgy, ring-encrusted hand and to grab kickbacks and commissions with the other. Amin tensed as the President spoke.

'My son, a little bird has told me that the news that we had a crop shortfall had leaked out.'

Amin answered cautiously. 'Y-yes, Pak.'

The President continued. 'One would normally expect the market to go up on a piece of news like that. However, the sugar market has been falling like a rock…'

Amin concentrated, but couldn't detect anything too dangerous as yet. Surely he couldn't be held responsible for the movements in the international sugar price? Cautious assent seemed to be in order.

'Y-yes, Pak.'

The President looked pleasantly at Amin and carried on speaking. 'As you know, I'm not a market man and I don't

Back Trap

understand the first thing about sugar…'

Dr Amin suppressed a shudder as he felt a trap being set. He had worked with the kindly old uncle for too long. He had seen better men than himself lured into the snare by the smiling face and honeyed words. And had seen them twitching out of control with their backs broken when, with the drop of a smile, the kindly old uncle had snapped the jaws closed. Dr Amin's mind worked in overdrive. At all costs he must tread carefully. His job, and more importantly several million dollars of commissions to be paid into his newly opened Swiss bank account, hung by a thread.

'So,' the president continued, 'can you explain what is happening? I thought the Fangs were supposed to be keeping everything secret?'

Dr Amin coughed. It was no good, he would have to start somewhere. He spoke slowly, choosing his words with extreme caution. Each one selected to convey the required degree of clarity while being sufficiently vague to allow him to take cover as soon as the jaws of the trap trembled.

'Er, it is true, Pak, that… that we are using the Fangs for secrecy…'

'Of course it's true. If you recall, it was I who instructed that they should be used for that very purpose. My question is, what bloody well happened?'

Dr Amin was taken back momentarily by the uncle's sudden outburst. This wasn't what he had anticipated. Normally the uncle kept up his pretence of friendliness for longer than this. Dr Amin decided that honesty was the best policy. 'To be honest, Pak…'

'I hate sentences that start like that. They are inevitably followed by a lie.'

'Pak, I have no interest in telling you anything but the truth,' protested Dr Amin with exaggerated honesty.

'Get on with it.'

'As I was saying, I honestly don't know what has happened. I have finally spoken to the young Fang—'

'—Even more of a crook than his father,' grumbled the kindly Uncle.

'Pak, I tend to agree with you…'

Back Trap

'You better had, otherwise you will find yourself an ex-Minister of Agriculture before you can blink.'

'Of course I agree with you, Pak,' added Amin quickly and truthfully. If he had any intention of disagreeing with the kindly Uncle he wouldn't be doing it then and there. 'What I meant was, er… that I believe your assessment of the younger Fang is extremely accurate. He's a crook. But he is, um… normally on our side.'

'What do you mean "normally"?' demanded the uncle. 'Given the amount he must make out of us he should always be on our side.'

Dr Amin sighed to himself and tried to preserve an aura of calm control. Ever since he had received the curt phone call earlier that morning summoning him to the uncle's office he had known this was going to be a bad day. He had hoped against hope that the old devil would remain unaware of what was happening in the sugar market until James Fang had phoned Dr Amin back and given him a full briefing.

'Well, you know… with these Chinese, you are never sure,' said Dr Amin, playing the old Chinese card again in an effort to build some common ground between himself and his tormentor.

'You can say that again,' grumbled the old uncle.

Dr Amin smiled quietly to himself and quickly launched a counter attack.

'Well, Pak, I regret to say that despite the plan to use the Fangs to help us in this instance…' Dr Amin hoped the kindly uncle would recall his outburst a few minutes earlier when he specifically took responsibility for employing Fangs in the first place. In cases like this, however, the uncle tended to have selective memory.

Dr Amin continued, 'I fear that they may be trying to play us out in typical Chinese style.'

The uncle looked thoughtful. 'What do you mean, "play us out"?'

'Well,' continued Dr Amin feeling that he was skating towards thin ice, 'I'm not sure exactly what their game is. But, like you, Pak, I was horrified when the news appeared on Reuters, and expected to see the price going up. I tried to call the Fangs but

Back Trap

couldn't get them. I think they were avoiding me.'

'Brilliant,' sneered the uncle. 'I can see how you got a doctorate.'

Dr Amin bit his tongue. Direct insults were not a problem. They would not cause fatal damage. He was far more worried by the unanticipated U-turn from an Exocet armed with a nuclear warhead.

The uncle spoke quietly. 'Tell me, my son, why we shouldn't be worried that the market won't turn round when it realises that we really are short of a million tonnes of sugar. And we have to spend a large proportion of our national reserves buying the bloody stuff.'

Dr Amin felt a surge of joy. If this was the problem, he had the answer at his fingertips. He was safe. He puffed himself up a little and announced rather grandly, 'Because, Pak, I signed a fixed-price contract with the Fangs for the whole contract of a million tonnes at the old price level of $350.'

The room went silent. The old uncle raised his head and his eyes flashed. After a few seconds that seemed like an eternity he spoke softly, slowly and with icy precision. 'My son, are you telling me that because you signed a fixed-price contract to buy one million tonnes of sugar at $350 a tonnes, we are unable to take advantage of a drop in the market of $200?' As he spoke, the colour rose in the kindly old uncle's cheeks. 'Are you honestly telling me that because of your fucking stupidity we are going to be paying $200 million more than we need to? Because if you are, I wouldn't want to be standing in your shoes.'

Dr Amin's head swam and he broke out in a sweat. He felt weak at the knees. The trap had been sprung and the sharp jaws had snapped around his tubby body. His back had been broken and he knew he was dead meat at the mercy of the cruel hunter masquerading as a kindly uncle.

Dr Amin stuttered. 'Pak, I... er... Fang... er...'

'Stop spluttering and sounding pathetic,' barked the uncle. 'Who exactly have you signed this contract with?'

Dr Amin slumped unbent into a chair and started to say 'The Fa...,' but stopped in his tracks. What a bloody fool he was. At the end of the day he hadn't actually signed a contract with anyone!

169

Back Trap

That slob Hartono had signed a fixed-price contract with Clyde and Clyde using the Fangs as an agent. All Dr Amin had done was to create the strong impression in the mind of Hartono that the Indonesian Government would eventually buy the sugar from him. Nothing, absolutely nothing, had been put in writing between Hartono and the Government. Not a word. And if he, Dr Amin, the Minister of Agriculture, didn't want to buy from Hartono then the Government wasn't committed. It was as simple as that. His back wasn't broken! Dr Amin was cleverer than he had ever thought. Turning to the uncle, he spoke deferentially but firmly.

'Pak, with every due respect, I don't think I am sounding pathetic. Neither have I prevented us from taking advantage of the fall in price. As you know, the system is that we always route our purchases through a vehicle…'

'Yes, yes, I know,' said the Uncle, sounding on edge and not wishing to have the existing system examined in too much detail. 'So bloody what?'

'Well, Pak, the way I have always seen it,' said Dr Amin lying through his teeth, 'is that this is the same as giving us an… an… option.' Dr Amin had read a lot about options recently. He felt they sounded rather grand without being too sure exactly what they were.

'Stop talking in riddles.'

'Pak, what I mean is that, since the Government has not signed a contract with Hartono, we are not obliged to agree to anything we don't like.'

The President looked quizzically at Amin and said slowly, 'You mean, if the price at the time delivery is supposed to take place looks good then we actually take the sugar. If, on the other hand, the price looks too high versus what we could buy for in the open market, then we don't?'

'Exactly, Pak,' said Dr Amin, trying to sound as though something he had just thought of had been the basis of his way of working for years. 'Heads we win, tails we don't lose.'

'Hmmm. We have never had to use the "tails we don't lose" option before?'

'No, Pak, because the price has never dropped this much

Back Trap

before. But it has always been at the root of my thinking.'

Dr Amin began to feel guilty about telling two such whopping great lies in as many minutes. He quickly put any guilt feelings to the back of his mind when he weighed up the alternatives.

The uncle smiled once more and looked at Dr Amin. 'Amin, it seems that even after all these years I have underestimated you. You plan is excellent. Tell Hartono he had better start taking more sugar in his coffee if he is ever going to use up all that sugar he has ordered. He certainly won't be selling any to us at $350!'

★

Hartono sat in front of Amin's desk. His jaw dropped.

'You can't do that.'

'I'm not. The old man is.'

'Then you're both nuts.'

'You can tell me that, but I wouldn't advise telling him. The mood he is in he might not like it.'

'So what do you expect me to do about it?'

'To be honest, Hartono, I don't know. You could be a good boy and take the loss of renegotiating the, er... understanding with the Government.'

'You mean you.'

'Me as a simple servant of the Government.'

'Bastard.'

'Or you could rat on your purchase contract with Clyde and Clyde and buy again from someone else at a lower price. It's up to you. However, knowing you as I do, I would think ratting was the most likely route.'

'Double bastard.'

'Look Hartono, the only thing you have to bear in mind is that I have a big incentive to support whatever course of action you decide to take. Unless this bloody contract goes through neither of us get any Swiss chocolates. And don't forget, I still have you by the balls. So please stop calling me names.'

'I knew as soon as you started to take too much of an interest in the way this business works we would have a problem. I just never thought it would be this big.'

171

Back Trap

'Why don't you look at it as an opportunity to make more money than you were making previously? All you have to do is explain to James that it has just been made clear to you that you didn't have the authority of the Government to sign the contract with Clyde and Clyde. Very sorry and all that but your signature was invalid. However, you are sure that you would be able to obtain the necessary authority to sign a replacement contract at a lower price. I expect they would all understand.'

'You're mad. Do you really think Clyde and Clyde are just going to renegotiate a contract like that? They're not a bloody charity you know!'

'The way I look at it, it's not really renegotiating. They don't actually have a sales contract. All they have is a piece of paper signed by you that isn't worth peanuts. And certainly not one million tonnes of sugar.'

'Jesus, you are bloody mad,' said Hartono realising he didn't have a leg to stand on and slamming the door as he stormed out of Dr Amin's office.

Singapore, Thursday, 27 April '95

James felt sick as he put the phone down. He bit his expensively manicured fingernails as his brain analysed what he had just been told. Hartono was ratting on the deal. He started to sweat. There was no way this deal could be allowed to fail. His whole life depended on it. Or at least it depended on the first shipment taking place. The first shipment that would contain one tonne of rather special white powder. If Hartono got to Clyde and Clyde first and told them what he had just told James, God knows what would happen. But whatever it was, it wouldn't be nice and it certainly wouldn't improve the chances of the transaction going through. The whole plan would come unstuck.

James punched the table and willed his brain to work quicker. For God's sake, what were the options? Think, dammit, he had to think. If Clyde and Clyde lost their sale to Hartono they would be left with one million tonnes of sugar that they had bought from Somboon at $250 a tonne. And given the way the market had continued to fall this was worth only $150 at today's market price. Heaven knows how low the market would be tomorrow. If they

Back Trap

had to resell the sugar at today price Clyde and Clyde would be looking down the barrel of a $100 million loss. This combined with the earlier losses they had surely made because of the unanticipated price drop, must certainly be enough to bankrupt the company. And a bankrupt company wouldn't take any sugar shipments, let alone the all-important first one. Shit, he had to think...

It wasn't difficult to guess the reason behind Hartono's decision to back out of the deal. He must be looking pretty stupid having signed a contract to buy at $350 a tonne when the price was so low today. There would be no way that he could persuade the bloody old shark to revise his decision and perform even if he wanted to. Even if he was able to arrange an even larger commission payment for Hartono, James guessed that wasn't the key problem. No, the real difficulty was the political unacceptability of Indonesia being seen to be buying sugar at such a high price compared to the current market.

The only way to save the situation would be to work on Somboon to get him to accept a price reduction. And God knows that would be nigh on impossible. The miserable bastard was still fuming at having been ripped off by Clyde and Clyde. But, it was the only way; it had to work.

First things first: he had to get to Robbie before Hartono did. He picked up the phone and punched in Robbie's private-line number.

On the Road Again

London, Thursday, 27 April 1995

Robbie sat in his swivel chair feeling elated. He was still thinking about the call he had received from Julia on his private private line two hours ago.

'Robbie, we've... I mean, I've... Oh damn, I don't give a shit, we've bloody well done it! I just spoke to the last broker. He's just bought back all those thousands of tonnes of futures things that we... er, I mean, I sold without having them. Robbie, we sold at an average of $300 a tonne and bought at an average of $200 a tonne, which means that on 50,000 tonnes we've made $5 million! Robbie – $5 million! That gives us your drop dead money twice over not to mention the other bits and pieces we've managed to tuck away. You can tell Clyde and bloody Clyde together with all your horrible trading clients to go to hell and retire today. Robbie, just think of it... five million...'

Robbie, was silent for a few seconds.

'Robbie, are you still there?' demanded Julia, wanting him to share in her excitement.

'Yes, sweetie, I'm here. J-just thinking about it as you said.'

'So will you tell Charles to go to hell today?'

'No, not yet.'

'You're crazy. Why not? I don't think you should stay in that office a moment longer than you need to.'

'It's not that simple, love. First of all, when this Indonesian deal is all through I should get a bonus of anything up to half a million quid. I certainly won't get that if I tell Charles to eff off.' Robbie hesitated and Julia jumped into the conversation with cold scientist's precision.

'And secondly?'

Robbie hesitated again. 'Well, love, it's not that easy to explain... and I don't want to get into it over the phone... But

On the Road Again

there's another big reason why I've got to see this deal through…'

'Robbie, you're talking in riddles…'

'I know, love. But I promise, I won't stay any longer than I need to. Honest. Trust me.'

They talked for a few minutes more and then Julia rang off, completely fed up that Robbie was putting such a dampener on her enthusiasm.

On a couple of occasions during the past week Robbie had allowed himself a daydream about how to deal with the money they hoped to make on their futures dealing. He had hardly dared to believe the cash would really be theirs. But now it was and he had to act fast. He would have to be extremely careful how he played his cards. Whatever happened he didn't want people asking any awkward questions. Everyone knew he didn't come from an affluent background. When he finally quit, the official line would be that a rich relation of Julia's had just left her a chunk of money. This combined with the bonus he had received from the Indonesian deal gave them enough to live on.

His conscience would just about allow him to live with the fact that he had used Clyde and Clyde's weight in the market to allow him, or at least Julia under his direction, to take a position that had made them a fortune. At the end of the day, their little flutter was peanuts compared to the total amount being bet by Clyde and Clyde. And anyway, he had made Clyde and Clyde twenty times as much as he had gained on the whole exercise. An investigation from the firm's compliance officers, however, might not take such a liberal view. No, he would have to be extremely careful.

He had discussed all this at length with Julia last night. Today he would start putting their plan into action. He picked up his private private line, dialled Banque du Rhône, turned his back to the dealing desk and spoke quietly into the phone.

'Hello, Victor. How's life?'

On the other end of the line Victor de Gruchy quickly tried to think of all the possible bad reasons for an unsolicited phone call from Robbie. On the spur of the moment he couldn't think of any, which annoyed him and put him on the defensive.

'Well, I was all right until I received a call from one Robert

Smith, tycoon of the sugar trade. You know how unrequited phone calls from you always make me nervous. Put me out of my misery; what's up?'

Robbie grinned to himself. 'I never knew I had such power over bankers. I'll have to use it more often in future. Anyway, this isn't a call from a sugar tycoon, whatever one of those is. It's from a rich husband.'

Victor felt lost. 'Glad to hear it. I've been trying to become one of those for ages; however, my wife always gets in the way!'

'Well, mine did until her great Aunt Min, or whatever the wonderful woman's name was, popped off and left Julia a chunk of money. My plan is to put it somewhere safe before she gets stuck into it. Mind you, she would have to try pretty hard to demolish the whole lot.'

'Congratulations, I never knew Julia was such a catch,' said Victor, fishing.

Robbie started to tell the story that he and Julia had rehearsed the previous night, hoping it sounded credible.

'Well, actually…'

God, never use 'actually'; it's a dead giveaway, Robbie thought as he heard himself talking.

'…Neither did I. Nor, for that matter, did she. Its not one of those t-t-total mysteries where the lucky person is phoned up out of the blue by a solicitor to tell them that they have been left millions, but it isn't far off.'

'You're kidding!'

'Happily not.'

'So what happened?' said Victor sounding genuinely interested but noting that Robbie was beginning to stutter. He had known Robbie for years. The stutter only appeared when he was under stress. He guessed that receiving a fortune out of the blue was stressful, But still…

'Well, great Aunt Min is actually Aunt Shirley who is, or was bless her, Julia's mother's elder sister. She married an older man who had made a lot of money in the East after the war as a r-r-rubber broker. Anyway, they never had children and rather adopted Julia when they were home in England during their long holidays.'

On the Road Again

Victor groaned. 'Don't tell me, let me guess. Hubby pops off a long time ago and Julia, quite innocently, keeps in touch with her rich, widowed aunt who finally falls off the perch leaving her all to Julia.'

'You've h-h-heard it before!' said Robbie, hoping that the trite story was sufficiently plausible through its simplicity.

'Lucky bastard,' said Victor with feeling.

Robbie smiled to himself. Success: Victor was hooked.

'Go on,' said Victor, 'make my day thoroughly miserable. How much was it.'

'Gross or n-n-net?' asked Robbie beginning to enjoy himself but wishing to God his stutter would go away.

'You know, I could really get to dislike you,' Victor paused. 'Net, of course. To be honest, I don't really care that the tax man has put his hand in the till.'

'In round figures, five million.'

'Pounds?'

Robbie winced at his stupid mistake. Of course Aunt Shirley would normally leave them a fortune denominated in pounds. He quickly tried to patch over the inconsistency in his story.

'No, unfortunately n-n-not, it's in d-d-dollars. The old man got so fed up with the UK when he returned from the East that he shifted all his portfolio into dollars.'

'Oh well, that's okay then. I'll still talk to you. If it had been sterling I'm afraid my jealousy would have been too great!' said Victor, only half joking. 'So I guess the good news for me is that you'd like to employ the services of Banque du Rhône to look after your newly acquired fortune and to ensure that Julia doesn't spend all of her money. By the way, isn't that a bit unfair? After all, it is her money!'

'Don't worry, I'm not hijacking it,' laughed Robbie. 'She will happily fill in any forms you want. To be honest, I think she's more worried about keeping the cash than I am.'

'Honest woman!'

'Yes, and honest cash too,' said Robbie seizing the opportunity to ram home the point. 'I would guess that the origins of the money are slightly more straightforward than some of the cash you look after.'

On the Road Again

'No comment,' said Victor sounding stern. 'Why don't the two of you pop over here for a day soon to sign a few bits of paper? In the meantime, I'll set up an account for you so we can look after the cash as and when you get your hands on it. We'll look after it carefully. Along with all the other money from quite legitimate sources that we care for!'

Robbie winced as the banker delivered his last line, signalling that in his heart of hearts he didn't believe Robbie's story. However, Victor had enough background on file to justify keeping the deposit, which was all he was required to do. There was no need to be more royalist than the King.

★

Robbie sat back in his chair, stared at St. Paul's and wondered whether he could trust de Gruchy. Or indeed whether he had any other option but to trust him. Bloody bankers. They were a nuisance when you wanted to borrow money and almost as much of a pain when you wanted to deposit it. The cut-throat world of sugar trading was far more straightforward by comparison! Robbie was jolted out of his daydreaming by his private line ringing. James was on the other end sounding unusually agitated.

'Robbie, thank goodness I got to you.'

Robbie tensed. Perhaps sugar trading wasn't so easy.

'James, what's happened?'

'It's that bastard Hartono, he's reneging on the contract.'

'Wha'd'ya mean?'

'Exactly what I said. He's ratting on the bloody contract.'

'He can't – he represents the Indonesian Government. Governments don't default just like that.'

'But that's just it,' said James sounding beside himself with anguish. 'As far as Hartono is concerned, he says he's just an agent of the Indonesians. And the Indonesian Government is pretty unimpressed about paying $350 a tonne for their sugar when the market price is one hundred and fifty. They say that Hartono had no right to bind them to a contract of such size and at such a price without their specific instruction or agreement. Furthermore I'm bloody sure they'd swear blind that Hartono isn't their official

178

On the Road Again

agent as such – which is probably quite true as far as the letter of the law is concerned.'

'James, what do you mean…' snapped Robbie.

'It's quite simple, Robbie. When Clyde and Clyde sign a contract with Hartono that's just what it is – a contract with Hartono. There is never any mention of the Indonesian Government.'

'But everyone knows he's the s-s-same thing as the Indonesian Government. He's been representing them for years. We've done millions and m-m-millions of dollars worth of business with them through him…'

'I realise that, Robbie. But that's not the point…'

'Well, what the hell is?'

'The point is that, like it or not, when Clyde and Clyde sign a contract with Hartono, you're dealing with him as an individual, not the Indonesian Government. If the Government choose to buy from him, that's their business. Same as if they choose not to buy from him. Which is what's happening now. Catch twenty-two.'

'Like bloody hell it is,' snorted Robbie. 'They've been doing b-b-business this way for ages. They can't just change the r-r-rules when it suits them.'

'Well…' said James nervously. 'I know what you mean but I think you're viewing the problem from the Western end of the telescope. From their point of view, I think they would say that it's unrealistic to expect their Government to pay millions of dollars more for sugar than they would have to pay if they bought at today's price. And the fact that Hartono is in the middle gives them the almost perfect excuse for not going ahead with the old contract. In fact, from their point of view there isn't an old contract. The only contract that exists is between you guys and Hartono. Finito.'

Robbie exhaled slowly and tried to think. He must take it slowly. No point in becoming over-emotional.

'James, do you have any evidence on file linking the Indonesian Government with H-H-Hartono. Anything at all?'

'I think so… as far as previous deals are concerned.' James went quiet for a little and then continued 'But then, I'm not so

On the Road Again

sure. You know how it's always been before. Hartono has always performed. We know he's been paid by the Indonesian Government. But I suppose we've never had any hard evidence where the money's actually come from. Neither do we have any agreement between him and the Government. I mean, it never seemed necessary...'

'Jesus, James...'

James continued, 'And what's more, even if we had asked for one we wouldn't have got it. Everyone knows how the system works, how Hartono fits in, and that he's the conduit we have to go through. That's it. Ask no questions.'

'But tell a shitload of l-l-lies.'

'I guess so.'

Robbie closed his eyes. This was the scenario that the auditors always pointed out and against which he had always argued so vehemently. Of course, on paper this was the risk. But it was only a risk because they as little bureaucrats didn't understand how the business worked. Now if they would kindly get out of his hair and let him continue running his business he could go on making millions for the company like he had always done... That bastard Hartono... now perhaps the little bureaucrats would have a chance to get their own back!

Robbie reviewed the situation quickly. It really looked as though they could be losing their buyer. Or, at least, at the price previously agreed. As far as James knew, this left Clyde and Clyde exposed to a loss of one hundred million dollars. They would have to resell one million tonnes of sugar for a price of $150. Sugar that they had finally bought from Somboon at the price of $250 that he had negotiated in Bangkok earlier this week. No wonder James was wetting himself. But what James didn't know, and must never know, was that Clyde and Clyde was already sitting on a cool $100 million got from riding the roller coaster. The last thing Robbie wanted was to lose this money, and along with it his bonus. On the other hand, it did mean that the little games being played by the Indonesians would at worst have no impact at all on Clyde and Clyde. If they really defaulted, there would be a lot of lost potential profit – but that was all in theory. In practice, he was buggered if he was going to let the Indos off

180

On the Road Again

the hook so easily. It was just too simple for them. Now was the time for James to start earning his commission. Robbie spoke slowly.

'James, you know what this could mean?'

James thought carefully how he should answer what on the face of it was a simple question, but in fact opened a Pandora's box of repercussions. He decided to go for the straightforward approach. 'Yes, one hell of a big loss.'

'Not just that, my friend. Clyde and Clyde goes bust, I l-l-lose my job and my bonus and you don't get a cent of commission. Somboon loses his sale and the profit, which he fought for so much in B-B-Bangkok. The Chinese lose their rake-off for putting the deal through their shady Hong Kong Company. As for you, in addition to losing your commission from us, you also lose whatever share of Somboon's profit you have negotiated behind the scenes...'

Robbie paused. Time to get tough. He continued, 'Together with whatever kickbacks you were supposed to get from the Chinese and H-H-Hartono. Not only that, but you might want to consider increasing your life insurance premiums as far as the Chinese are concerned. They seem to have a major sense of humour failure as far as losing m-m-money is concerned.'

James started to protest and then decided not to. Now wasn't the time to protect his reputation. In any event, bloody Robbie was absolutely right. This guy was more Chinese than a Chinese. All James was interested in was somehow keeping the deal afloat, at least for the first shipment.

'Look, Robbie, I know the situation looks bad but I don't think it helps to get personal.'

Having made his position clear, Robbie could afford to back off. 'No, James, you're right. Sorry. But I think you get the p-p-point. At the end of the day, the only way I can see of salvaging any of this is to negotiate something with Somboon and the Indonesians. We can and will make all sorts of aggressive noises towards the bastards about d-d-defaulting, but the bottom line is that I don't think we have much of a leg to s-s-stand on. Our only hope is to come up with a reworked deal that gives them enough of a price reduction to make them feel they are not getting ripped

181

off, and at the same time make them able to honour their purchase contract.'

'Yes, but that price will have to be pretty near today's market,' butted in James. He knew what Robbie was driving at but didn't want him to make it sound too easy.

'Look, James, basically the bottom line for Clyde and Clyde has to be performance at a price that allows us to pay Somboon and receive enough money from H-H-Hartono to more or less cover what we owe. I'm sure we can put our hands in our pockets a little bit. But not to the tune of $100 million. You are really going to have to earn your commission talking to both Somboon and the Indonesians. The Chinese won't care what price the contracts are fixed at – they are only getting a fixed commission anyway.'

Robbie paused, waiting for James to respond.

Finally James said quietly, 'Do you really think it can still work?'

'Yes, provided we all give a bit. And that means you too, James. Just think of all the commissions you and your father have earned from our d-d-deals over the years. Now it's pay day. As far as I can see, for the moment the main problem isn't going to be any of Somboon, the Indonesians or the Chinese.'

'What do you mean?' asked James, truly perplexed.

'It's going to be the Swiss. Imagine what Banque du Rhône is going to say when they discover that because of the Indonesians falling out of the picture, they've just lost most of their collateral! They've opened l-l-letters of credit to buy sugar for $250 a tonne that is now worth only one hundred and fifty. Shit!'

'Oh God. I see what you mean. What can you do about that?'

'I honestly don't know,' lied Robbie. 'But what I do know is that I had better t-t-talk to them before they find out from the market what's going on. These guys have ears everywhere. In the meantime, you'd better start working on your dear cousin Somboon to explain the facts of l-l-life. I can tell you for nothing that if Clyde and Clyde goes bust then Banque du Rhône is going to go over any documents that Somboon submits to them in order to claim under the letters of credit with the finest of fine-toothed combs. The chances of him getting any money out of

On the Road Again

them, letter of credit or no, is probably less than zero. In this game no one wins but the b-b-bank.'

'Same as usual,' grumbled James. 'Give me a couple of hours to work on Somboon and I will get back to you. Wish me luck.'

'As always. Just think of your commissions. That should help.' The line went dead and Robbie started to plan the conversation he was about to have with Victor.

★

'Robbie – twice in one day. Don't tell me bad health and good luck is beginning to run in the family!'

'Victor this is s-s-serious,' said Robbie. It was important that he kept the banker where he wanted him.

'I told you I didn't like your uninvited calls. What's the matter?'

'The Indonesians are r-r-reneging. They say the contract never existed.'

'And does it?'

'Sort of.'

'Robbie, stop jerking me about. Is there a bloody contract or not? You swore blind to me over the phone the other day from Bangkok that the deal was structured like all the others and that you had sold to the Indonesians through Hartono as normal. Gordon sent me copies of all the documents.'

'We did sell to Hartono. It's just that Hartono has decided not to honour his contract. He's arguing that he didn't have the right to s-s-sign a contract on behalf of the Indonesian Government in the first place. So all we have is a contract that begins and ends with H-H-Hartono himself. No Government backing. And there is no bloody way Hartono can or will perform if the Government isn't in the picture.'

'Bastards.'

'Agreed. But at the end of the day we d-d-don't have anything in writing direct with the Indonesian Government. If they or Hartono want to shaft us they can.'

'And are!' said de Gruchy angrily. 'God, what a fucking mess this could develop into. You realise that I virtually forced the

183

On the Road Again

board to approve opening your letters of credit based on the backing of the Indonesian Government purchase. They will go completely bloody crazy if they discover that I was having them on, albeit inadvertently. Holy shit! I'm dead meat! Christ almighty...'

Robbie was taken aback at the way Victor was losing control. This was completely out of character. What was the matter with him?

'Look, Victor, it needn't be as bad as all that.'

'Are you completely bloody mad? What could make it better?'

'Cash collateral.'

'Robbie, give me a break. Your dubious Aunt Min left $5 million. Here we are talking about $250 millions. Unless you have fifty more Aunt Mins lurking around, or are preparing to tell me the truth about where your money really came from, I don't see it.'

'Victor, keep Aunt Min out of this,' said Robbie sharply. 'That's my private business and has absolutely nothing to do with Clyde and Clyde.'

'If you say so... Anyway, Robbie, you're quite right. Sorry. I'm getting a bit worked up...' Victor breathed deeply and tried to get a grip on himself. It was getting well past the time for his next fix.

'It's just that... it's the thought of going to the board with news of misleading them about $250 million.'

Robbie was becoming more and more puzzled by de Gruchy's erratic behaviour. He was almost glad to be able to let the poor guy off the hook.

'Victor, you won't have to. But this has to stay between you, me and the board. Is that clearly understood.'

'Yes, yes, of course. What are you talking about?'

'Okay, you remember I told you we were making out like bandits by taking a position against Somboon?'

'Yes...'

'Well, we've closed out and made $100 million.'

'My God.'

'Obviously Somboon doesn't know, otherwise he would blow a fuse.'

'I can imagine!'

184

On the Road Again

'Well, that money is sitting in cash and can be moved to your bank on the strict understanding that it backs up the letters of credit. Since the market price of the sugar is currently about $150 million, this, plus the cash deposit of one hundred, gives you dollar-for-dollar cover for your purchase commitments of $250 million. Something even your credit committee should find attractive.'

It was some time before Victor de Gruchy spoke. His voice was thick with emotion. 'Robbie, I... I don't know why you're doing this... but thanks. You know without it I would be for the high jump.'

'Let's just say we're friends. Remember it's just between us girls.'

As Robbie hung up he heaved a sigh of relief. This deal had to go through. More than just his bonus depended on it.

*

The line between Bangkok and Singapore sizzled, as James explained to Somboon why he shouldn't have to worry about accepting a much lower price than originally agreed. To James' amazement, Somboon finally accepted the logic regarding the money they would make from the first shipment and therefore the importance of preserving the structure of the whole deal. Why had he changed his mind all of a sudden? This was most unlike his pig-headed cousin. Anyway, changed it he had.

*

'Robbie, I'm still not really sure why he agreed to take a cut given all the fuss he was making the other night. In fact, he hasn't fully agreed yet. He wants to talk to you first...'

I bet he does, thought Robbie, *And I bet I know why he agreed to the cut.*

'You mean to hear me crawl?' Robbie asked sharply.

'Don't put it like that. You are asking him to give up a profit of several million dollars in order to keep the deal afloat and to prevent Clyde and Clyde going bust. The least you could do is to

185

On the Road Again

ask him personally.'

'I suppose you're right. How much is he prepared to come down?'

'He wants each party to lose equally. If we assume that there's a difference of about $200 a tonne between the price the Indos originally bought at…'

'It's not what they *originally* bought at,' interrupted Robbie, 'it's the *real* price they bought at – before they bloody well defaulted. You're beginning to sound like them!'

'Look, Robbie, it's no good getting on your Western high horse. The reality of the situation is that they aren't going to back up the original deal – whichever way you bloody well want to look at it.'

Robbie tensed. 'I know, I know. It's just that it makes me bloody well puke to think how easily they just default and then we all run around like idiots trying to make things nice for them. Bastards.'

'Reality of business in Asia,' said James coldly. 'You should be happy we aren't trying to deal with the Vietnamese! Then you'd really find out what a contract wasn't worth.'

'Don't even think about it, James.'

'Right, so the loss between the first price and today's market is about $200. Split three ways this comes to about $66 a tonne each.'

'It should be four ways. What about your share?'

'Don't worry… I'm having to subsidise Somboon in this.'

'Hmmmm… What do the bloody Indonesians say?'

'I've had a word with Hartono. I reckon he'll put his hand in his pocket – or at least in the Government's – for his share. If they can get a reduction of $120 million they will reinstate the contract. That means that you will have to cough up the same. What do you think?'

Robbie went silent. That would reduce their extra roller coaster gain to less than fifty million. Still not a bad haul in the circumstances. Plus, if the deal stayed alive, they would still make their original profit from the deal itself – that was another fifty million.'

Robbie spoke thoughtfully. 'This whole thing really makes me

On the Road Again

sick. It's not just what I think, the board will have to agree. They'll go berserk... I can't promise anything, but I suppose it will have to be acceptable...'

'Right. It's better than going bust.'

'That's the argument I shall use to the board,' said Robbie flatly. I just don't know. Anyway, I've sorted the bank out. Don't ask me how, but I wouldn't approach them for a loan for the next few days.'

'Robbie, you're a genius.'

Both men went quiet. James spoke first.

'I guess that means that the deal is probably still on the road?'

'Yup. But I don't want another day like today!' He hung up.

Robbie closed his eyes, leaned back in his chair and breathed deeply. *On the road, but where to?* He thought to himself as he prepared to make one final call on his private private line before leaving for home. It was time for him to talk to Slade.

Sea Sore

South China Sea, Monday, 29 May 1995

The Chinese rust bucket creaked, groaned and shuddered as she changed course slowly, to face again straight into the eye of the tropical storm. The ancient vessel wallowed and rolled in the surging sea, her spent engines pounding as they fought against the screaming typhoon that tortured her rigging and the squalls of rock-hard rain that lashed her hatches. Hatches which the *Double Jade*'s unshaven, hollow-eyed captain knew protected 300,000 bags of sugar. And another twenty bags of an extremely special cargo. The captain swore bitterly as the wind shifted again. He barked an order into the greasy intercom.

He had not been told what the extremely special cargo was. What he *had* been told was that if anything happened to it his throat would be cut. And he had seen enough of life in charge of a rust bucket plying the seas in the Far East to take the threat seriously. Nothing untoward was going to happen to the special cargo if he had anything to do with it. Neither was his throat going to be cut. Somboon's brother Kriangsak, standing next to the captain on the bridge, would be witness to both facts.

The crew down below hung onto whatever piece of secure metal they could find and speculated as to what was happening on this strange voyage. When they had left Bangkok this storm had been forecast. They knew it. The captain knew it. Normally he would have seized this golden opportunity to prolong their stay in the sex capital of Asia. But not this time. This time they had set sail smack into the face of a severe tropical storm, which had hit them as they had steamed out of the Gulf of Siam and into the South China Sea.

And that was another odd thing. Normally they would have followed the coastal shipping lane, which hugged the Vietnamese coast. When you were in a vessel as old and badly maintained as

Sea Sore

the *Double Jade* there was little point in taking excessive risks. But on this trip they had set a course into the middle of the South China Sea, miles from anywhere and as far removed from passing ships as you could imagine. If they had a problem now, they were doomed.

With each change of direction and shriek from the tortured ship the crew reconsidered their position and cursed the captain and whatever damned game he was playing.

For his part the captain had no illusions. He had been given extremely precise instructions and the promise of a large sum of money to encourage him to follow them to the letter. He pored over the chart covering the remote part of the South China Sea into which he had been told to sail. They were exactly where he had been told to be, at exactly the time he had been told to be there. He cracked his finger joints, hawked and then cracked a half-toothed smile at Kriangsak who didn't respond. The captain spoke in the Chinese dialect that they had in common.

'What's the matter, honourable friend? Are you feeling sad that you won't be able to cut my neck?'

'To be honest, I don't give a shit about your sacred neck. I just earnestly wish this heap of junk you call a ship would stop moving around. I think I'm going to throw up.'

'Well, don't do it on the bridge, honourable friend. It might not look much, but this is an extremely clean ship. Go outside… You might get blown overboard!' The captain cackled, hawked again, swore at yet another wind change and shouted an order in Chinese to the engine room.

He looked at the forlorn Thai. 'Don't worry, honourable friend. Unfortunately you won't die. The *Double Jade* won't sink and this lady will have departed in an hour or so. That is the way of women and tropical storms. Don't you agree?'

In the final analysis, it took three hours for this particular lady to leave. However, the wind finally dropped, leaving behind a legacy of a long-rolling swell. The *Double Jade* settled down into a rhythmic, sickening, see-sawing motion. The captain checked their position for the tenth time, looked at the late-afternoon sky and scanned the sea through a pair of binoculars. Suddenly he stiffened.

189

Sea Sore

'She's here.'

'Where? Show me,' said Kriangsak, forgetting his seasickness and grabbing the binoculars from the captain.

'About a mile away over there. Heading straight for us.'

'I can't see a thing.'

'That's why you need me, honourable friend,' said the captain.

The two men waited in silence. The *Double Jade*'s engines throbbed steadily, far happier now that they no longer had to compete with a tropical storm.

Suddenly the sea, about 600 yards away, began to boil. The conning tower and then the black threatening hull of a submarine burst out of the sea. Water streamed off the massive shiny hulk, which dwarfed the *Double Jade*.

'Shit, it's enormous,' gasped the captain, staring at the 300-foot-long submarine. 'I never thought they were so big.'

'Get nearer,' commanded Kriangsak.

'My honourable friend, with all due respect to my neck, you know fuck all about the sea. That monster is far more manoeuvrable than we are despite its size. Our job is to stay still. They can do the moving.'

As he spoke, a figure dressed in dark blue or black appeared at the top of the conning tower. He shouted an instruction in heavily accented English into a megaphone.

'Hold course... speed... Not move unless we tell you. Get ready boarded.'

The captain gave a Chinese translation of the instruction into his intercom as the submarine slowly approached the *Double Jade* like a glistening, panting mammoth.

'Secure boarding line,' commanded the figure on the conning tower as a flare with a rope attached was fired in the direction of the *Double Jade*.

'I don't like this... very dangerous... The sea is still rough... We could be damaged. This is an old ship. I don't think we should do this...' complained the captain as he moved around the bridge checking the position and status of his ship.

Kriangsak looked directly at him and spoke sternly. 'I don't give a shit what you think. Just do what the man with the megaphone says.'

Sea Sore

Still grumbling the captain gave an order to fix the line between the two rolling vessels. As soon as the line was secured, a burly figure dragged himself along it commando style on a pulley, seemingly fearless of being crushed between the two vessels or dropped into the frothing grey sea.

'This man is very strong,' muttered the captain with a mixture of awe and fear. 'In all my time at sea, I've never seen anyone do that before.'

The figure arrived at the *Double Jade*'s deck rail, pulled himself over it with incredible agility for someone so thickset, and landed nimbly on the deck brandishing a revolver. He was followed close behind by another equally thickset man armed with an Uzi machine gun.

'Welcome aboard. No need for guns,' said the captain nervously to the first arrival.

'Shut up!' replied the first arrival. 'Where is it?'

Kriangsak moved forward slightly. He spoke with more authority than he felt he really had in the face of the gun-toting figures in black. 'Down below.' He gulped slightly. 'And that's where it's going to stay until the money is transferred.'

'Who you?' demanded the second arrival, pointing the Uzi at the jittery Kriangsak.

Kriangsak took a breath. 'Somboon's brother. And please put your guns away otherwise we won't get far.'

Neither arrival moved. 'Where Somboon?'

Kriangsak looked at the first man. 'He was unable to come at the last minute... so, er... he sent me.'

'Don't like it. Already rules changing,' grumbled the second arrival.

Kriangsak stared at the two men. 'Look, I don't think it makes any difference. It isn't either Somboon or me that you want... it's the goods. And the agreement was cash on delivery. So please start organising it.'

The two arrivals remained motionless. The first one spoke. 'Not so fast. First we want to inspection goods. Then tell bank pay $250 million. That half total $500 million. Move goods to sub. Test in lab on sub. If okay, we tell bank transfer rest.'

Kriangsak scowled. 'That wasn't the original deal.'

191

Sea Sore

'We know,' continued the first arrival. 'No matter. Boss changed deal. Wanted more protection. And you wrong 'bout not want Somboon or you. We do. You come with us until final test on the sub okay. Only few hours. Chance you learn about submarines!' The first arrival smiled nastily as he said this, revealing a row of gold-capped teeth.

Kriangsak went green at the thought. 'I don't want the chance. I'll talk to Somboon and see what he says.'

The first arrival continued talking. 'Up to you. But don't forget bank in Switzerland close five-hour time. After that, too late in Europe and we wait until tomorrow.'

Kriangsak grunted and tried to sound brave. 'What's your name?'

The first arrival said nothing for a few seconds while he calculated whether or not to reply. 'Kielski.'

Kriangsak grunted again and then disappeared to raise Somboon on the ship to shore radiotelephone.

Kielski and the second arrival sat down. 'Drink,' commanded Kielski.

'What?' asked the captain.

'Give drink. Now.'

The captain swore under his breath and sent a crew member off to find a bottle of Mao Tai to keep the unpleasant visitors happy.

By the time Kriangsak returned, the two arrivals were already onto their second large shot of Mao Tai and beginning to flush up.

'So,' asked Kielski belligerently, 'do we have deal?'

Kriangsak spoke slowly. 'Somboon has spoken to Fang who has spoken to your boss. We are all totally pissed off that the deal has been changed in this way.'

Kielski looked restless. 'Get to point; do we have deal?'

Kriangsak glared at Kielski. 'We have nothing to hide. We don't agree to release the goods for less than $400 million. When we have confirmation of $200 million being received into our account we will release ten bags. Once the second $200 million is received we will release the second ten bags. At the same time your boss will give instructions for the balance of one hundred

192

Sea Sore

million to be held by the bank in the bank while we wait for your test results. I will go with you on your damn submarine to ensure fair play. Once the final balance is paid you will return me immediately to this ship.'

'All that agreed with boss?'

'Yes.'

'I check. You drink.' It was a command, not an invitation.

'No. You just check.'

Kielski smiled another nasty, gold-filled smile and spoke in a harsh language into a small walkie-talkie while keeping his eye fixed on Kriangsak. After giving brisk instructions he switched off the walkie-talkie and sat down.

'Wait. Drink.' This time an instruction to the captain.

After five minutes of tension-filled silence, Kielski's walkie-talkie bleeped. He grunted into it several times and then turned to Kriangsak. 'Okay. Boss agree. Show first ten bags.'

Kriangsak climbed down into the hold with the captain, and two selected crew. The twenty special sacks were stacked inside a stout wooden cage, which was padlocked and lashed between two pillars to prevent it moving. Kriangsak undid the lock, and the two crews prised open the cage door. He counted out ten sacks, which were placed carefully beside the cage. Lastly he re-locked the cage and ensured that the hatch was itself re-locked as the bags were carried delicately into the ship's lounge and lined against one wall.

Kielski looked at the grey, woven polypropylene bags and cracked his fingers.

'Open.'

Kriangsak delicately slit open the top of the first bag and revealed a thick, clear-polythene liner. Kielski bent over the bag, took the liner between his two hands and stared intently at the pure white contents and spread the grains between his fingers. He grunted and handed the bag over to Kriangsak who even more carefully made a small incision in the top right corner of the liner. He then took a straw, pushed it delicately through the slit into the snowy powder, put his thumb over the end of the straw still in his hand and withdrew it. He motioned to Kielski to hold out his hand and then let the few small white granules fall into it. Kielski

193

Sea Sore

moistened his little finger, picked up one of the granules and touched it onto the tip of his tongue.

Silence.

Kielski slowly raised his eyes, looked at Kriangsak and nodded. Kriangsak returned the excess powder to the polythene bag, carefully folded the corner several times and taped it down with parcel tape. He then did the same with the outer bag and moved on to the next bag in the line.

As if engaging in some religious ritual, Kriangsak and Kielski carried out their precise testing of the remaining nine bags in total silence while the second arrival from the submarine blessed the proceedings with his Uzi.

After half an hour the ten bags had been tested and approved.

'Now arrange the first 200 million,' said Kriangsak. As he spoke he saw the second arrival flinch and his finger tighten on the trigger of the Uzi, which he still carried in front of him. Kielski also saw the movement and smiled.

'Money transfer will happen. Don't upset friend. He get nervous.'

Kriangsak looked straight at Kielski.

'We have taken two of the available five hours. No money, no goods. Please get on with it.'

Kielski spoke into his walkie-talkie. 'Wait confirm,' he commanded, sitting down and taking another slug of Mao Tai. Kriangsak wondered what was going to happen to Kielski as he continued to take multiple minute portions of heroin and wash them down with Mao Tai. So far the brute showed no outwards signs of ill effects.

After ten minutes, Kriangsak received an excited call from Somboon, which he took in the captain's cabin.

'It's there,' gabbled Somboon. 'Banque du Rhône called. The bloody money's there!'

Kriangsak felt his heart stop. It was working! Then he paused.

'Is there anything that can go wrong with the money clearing?'

Somboon chuckled. 'No, that's the incredible part. I asked the same question and the clerk let slip that it was an internal book-keeping entry – the bloody Ukra... buyers also have their money with Banque du Rhône! Small world. It's just a question of the

Sea Sore

stroke of a pen – or I guess a computer key these days – to transfer the money from one account to another.'

'I guess there aren't many banks these days, even in Switzerland, which will handle this business. Anyway, it makes life simpler. So I should let the first ten bags go?'

'Yes. And hurry up with the second ten; we're getting tight on time.'

Kriangsak returned to the lounge.

'Okay, you can have them.'

Kielski turned to the captain.

'Load sacks into cradle… If lose one, you're dead.'

The captain was convinced from the look of Kielski that he wasn't joking.

One by one the precious sacks were fitted into the breeches buoy and winched carefully along the floodlit line connecting the two rolling vessels.

As the last sack arrived safely aboard the submarine Kielski turned to Kriangsak. 'Okay, start again.'

For the next hour the scene was re-enacted. The tension rose as each sack was tested and approved. As the contents of the twentieth sack received a blessing, Kriangsak snapped at Kielski.

'You'd better hurry up and arrange the second $200 million plus the balance of one hundred in the security account. There's only half an hour left of European banking time.'

Again Kielski spoke into his walkie-talkie and fifteen minutes later Somboon called.

'The second two hundred has been transferred and another hundred in the safe account. Let the second lot go and you go with it. Once they've completed their tests and instructed the bank to release the balance then you nip back onto the *Double Jade* and celebrate.'

'Somboon,' retorted Kriangsak, 'I don't think you've ever been on a ship for longer than an hour – let alone swung in the middle of the night forty feet above horrible choppy black water from one onto a goddam submarine. So don't tell me what I've got to do. I know, and I don't bloody well like it. And what's more, I shall have to spend the night cooped up in that revolting Ukrainian tin can until the start of European banking hours tomorrow.'

195

Sea Sore

'Well, look at it this way,' said Somboon, feeling irrepressibly richer by $200 million, 'they've probably got good quality caviar and Vodka.'

Kriangsak hung up before he threw up and grumpily returned to the lounge. He still had to complete his part of the job before he could feel irrepressibly rich.

As the last bag left, Kielski motioned to Kriangsak with his revolver.

'You next.'

Kriangsak looked warily at the thin cord strung between the two vessels and then down at the sea many feet below. He felt his legs getting weak.

'Are you sure I won't fall in?'

'Shut up and hurry up,' snarled Kielski. 'You might get bit wet. Nothing more. Follow him,' pointing to the Uzi carrier. 'I follow you. He pull you… You too weak!' The last part was added with a curl of his lip.

Somboon turned to the Chinese captain. 'You wait here. Don't move an inch until I get back tomorrow. Understand?'

'Sure,' nodded the captain, happy at the thought of seeing the special cargo, Kriangsak and the unpleasant strangers disappearing from his ship one after another along the thin line.

★

Kielski landed deftly on board the submarine and immediately pushed the shaking Kriangsak roughly down the metal steps into the airlock inside the conning tower.

'Get down quick. Must move.'

All three men slithered down the steps, through the airlock and into the stale, oily air of the submarine. As soon as he entered, Kielski snapped out a series of questions in a foreign language to the burly crew and nodded in satisfaction to the answers. He pointed to a metal seat.

'Sit. No move.' Kriangsak looked warily around the inside of the submarine. It seemed a mass of pipes, dials and long thin corridors. Menacing, thickset crew moved swiftly around the cramped interior with the grace of ballet dancers. These men were

Sea Sore

trained. Nothing for it but to do as he was told. Kriangsak sat down on the metal chair.

He didn't even see the butt of the Uzi as it cracked on the back of his head knocking him unconscious and sending him sprawling onto the greasy, cold floor. Kielski looked with disdain at the unconscious Thai. He snapped a command and two of the ballet dancers picked up Kriangsak as if he was a paper doll and threw him back onto the chair.

When he regained consciousness Kriangsak found himself gagged with his arms and legs tightly bound to the metal seat. He tried to move but could not. His head throbbed and the gag cut into the back of his mouth making him feel even more sick than he had done on the *Double Jade*. He started retching and some of the crew turned round, noted that he was conscious, and carried on with their duties.

Kriangsak guessed he hadn't been blacked out for too long. He could feel the submarine beginning to move and then diving gently. His chair slid slightly along the metal deck.

After a couple of minutes Kielski spoke to the submarine's commander, who gave some clipped instructions to the crew. Kriangsak could hear a lowering in the note of the engines. The submarine was stopping. The commander took the periscope, twisted around, focused on something and then barked into a microphone what sounded to Kriangsak like figures. Ten seconds of silence, then another curt command, after which five sickening jolts sent judders throughout the submarine.

★

The unshaven, hollow-eyed captain did not see the five streaks of foam that sliced through the black night water towards his stationary ship. He hardly felt the simultaneous explosions as five warheads ripped through the *Double Jade*'s rusty skin and detonated deep in her sugary guts. The ancient ship split open like an over-ripe banana. Within three minutes her bow was in the air and she had started to slip backwards into the shark-infested South China Sea.

Those crewmembers who were still alive frantically tried to

197

Sea Sore

launch the *Double Jade*'s lifeboat but were defeated by years of rust.

Down below the unshaven, hollow-eyed captain did not stir. He lay sprawled on his back, his body wracked by the impact of the explosion that had split his throat from ear to ear, satisfying the curse muttered by Fang Hock Joo against the captain's father in Singapore so many years before.

Flour Power

South China Sea, Tuesday, 30 May 1995

Kriangsak rocked backwards and forwards on his metal chair trying to shout through the tightly bound gag, which pinned his tongue to the floor of his mouth. The rocking made an unusually loud sound in the submarine as it hung in the water, its engines idling, waiting the torpedoes to strike. Kielski turned away momentarily from the periscope that he was cradling and snarled at Kriangsak.

'Shut up. Bastard.'

As he spoke, they were rocked by five almost simultaneous explosions which sent shuddering shockwaves through the submarine. A ripple of congratulation started to spread through the crew but was cut short by a vicious look from the Commander. For ten minutes Kielski remained glued to the periscope turning slowly from side to side to scan the whole length of the crippled *Double Jade*. The crew of the submarine stood motionless, straining to hear and feel the death throes of the ship not far above them. A series of small explosions from the *Double Jade* sent further judders through the submarine and then finally one long, desperate, shrieking boom as the stricken vessel slid below the waves, past the submarine two miles away and onwards, down towards the sea bed thousands of feet below.

Kielski stood up, stretched his back and spoke briefly to the Commander. A few more commands and the submarine hummed back into life, resuming its descent behind the *Double Jade*. Kriangsak once more started rocking and glaring at Kielski who nodded at a crew member to remove the gag. Kriangsak gulped in the oily air.

'You've… you've blown them up, haven't you?'

Kielski looked down at the small Thai with an unpleasant look of amusement in his eyes. 'Very clever. Yes.'

Flour Power

'But why? They hadn't done anything to you. That wasn't part of the deal. Did the crew escape?'

'No. Dead.'

Kriangsak started to shout, 'But why? We've known the captain for years... they wouldn't have said anything.'

Kielski slapped Kriangsak viciously across his head and the chair toppled over onto the metal floor. Kielski looked down at the figure pinned like a butterfly to the chair with blood beginning to drip from his nose. He kicked Kriangsak viciously in the stomach. Kriangsak retched onto the floor but nothing was left inside him from the earlier bout of seasickness.

'You shut up. Don't care about captain. Now he no talk. Better like that for us and you.'

For a moment it looked as though Kielski was going to kick Kriangsak to a pulp. Then he thought better of it, spat down on him and walked off muttering in the direction of the laboratory.

★

'How long will it take now?' asked Kielski looking around the laboratory at the racks of glass tubes and the two flickering green screens

'It depends how much you and your fellow thugs disturb me,' replied Chief Chemist Bizel, not bothering to look up from the work surface. He wore the air of a man who had nothing in the world to fear from the killing machine standing opposite him. 'I have told Mr Kroll I will be able to give him a complete analysis on the whole shipment in about ten hours.'

Bizel looked up.

'Provided I am not disturbed. Analysing one tonne of anything is not easy. One tonne of heroin in cramped surroundings is particularly difficult. Now please go away.'

Kielski grunted and left. He knew that the relationship between Kroll and Bizel was extremely close. Bizel was the brains and Kielski was the brawn. And Kroll knew perfectly how to play them off against each other. In fact, if at that moment Kroll hadn't been too preoccupied with his second 'wife' Zora, he would have been savouring the thought of his two most reliable lieutenants

Flour Power

who hated each other's guts cooped up together in a metal cigar tube hundreds of feet below the surface of the sea. As it was, Zora had his attention.

Bizel worked his way through each bag efficiently and quietly, helped by two laboratory assistants who did their best to keep out of the way of the master. After two hours, one of the assistants sat back and stared in amazement at the reading he was getting from the computer screen. He punched in some more commands. Results unchanged. He quickly and carefully changed the sample and waited for the computer to register the new result. No change. He went cold, then quietly motioned his colleague to look at the screen. Bizel looked up at the two young men. 'What is it? Why are you whispering like two conspiring schoolgirls?'

'Sir... it's just that, er...'

'Stop stammering. What is it?' Bizel moved over to their bench and pushed them roughly aside. He stared at the screen. 'Shit.'

'Exactly, sir, shit – but not heroin.'

'Where did the sample come from?'

'Mid-bag sample from the third bag.'

Bizel stared at the screen again 'Shit. What exactly is it?' he demanded.

'Sir... I'm not sure,' said the first technician warily. 'But it... it... looks like some sort of flour. I would guess something like tapioca but I will need a couple of minutes to be sure.'

'Be sure. And quick,' snapped Bizel, sitting down heavily, mopping his brow and considering the consequences of what it looked as though they were discovering.

After five minutes the first assistant looked up triumphantly. 'I was right: tapioca flour. The mix is approximately ten per cent heroin and ninety per cent tapioca flour.'

'Oh God,' said Bizel quietly. 'They really have gone and done it. They must be completely fucking crazy. They're dead meat. Stuffing Kroll, with tapioca flour. They would be better off dead.'

As he spoke, Bizel also considered the unenviable position of being the messenger who told Straff Kroll that he had just paid $400 million for just under one tonne of adulterated tapioca flour. He bent down and paged Kielski on the internal address system. It would be better to share the burden of delivering this type of message.

★

Straff Kroll paced like a caged animal around the large room leafing through faxes and grunting. His energetic movements and trim figure belonged to a thirty year old. His half-moon glasses and streaks of grey in his close-cropped hair gave a hint of his real age of fifty-two. He wore beige slacks and a shiny silk shirt, which managed at the same time to be trendily baggy and figure hugging. The first three buttons were undone revealing the beginning of a muscular hairy chest and a gold-chained medallion. A male secretary sat waiting patiently for instructions. Zora, his previous secretary, lounged on a sofa and leafed through a fashion magazine, keeping one ear open to the latest developments in her 'husband's' business empire. An empire with which she was intimately familiar. And which she now considered half her own. There was no way Kroll was ever again going to have another female secretary. And since Zora knew better than anyone that Kroll was demonstrably un-queer, she felt like a cat with the cream.

Zora glanced up. 'What's happening to the Asian shipment? Isn't it about time that that creep Bizel finished his analysis? We need to get the stuff into the network.'

Kroll looked up from his faxes and stared at Zora. She was developing an annoying habit of thinking of things before he did. And no one was supposed to be quicker than Straff Kroll. At times he appreciated her more in bed than fiddling around in the business. And this was one of those times. 'Look, pussycat. The sub won't go any quicker just because Bizel has done his analysis. In fact, the only immediate result will be that I shall be one hundred million worse off since the balance of the payment will be transferred out of the bank in Switzerland.'

Zora continued leafing through her magazine. 'You seem to be pretty sure we are getting what we have just paid for.'

Kroll winced internally at the 'we'. 'He' had just paid for it dammit, not 'we'. It was his business, built up over the years from

Flour Power

small-time racketeering to one of the biggest drugs empires in Europe and possibly the world. It was getting to the stage when she would have to go. But then, she was exceptionally good in bed... and she did have this annoying capacity to be right.

'I am. I have been dealing with the Fangs for years on different projects. They have supplied two shipments, which went like clockwork. Good quality stuff. No problems. They are getting a good price and they have the source in the family. Why should it go wrong?'

'Dunno. Just call it female intuition. I will be happier when I know our money has been well spent.'

Kroll carried on pacing and looking at his faxes. Only now he was also thinking about the supply. Would the Fangs dare to rip him off? He, Straff Kroll, with a hard-earned personal reputation for vicious cruelty above and beyond the call of duty? Surely not. But then...

'Bizel said it would take him at least ten hours. He has only had...' – Kroll looked at his gold Rolex – '...maximum of... four ...so we will just have to be patient.'

The phone rang and was answered by the secretary. 'Mr Kroll, it's the submarine...' Kroll tried to walk slowly to the phone but ended up bounding. Zora was there before him and switched the phone onto the loudspeaker.

'Who is it?' barked Kroll.

There was a silence and then Kroll could hear Bizel's distorted voice coming through the static over the phone.

'...It doesn't... good.'

'Bizel, talk slowly and loudly; I can hardly hear you,' shouted Kroll.

'I... have... finished... some... of... the... analysis... and... it... doesn't... look... good.'

'What the hell do you mean?' shouted Kroll.

There was a period of distortion and static, then Bizel's strained voice could be heard again.

'...Only ten per cent heroin ...rest is... is... tapioca flour.' Zora started to swear fluently and vulgarly as Kroll's brain went into overdrive.

'Bizel, are you sure? Where is Kielski?'

203

Flour Power

'Here, boss.'

'Kielski, what the hell does this mean? You did a tongue test on each bag. Can't you tell the difference between heroin and tapioca flour?'

'The top quarter of each bag is okay, boss. It's the rest which is... is...'

'Shit,' screamed Kroll. 'You bloody idiots have made me pay $400 million for three quarters of a tonne of shit.'

Zora and the secretary backed away. They had both seen Kroll out of control before. Nothing and no one was safe. Kroll let out a blood-curdling roar and brought his fist down on the glass-topped desk, splitting the glass and showering the contents around the office. He lashed out with his right foot at a table lamp and sent it sparking and spinning across the room and slamming into the wall. He wrenched up a potted shrub by its leaves, spun it round its head and bought it crashing to the ground. 'You are all... completely... bloody... incompetent...' he screamed at the top of his voice. 'I will personally rip your goddam guts out.' Then he paused.

'Kielski...'

Kielski's unsteady voice came up from under a pile of earth-covered paper.

'Boss?'

'Is that little Thai shit still alive?'

'Yes, boss.'

Kroll smiled. 'Well, teach him that no one, but no one, short-changes Straff Kroll. And do it well. Very well. Make sure Fang and Somboon go the same way. Very public. I want the world to see the message. Tell the captain to get that bloody submarine back here quickly. I want the quarter that is still good. Do it now. And pray that I have calmed down by the time you get back.'

Kroll turned to Zora who was still cowering in the corner of the room.

'Shut up.'

He then walked over and grabbed her by the arm and pushed her roughly in the direction of the bedroom. He needed to relax.

★

Flour Power

Kielski walked into the room where Kriangsak was still lying on the floor and pointed at the two sailors who were on guard.

'Undo him.'

Kriangsak stood up stiffly and looked in fascination as Kielski flicked his knife across his cheek, drawing blood.

'You really think you get away with it?'

Kriangsak started to snivel. 'I... I... don't know what you mean. Please don't hurt me.'

'You really think you rip us off?'

Kriangsak didn't see Kielski's knee come up into his groin.

'You die first. Then your brother.'

By the time Kriangsak's broken body was flushed out into the South China Sea through a torpedo tube it was unrecognisable. Kielski had done it well. Straff Kroll would have been proud of him.

Hot Shot

Bangkok, Wednesday, 31 May 1995

Somboon was feeling extremely happy and rich. Everything was right in the world. He slid his hand up between Lee Lee's thighs and looked at his watch. Bloody Bangkok midday traffic jams. He couldn't wait to get to the flat he maintained for Lee Lee. He told the driver to turn up the air-conditioning and play his favourite Chinese love songs. Not much longer now, surely the damn traffic must start moving soon.

Somboon heard the big motorbike manoeuvring up beside them. Perhaps he should also get one to cut through jams like this. But then he wouldn't be able to slip his hand up Lee Lee's thigh. He pushed his hand to the top of her leg, hiking her miniskirt in the process, and turned smirking to see if the motorcyclist had noticed. The un-helmeted rider leered in at him through the darkened glass. Somboon tensed. Something was unusual. Then the bike pulled forward a little and Somboon began to relax.

He had no time to scream as the smiling pillion rider pulled out a snub-nosed machine gun and lazily emptied it into Somboon, Lee Lee and the driver before the bike pulled away swiftly through the stationary vehicles.

One minute later the lights changed and the traffic started to move. Somboon's car remained motionless as the tropical sun beat down on it. The jammed cars began hooting.

The young policeman stared at the stalled car blocking the midday traffic. He sighed, climbed down stiffly from his small bandstand in the middle of the junction and walked officiously towards the motionless Mercedes…

Morning Calls

London, Friday, 2 June 1995

Robbie turned over in bed and tried to swot the bee buzzing in his ear. It wouldn't go away. Julia stirred and mumbled 'pho…'

Robbie grunted. 'Uuh?'

'Pho…'

'Oh God.' Robbie scrabbled around on his bedside table and found the phone. As he pulled the handset towards him the body of the phone clattered onto the floor. Robbie mumbled into the handset.

'Ho.'

'Robbie, is that you?' Robbie began to wake up and feel extremely bad tempered.

'No… the Pope. Who's that?'

'Who's 'at?' echoed Julia, turning over and pulling the duvet off Robbie.

'James,' said the distant voice.

'Uh?'

'James. James Fang. Robbie, wake up.'

'Christ, James, it's the middle of the night,' snapped Robbie, looking at the radio alarm which showed six fifteen.

'Robbie, I'm sorry to disturb you but it's important.'

'I'm glad.'

'Robbie, you won't be,' said James earnestly.

Robbie pulled his thoughts together. For James to phone this early it had to be important.

'James, what is it? I'm more or less awake now.'

'Robbie, it's Somboon.'

'What about him?'

'He's dead.'

'Whaaaat?' Robbie sat bolt upright. 'You're kidding.'

'Robbie, I wish I was. But I'm not. He was shot yesterday in

207

Morning Calls

Bangkok. A hit job. They got him in a traffic jam.'

'Oh God,' mumbled Robbie.

There was a long pause. James spoke slowly.

'Robbie, they also got Lee Lee and the driver. I'm so sorry.'

'Oh no,' said Robbie, his mind beginning to race. James must have known about Lee Lee. 'How? Was he set up?'

'Robbie, what is it?' said Julia, sitting up in bed and pulling the duvet around her.

'Somboon's been shot. Dead.'

'Sorry?' said James. 'I can't hear you.'

'Nothing. I was just telling Julia what's happened. Do you know who did it? And why?'

There was a pause as James weighed up what to say. He realised he was in shock. He had to be doubly careful.

'I'm… I'm not sure. You know Bangkok is a pretty rough place and Somboon had a lot going on. For sure, he must have trodden on someone's toes. But he was a fairly shrewd guy and he knew the score…'

'Is it to do with our deal?'

'No,' said James a bit too quickly. He paused. 'At least, I don't think so. But I'm not sure. To be honest I'm getting a bit worried. Our ship has gone off the map. Hasn't been heard of for two days. We have the coastguard on alert but so far nothing. She's simply vanished.' There was another pause. 'Robbie, I'm worried.'

'I'm not surprised! Look, James, I'm sorry about Somboon but I guess, as you say, he must have upset someone locally. You've always told me how cheap it is in Thailand to have people knocked off. If I were you I wouldn't go jumping to conclusions and linking our contract to this or the disappearance of the ship. You know as well as I do that it's an old rust bucket. I'm sure we'll find it's just broken down somewhere and the radio is out of order.'

James made acknowledging noises. If only Robbie knew what was really being shipped he wouldn't be so damn cool and logical! If the ship had just broken down Kriangsak would have found a way to get a message through one way or another from the submarine. As it was, there had been no message from either the ship or Kriangsak for two days and no transfer of the balance of

Morning Calls

the money. Presumably Kriangsak must still be on the submarine waiting for the test results and making sure the funds were transferred. Ten times, James's hand had hovered over the phone as he debated whether or not to call Kroll and complain about the delay. That was before he had heard the news about Somboon. Once, he had got as far as dialling Kroll's number, but then had hung up. Kroll not only had Kriangsak hostage on the sub but also the heroin. For better or for worse, James and Somboon had decided that this was the only way to satisfy Kroll that he was getting good-quality goods. After all, he had paid up $400 million based on a visual inspection. The heroin was of excellent quality. If anything better than the shipments that James had supplied previously. There was no point in pushing Kroll unnecessarily. But that was before James had heard the news about Somboon. Was he jumping to conclusions linking Kroll with Somboon's murder?

'James, are you still there?'

James snapped out of his reverie. 'Yes, yes... sorry... I'm a bit shocked.'

'That's understandable.' Robbie paused. 'Look, James, I'm sorry to be practical at a time like this, but is this ...this horrible thing going to interfere with the rest of the shipments? What does Somboon's brother say? What's his name? Kry something or other.'

'Kriangsak. I dunno. He's just disappeared. I haven't heard from him,' said James, being truthful but misleading.

'Presumably he's gone underground. He must know what Somboon did to upset whoever it was.'

'Presumably. Without either Somboon or Kriangsak around nothing much is going to happen for the other shipments. You know it's a typical Chinese family business. The boss takes all the decisions.'

'Can you help?'

'Wrong side of the family. It would take my father to intervene, and I wouldn't want to do that just yet. But we have another problem.'

'Great. What's that?'

'The Chinese. They have read about Somboon in the Chinese

209

Morning Calls

press – these types of things happening to overseas Chinese around the region are always reported much earlier and more accurately in the regional Chinese language press than in the English papers.'

'Presumably that nice Mr Jiang Yong Ruen is worried that his vehicle Ever Rich in Hong Kong might not be as rich as he is hoping?'

'Exactly.'

'Greasy little bastard.'

'He always was. But we need the Chinese linkage in the deal to keep things confusing. And he knows it. Can you call him, Robbie, and assure him that the problem with Somboon will not affect the deal from Clyde and Clyde's perspective?'

'I could. But I wouldn't be telling the truth, would I?'

'I always thought you said that Clyde and Clyde would have to honour its contracts whatever happened to the supply or off take?'

'Don't play games with me, James. It's too early in the morning. If I call Jiang it will be purely to keep him sweet. The pressure is still on you to perform on the supply side. And I don't care whether you will have to go crawling to your father or not. That's your problem. Clear?'

James bit his tongue. He was in no position to argue.

'Okay, Robbie. Keep your hair on. It's clear.'

'Good. Has there been any reaction from the Indonesians?'

'No. No reason to be. As far as they are concerned the sugar is coming from China. Somboon wouldn't mean anything to them. And in any case they don't read the Chinese press.'

'At least that proves why we have to keep Jiang happy. Let's do it this way. You keep the pressure on the coastguard to contact the *Double Jade*. If you can't find Kriangsak, you had better talk to your father to get him to step in. For my part, I'll call Jiang to butter him up, and the insurance people and the bank to warn them.'

'No,' said James, too quickly. 'I mean… is it really necessary? To call the bank, I mean?'

Robbie paused and wondered why James was reacting in this way. The banking side was Robbie's problem, not James's.'

'Why not? And what's it got to do with you anyway? Victor de

210

Morning Calls

Gruchy is my problem. Chinese press or no, I can tell you that he won't be slow in picking up on the fact that the supplier for his client Clyde and Clyde in one of the largest sugar deals ever has just been knocked off. Bankers don't like surprises. Much better that I give him some warning and make soothing noises before he finds out by himself.'

'I suppose you're right. It's just that I wonder if it is too wise to rock the boat before we know the facts.'

'In all of this confusion, one of the main facts is that Somboon has been murdered.'

'Yes, yes, I suppose you are right.'

'Believe me, James, I am. Now go and organise your part of the deal and ring me as soon as anything happens.'

Robbie hung up and lay back in the bed.

'Was that supposed to happen?' said Julia, throwing part of the duvet over him.

'Which bit, Somboon getting murdered or the ship disappearing?'

'Either. I mean both. I don't remember either being in the plan you told me about.'

'You're right. They weren't,' said Robbie looking worried. 'And I don't like it. None of this was in the original game plan at all.'

Robbie swung himself out of bed and pulled his dressing gown on.

'Something is going horribly wrong. I had better make some calls. Why don't you go back to sleep for another hour. I'll wake you when it's getting-up time.'

★

The doorman looked up in surprise and then glanced involuntarily up at the clock on the reception-area wall.

'Don't say it, Fred,' growled Robbie. 'As a matter of fact, I couldn't sleep.'

'Sorry, sir,' said the security guard-cum-receptionist. 'Didn't mean to be that obvious. It's just that it's only seven thirty.'

'I know,' said Robbie disappearing into the lift. 'It feels like it.'

Morning Calls

As he sat in his leather chair staring out over St. Pauls, shimmering in the early morning sunshine, Robbie turned over yet again the facts that James had given him. He thought of Somboon and Lee Lee lying dead in Somboon's Mercedes. Victims of some crime, which he didn't understand. He thought of Lee Lee only a few weeks earlier in the Oriental Hotel and felt sick. The calls Robbie made earlier in the day hadn't clarified anything at all. Robbie sighed, and looked at his watch. Eight o'clock, which made it seven in Geneva. He had better call de Gruchy at home before he heard the news from someone else.

Victor's voice as he answered the phone sounded rather too clear and alert for someone who had just woken up.

'Victor, it's Robbie. Sorry to disturb you so early.'

'Don't worry,' said Victor, 'you just beat me to it. Are you in the office already? It's only just past eight your time.'

'Couldn't sleep. Anyway, what did you want to call me about?' asked Robbie. Surely de Gruchy couldn't know about Somboon yet. And if he did, he didn't sound too worried.

'This is a bit like a party game,' said Victor sounding perky. 'You disturb me in my bed and then ask me why. Anyway, surely the answer is our dear late Somboon.'

Robbie was stunned for a few seconds. 'You know about him then?'

'Me and a few million others. It's all over the press in Asia.' De Gruchy paused and then asked slowly and deliberately, 'What do you think he did wrong?'

'Blowed if I know,' said Robbie truthfully. 'I only heard from James Fang early this morning that he had been murdered. How did you hear so early? Perhaps I should be asking you what he did since you seem to know so much.'

De Gruchy paused and laughed softly and rather unpleasantly. 'Banks know lots of things. It's their job. But they never tell anyone any of them otherwise they wouldn't hear the things in the first place. Anyway, I should be asking you the questions. How do you think Somboon's rather abrupt disappearance from the stage will affect your deal? Do you think Somboon's company will still supply the balance of the sugar?'

Robbie chose his words carefully. 'To be honest, Victor, I

212

Morning Calls

don't know. James says that Somboon's brother Kriangsak has disappeared. Presumably he is scared stiff that the same thing will happen to him…'

'Probably a pretty good presumption.'

'Which means that there is no one left who will run the company. The next of kin, as it were, is James's old man and James is none too willing to get him involved at the moment.'

'Mmmm,' muttered Victor. 'Which means that Clyde and Clyde could be in the shit if Somboon's company doesn't deliver the rest of the sugar that you have sold to the Indonesians.'

'In a word, yes. Does that give your bank a problem?'

'Not at all,' said Victor with a rather unpleasant smugness. 'If there's no delivery by Somboon's company then there's no claim against the letters of credit we issued in their favour. We won't have to pay out anything and we will have earned a nice fee for nothing!'

Robbie realised how much he really disliked de Gruchy. He searched around for a way to get at him. He had a juvenile desire to hurt this too smug banker. 'Did you also hear that the first shipment had gone astray? Ship hasn't been heard of for two days. Your collateral has, to all intents and purposes, disappeared.'

'Yes, but that's only worth $3 million. I don't think we would worry about that too much given the fact you were kind enough to deposit $100 million cash with us when the Indonesians defaulted.'

Bastard, thought Robbie. *He's right. As always, the bloody bank was sitting pretty.*

'Okay,' said Robbie sounding matter of fact. 'Can I take it, then, that in all of this mess I don't have to worry about the bank's support?'

'Always behind you,' said Victor.

Until we really need you, thought Robbie as he hung up.

★

James waited to be connected to Kroll. Finally the heavily accented voice came on the line.

'Kroll.'

213

Morning Calls

'Mr Kroll, this is James Fang.'

'Mr Fang, I am surprised to hear from you.'

'I would have thought you would have been expecting a call.'

'I don't usually get calls from dead men, Mr Fang.'

'What do you mean?'

'You are a dead man, Mr Fang. As dead as your little relative Somboon.'

James started to sweat. 'Do you know about Somboon?'

'He's dead. Just as you will be very soon. No one, but no one, gets away with cheating on Straff Kroll.'

'Did you kill him, Kroll? What do you mean, cheating?'

'Don't pretend to sound innocent, Mr Fang. You are already a dead man. You and your family decided to play out Straff Kroll and lost. That's all there is to it.'

'I don't know what you mean, Kroll,' protested James. 'We delivered the heroin just as we agreed.'

'Hardly as we agreed,' said Kroll quietly. 'I don't think we agreed that you would deliver three quarters of each bag full of tapioca flour with only the top quarter containing heroin. Although I must congratulate you on the quality of the top quarter. It is a shame that you couldn't have delivered the whole cargo like it. Never mind. You're dead.'

'I don't know what you are talking about... We never intended to deliver anything but the proper goods... I don't...'

'You are wasting your time, Fang. You're dead.' The line clicked.

James sat shaking. What had happened? Had Somboon cheated on him? As he sat there, panic rose in him. The phone rang and he jumped. It was the coastguard with two messages. The first, that they had discovered a large oil slick and debris, some of which could be from the *Double Jade*. The second, that a heavily mutilated body of someone who could be Kriangsak had been washed ashore fifty miles away from the oil slick.

James ran to the bathroom and threw up. Kroll's voice kept on running through his brain: 'You're dead... You're dead.' He had to escape. Now.

Courtesy of Her Majesty

Marlow, England, Monday 5 June 1995

Trevor Slade stood looking pensive opposite a discreetly positioned corner table in the main dining room of the Thameside Inn. A fit-looking grey-suited businessman walked purposefully up to him.

'It's all fixed. Works clear as a bell. You could hear a mouse fart.'

Slade rolled his eyes. 'Hopefully, Jones, it will pick up a bit more besides that.' He turned to the maitre d'hôtel who was standing next to him.

'Right, Mr Solveni, shall we run over the basics again?' he said, addressing the unhappy-looking maitre d'hôtel, who nodded his head sadly.

'Firstly, you are to assume that the restaurant is full, so please don't accept any more reservations for lunch today.' Slade looked at Solveni for some sort of acknowledgement and continued after he was given another despondent shake.

'Secondly, the guests of honour will sit at the corner table. You will keep empty all the tables between the corner table and the side door.'

Another shake.

'Thirdly, at two thirty, all the staff – and by that I mean all the staff including you, Mr Solveni – will go with this gentleman beside me to an upstairs room and wait there for further instructions. On no account are you to come down until you are told to. Is all that clear?'

The maitre d'hôtel looked ill at ease. 'Clear, but I still donna like it.'

Slade looked annoyed and began to sound edgy. 'Look, Mr Solveni, I'm sorry that what we're asking you to do is a bit out of the ordinary. The hotel's owner has already explained to you

215

that you are to give us your complete co-operation for the day. That's all you have to do. Tomorrow, it's business as usual.'

'I know, I know,' complained a distraught Mr Solveni, 'it's just dat... well, I never bin ask to do dees typa ting before.'

'Something to tell your grandchildren about,' said Slade walking away from Solveni towards the main entrance and adding under his breath, 'Not that someone like you is likely to have any.'

As Slade approached the door, Robbie walked in dressed in a blazer and slacks and looking serious.

'Good afternoon. I hope I'm not too early?'

'No, not at all, Mr Smith. Better early than late today.'

Robbie shook hands with Slade and wondered whether policemen ever called anyone by their Christian name.

'Let me explain the geography,' said Slade, sounding relaxed yet businesslike. 'The principal guests sit over there in that corner. You and I will sit opposite them in the other corner over here. You will be able to see the guests of honour when they come in, but they won't be able to see you. Once they are sat down, you'll be able to hear everything they say through this small earphone. There is a microphone hidden in the flower arrangement on their table. It is extremely sensitive...'

'Hear a mouse fart,' added the man in the grey suit helpfully.

'Jones, if you say that again I shall put you back on sniffer dogs at Heathrow,' said Slade, glaring at the grey-suited Jones, who disappeared to make some minor adjustments to his tape recorder.

'All we have to do is to sit here and enjoy an overpriced lunch courtesy of Her Majesty while our two guests tell sufficient juicy information to the flower bowl to have them put inside for a generation,' Slade continued.

'Once I think we have recorded enough we will introduce ourselves, spoil their lunch and clear up a few points that I'm sure will need it.'

Robbie nodded. 'What's this about guests, plural? Who will be here besides Fang?'

Slade grinned. 'Aha, Mr Smith. If you don't know, I think we should leave that as a surprise. Don't you have any idea at all?'

Robbie shook his head. 'Absolutely none. I didn't even know

Courtesy of Her Majesty

that Fang was here in the UK until you told me. His trip here is a complete mystery.'

'Oh come on, Mr Smith,' said Slade, staring hard at Robbie and sounding sarcastic. 'I don't think the whole thing is that much of a mystery. Bits, yes, for the moment at least, but not the whole thing. We wouldn't be here today if you hadn't started the ball rolling in the first place by telling us about the drugs shipment.'

'Don't take me too literally,' said Robbie, beginning to get annoyed with Slade's arrogance. 'What I meant was, I was unaware of Fang's arrival in the UK and this lunch... How the hell did you know he was in the country?'

'Well, let's just say that with the help of our Singapore and Thai colleagues we have known pretty much every detail of Fang's life for the past few weeks.'

'Amazing,' said Robbie.

'Not really,' said Slade. 'It's called eavesdropping. We do it on most of the people we are interested in.'

Robbie looked thoughtful. 'Including me?'

Slade smiled. 'Why would we need to eavesdrop on you, Mr Smith? Anyway, I think we should go and become diners – the restaurant is beginning to fill up and we need to be sitting down before the important guests arrive.'

Slade and Robbie sat down at a table in the corner opposite the main entrance and made small talk as they waited for Fang. He arrived at twelve forty-five, staring nervously around the restaurant before being shown to his place at the corner table by Mr Solveni.

'God, he looks so ill,' said Robbie to Slade in a low voice.

'So would you if you had had the conversation with Kroll that he had three nights ago. He knows he's on Kroll's hit list. Not a comfy place to be.'

'Does Kroll know he's in the UK?'

Slade smiled. 'You'll see. Can you hear through your earphone?'

'Yes, no mice farting but Fang has ordered a gin and tonic.'

Slade looked up towards the door. 'Here we go – your mystery guest.'

Robbie's jaw dropped as a tall figure appeared at the door.

217

'Christ, it's Victor de Gruchy!'

'You sound surprised,' said Slade.

'I am,' said Robbie weakly. 'Does that mean he's in on it too?'

'Up to his Savile-Row-tailored little neck.'

'I know he's greasy, but I thought he was just an ordinary banker,' said Robbie.

'Not quite just an ordinary banker, Mr Smith. Listen.'

As de Gruchy sat at the table, the microphone picked up his cultured voice.

'My God, Chink, you look like death. What's the problem?'

'Grouch, don't even say that. You know what happened to Somboon; well, I'm on the same hit list.'

Robbie leant over towards Slade. 'What's with this "Chink" and "Grouch" stuff? I know they know each other professionally but here they seem to be old buddies using nicknames.'

'That's just what they are,' said Slade. 'Old school buddies. Cranborough. That's where they met and first started taking drugs.'

Robbie sat stunned. 'I never knew that. I mean …either the school or the drugs.'

'Mr Smith, there's rather a lot you don't know. But if you listen our good buddies might tell you. By the way, Fang kicked the drugs some time ago, but de Gruchy didn't. He's a heroin addict.'

De Gruchy had ordered a drink and as the waiter disappeared the couple started talking again in low voices.

'But why you, Chink? Come to that, why Somboon? I thought everything was going okay. I transferred $400 million from Kroll's account into ours and was just waiting for the instruction to transfer the rest when all hell broke loose. I had Kroll on the line ranting and raving and threatening me. He wanted the original transfers back. I told him no way. Then he said that on no account was I to transfer the balance. He sounded completely beside himself with rage.'

'Grouch, I don't know what went wrong. Kroll said that we had supplied adulterated goods. Well, to be exact, a mix of some very good stuff which covered up a load of shit. As far as I know, my uncle only supplied top grade stuff to Somboon – you should

Courtesy of Her Majesty

know; it's what I normally send you.'

De Gruchy smiled. 'The best.'

Fang continued, 'I can only assume that Somboon tried to be clever and short-change Kroll. Perhaps that was why he wanted Kriangsak to go with the shipment and not himself. But I can't see the logic in it. We were, I mean we still are, making a hell of a lot out of the shipment. Why screw everything up for the sake of a bit more?'

De Gruchy was quiet as he thought. Finally he spoke. 'I agree it doesn't make sense, but there is no other logical explanation. Somboon did the dirty and paid the price.'

'And bloody well dropped me in it too,' wailed Fang. 'Grouch, I need to disappear quickly. I've got to get out of Kroll's reach before I end up like Somboon. The problem is, I don't know where to go – South America? I guess anywhere where I can change my identity. Will there be a problem getting part of my share transferred to wherever I end up?'

'Not at all. I mean, as long as there is a bank wherever you go. All we need to do is to ensure that your share is put into an account over which you have clear signing rights. We have to make sure that the whole thing is done properly. Now that we have the money I shan't hang around at the bank for too long. Just long enough to let things die down, then I shall slide away somewhere. Perhaps join you in South America!'

Robbie sat listening to Fang and de Gruchy's conversation as if hypnotised while Slade munched his way though his overpriced meal. With every sentence, Slade's case against the couple became stronger.

Their conversation stopped as a waiter served the main course, and Robbie spoke to Slade. 'So, de Gruchy is a banker to Kroll as well as running the drug money account for Fang and Somboon?'

Slade sat back and dabbed his lips with his napkin, obviously enjoying the opportunity to make Robbie look small.

'Mr Smith, your Mr de Gruchy is involved in almost every shady commodity deal possible. He finances the basic purchase and sale of commodities and somehow a little commission manages to find its way into his own account. He makes sure that Banque du Rhône's private banking department runs personal

219

Courtesy of Her Majesty

deposit accounts for the Ministers, military men and intermediaries from Africa to Asia who are issuing licences, turning a blind eye or generally helping the trade take place and receiving a 'commission' for their services. Now and again he is really lucky and people approach him with funds from a drugs deal which need a little laundering. If he can do a sufficiently good snow job on the directors of Banque du Rhône by mixing up, say, sugar and heroin, and misleading the board into believing that they are financing a legitimate deal then, bingo, black money becomes white. Again, with a not so small commission going to de Gruchy. He needs the money; he has big spending requirements – heroin is expensive.'

'So that explains why he is so interested in my sugar deals?'

'Exactly. But don't worry Mr Smith, we know you're clean. To answer your earlier question, we've had you under surveillance for ages. You're more or less clean. That is except for a little illicit private account dealing which looks horribly like insider trading. Anyway, that isn't the business of the drugs squad. But the fact that I know about it will, I'm sure, help your complete memory loss about this whole sordid affair as soon as today is over?'

Robbie coloured. 'Er, yes, of course.'

'Good. I thought it would. Please don't forget what we know. I wouldn't have a moment's hesitation to use the information to get you locked up if necessary.'

'I must say that I find your approach quite unpleasant,' said Robbie sharply. He paused. 'However, I can assure you that you will have no need to use the information.'

'Good,' said Slade. 'Just wanted to be clear.' He stood up.

'Come on, I think the time's come for us to introduce ourselves to our friends in the corner. Let's start the fun.'

James Fang was the first to spot Robbie as he approached their table. He looked dismayed at first but managed to hide it well as he rose to shake hands.

'Robbie! What a surprise. Fancy seeing you here.'

Slade replied before Robbie could open his mouth.

'Not really a surprise, Mr Fang; we're expecting you.' Slade turned to Victor de Gruchy. 'And you too, of course, Mr de

Courtesy of Her Majesty

Gruchy. Shall we all sit down?'

'Who the hell are you?' demanded James, looking wildly around the restaurant fearful of an assassination attempt.

'Let's just say I am someone who knows an awful lot about you, Mr Fang. But there's no need to panic; I don't work for Kroll so you are relatively safe for the moment. Now, shall we sit down?'

Fang and de Gruchy looked thunderstruck and sat down slowly.

Slade sat opposite James and spoke again in a conversational way. 'Mr Smith here didn't know that you two were acquainted. That rather surprised me.'

James ignored Slade. 'Robbie, what are you doing here? Who is this bloke?'

Again Slade jumped into the conversation before Robbie could answer. 'I'm not just an ordinary "bloke", Mr Fang. I already told you, I'm someone who is very interested in the reason why you two are here meeting in this restaurant.' Slade turned towards Robbie. 'And in case you really are wondering, Mr Smith is here because I invited him.'

'Robbie, is he telling the truth?' asked James.

'I'm not sure who's telling the truth around here,' replied Robbie. 'Certainly not either of you.'

Victor de Gruchy coughed and spoke. 'I am not sure what you mean, Robbie. Perhaps both you and Mr... er, Mr?'

'Slade,' said Slade.

'Right, Mr Slade could tell us what you are talking about, then we could clear up any mysteries.'

'I do hope so,' said Slade. 'Let's start with a question about your previous drugs shipments. Where did you source the stuff from, Mr Fang? Not from Thailand like this shipment, we know that.'

'I don't know what you are talking about, Slade,' said James hotly. 'My business with Robbie Smith concerns sugar, most of which comes from Thailand.'

'Mr Fang. This could be a rather long conversation. And from what I understand you have a pressing appointment with a flight to Buenos Aires later today. I think we could all save each other a

221

Courtesy of Her Majesty

lot of time and inconvenience if you assumed that we know you have been supplying heroin to Kroll for some time now. We know about the current deal, which is going wrong, but we still have some missing bits concerning earlier transactions. It would help us rather a lot if you could fill in the gaps before you disappear.'

'Are you police?' asked de Gruchy.

Slade laughed softly. 'Oh no, Mr Fang. They're much too nice. I'm from the drug squad. We're the ones who make Kroll look like Andy Pandy.'

'I think you're bluffing, Slade,' said James.

Slade sighed and looked bored. 'Mr Fang, we know that you were supposed to ship one tonne of heroin to Kroll hidden in the first of Mr Smith's sugar shipments aboard a vessel called the *Double Jade*. The heroin was transferred from the *Double Jade* to Kroll's sub, which then ungraciously torpedoed the *Double Jade*, which sank with no survivors. And that was even before Kroll discovered that you had short-changed him on the drugs. Which gives you an idea of the type of person he is. After he did discover about the adulterated drugs shipment he had Kriangsak ripped limb from limb and Somboon murdered along with his mistress. And you, Mr Fang, are next on the hit list. Now do you believe me?'

James Fang groaned.

'Since you know so much, tell us why Somboon adulterated the shipment,' said de Gruchy.

Slade looked at de Gruchy and Fang, smiled, and paused. 'He didn't.'

'Then who did?'

Slade smiled again. 'We did.'

'Whaaaat?' said James, Victor and Robbie in unison.

'I thought you might like to know that,' said Slade. 'Makes things a bit neater, doesn't it?'

'You mean Somboon delivered perfectly good heroin and somehow you switched it?' asked James.

'Not me personally,' said Slade, 'but some of our good friends in Bangkok.'

'But why?' asked de Gruchy in amazement. 'You got

Courtesy of Her Majesty

Somboon and Kriangsak killed.'

'Well, that's partly why,' answered Slade. 'You see, Mr de Gruchy, my job falls into two parts. Firstly, finding out about drug shipments, and then stopping them. I always reckon that one of the best ways to stop them is to get rid of the people making them. In this instance Somboon, Kriangsak and, of course, yourself, Mr Fang. We have plans for Kroll later on. However, before we get rid of him, we thought it might be useful if he helped us dispose of some of his suppliers.'

'You calculating bastard,' exploded de Gruchy.

'I hope so,' replied Slade coolly.

'But how did you know about this shipment?' asked James.

'I told him,' said Robbie, speaking for the first time.

'You! But all you knew about was the sugar. How the hell did you find out about the drugs?' demanded James. He paused. 'Wait a minute, it was Lee Lee, wasn't it!'

Robbie nodded. James continued, 'I told Somboon not to send her to you…'

'Do you mean her visit to my room was a set up job?' asked Robbie.

'Of course it was,' sneered James. 'You don't imagine she would have come of her own accord do you? You must be more arrogant than Somboon said you were. No, no; she was sent by Somboon. The clever sod saw you were interested in her and he couldn't miss the opportunity to get you in a position that would be useful to him later on. Only this time it cost him his life.'

'And hers,' added Robbie acidly.

Slade looked at his watch. It showed two thirty. 'Mr Fang, you really will have to be going soon. Are you sure you wouldn't like to tell me a little about the earlier shipments. I think you can see that we know quite a lot already about your business.'

Fang sneered at Slade. 'Go to hell. You are the one that killed my cousins and put a price on my head; why should I help you?'

Slade paused a little. 'It's just that where you're going it won't help you much, and the information could be extremely useful to us.'

'No way,' said Fang, looking towards the side door as it burst open.

223

Courtesy of Her Majesty

The motorcyclist looked steadily across the room, smiled at Fang and then slowly raised his right arm. Slade pushed Robbie to the floor as two muffled shots punched the air. The first hit Fang squarely between the eyes, blowing away the back of his head. The second ripped through his heart, throwing him backwards off his chair and onto the floor. Satisfied that he had done his job, the assassin turned and walked calmly out through the side door.

As the motorbike roared off into the distance Robbie scrabbled to his feet, he looked around the room expecting there to be pandemonium. His jaw dropped. The other diners were talking quietly among themselves as if analysing a play.

Slade climbed stiffly to his feet, brushed down his trousers and waved his hand at Jones, who held a revolver in his right hand. 'You can put your peashooter away – our friend was a professional. He doesn't need any help.'

Jones looked hurt and muttered, 'It's not so difficult with a sitting duck. He should try in a crowded London street.'

'Or a Geneva one,' said Slade, smiling at de Gruchy who sat terrorised next to James's crumpled body.

Slade walked towards the corpse and peered down at it. 'I told him he had to be going soon. Shame he wouldn't tell me anything before he went. Still I expect Mr de Gruchy will be a bit more helpful.'

Robbie pointed weakly towards the others in the room who were chattering quietly to each other. 'Wh... wh... who are they? Why aren't they panicking?'

Slade smiled. 'Part of the team. Isn't it amazing how far people will drive on a Monday to enjoy an overpriced lunch courtesy of Her Majesty.'

Water Bugs

Jakarta, Friday, 12 April 1996

'Where the hell's Omar?' grumbled the Minister of Agriculture, staring angrily at the empty space, which should have been occupied by his white ministerial Mercedes.

The hot afternoon sun beat down on the portly Dr Amin. He felt his temperature rising rapidly as a result of both the sunshine and his anger at the missing car. He turned to his aide. 'Abdul, go and find the lazy bugger. I haven't got all day.'

Abdul scurried back into the bleak Ministry building looking around wildly and hoping against hope to find the missing Omar lurking somewhere near the entrance. Dr Amin exhaled noisily. His right foot started tapping in annoyance. He felt his blood pressure rising. He tried to calm himself. He was at a dangerous age. The Minister added muttering to his outward signs of anger. He began to sweat.

Thirty seconds after Abdul's departure, the ministerial car crept around the corner into the driveway and drew up gently in front of the tapping, muttering, sweating Minister. Omar opened his door slowly, and creakily prepared to climb out.

Dr Amin glared at him angrily. 'Forget it, Omar. I want to get out of the sun before I either retire or get cooked like a lobster.'

Dr Amin threw open the back door and sank grumpily into the back seat.

'Omar, what is it with you drivers that you can never be where you are supposed to be when you are supposed to be there? Is there some sort of training course that you all go on?'

'Sir?' said Omar, fiddling with his hearing aid, which had started to whistle.

'Oh, never mind,' snapped the irate Minister. 'Just hurry up and drive. I don't want to keep the President's son waiting.'

Omar fumbled with the gearshift and the Mercedes crawled

225

Water Bugs

down the driveway, past the security guard dozing happily in the post-lunch sunshine and out through the Ministry's grand but rusty gates. The guard continued sleeping peacefully, draped like a worn overcoat over the uncomfortable metal folding chair that was his daytime home. His rice-tight potbelly undulated gently to the rhythm of his open-mouthed, contented breathing and his arms dangled like aerial roots by his side. His too tight uniform jacket ballooned open between the buttons that strained valiantly to tether it, revealing harlequins of a grubby, off-white sweatshirt beneath.

Five minutes passed. Finally Abdul ran out of the Ministry building looking hot and bothered. He peered up and down the driveway for signs of either the Minister, the car, or both. Nothing. 'Shit!'

He clenched his fists and finally made up his mind to ask for a transfer from the Ministry of Agriculture.

'Bloody drivers,' grumbled the bad-tempered Dr Amin, still mopping small beads of sweat from his nut-brown brow as the car rumbled down the eight-lane highway. 'Wish I'd kept that mad sod Akbar.'

Outside the cool, quiet Mercedes, a tangle of battered trucks, shining limousines, and noisy mopeds straining under the weight of whole families, jostled for space along the boulevard that glimmered in the heat of the sweaty tropical afternoon sun. Crowds of skinny honey-brown people picked their way along the deformed dusty pavements and past street vendors who sold everything from baseball caps to noodles and cigarettes from three wheeled carts.

The crowded roads and pavements were bordered by shiny modern glass-clad skyscrapers. Outside each building was a shrill whistle-blowing uniformed guard waving his arms in an authoritative and agitated manner at traffic, which, to a large part, ignored him. A loudspeaker boomed echoing instructions to snoozing or gossiping drivers to come and collect their masters.

A typical Jakarta afternoon scene.

★

226

Water Bugs

Dr Amin breathed in deeply through his nose and savoured the scent from the magnolia trees that hung heavy in the balmy tropical evening air. His domed, wet, brown belly glistened in the bright moonlight as he lay on his back, looking up at the stars, and gently flapped his arms and legs. He made slow but steady progress towards Mary-Jo at the shallow end of their new pool. Mary-Jo meanwhile did some lazy aquarobics exercises while she waited for her tubby husband to arrive. Dr Amin finally made it down the length of the pool. He let his feet sink slowly to the safety of the pool bottom and turned breathlessly to Mary-Jo.

'You know, it was easier doing that last year in the birdbath,' he said, shaking the water from his ears.

Mary-Jo laughed quietly. 'True, but in general life has been much easier since then.'

'You know, you're right,' said Dr Amin as he turned, hitched his arms over the poolside rail and let his legs float up.

'I suppose we were... I mean I was... wrong to buck the system for so long. I don't know why it is but it's been much easier to get on with everyone at work since I... um ...changed.'

'Do you think they know?' asked Mary-Jo quietly. She dropped her voice even further. 'About Hartono, I mean.'

Amin cycled his legs slowly and looked thoughtful for a moment.

'I really don't think so. I mean, I've never discussed anything with anyone apart from Hartono. And I don't think he blabs. It's not in his interest.' He stopped cycling and stood up. 'But you're right. It's a bit like everyone knows and that we're now part of some club.'

'Mmmm,' said Mary-Jo, as she thought about her new kitchen and the bathrooms, which had suddenly been renovated out of the blue. The 'sweet little stove' had gone along with all the other 'characterful' facilities which had filled her with so much embarrassment, particularly when her mother visited. In their place were the ultra modern fittings which befitted her husband's rank as a senior Minister, and after which she had hankered for so many years.

'But I still don't understand why I suddenly qualified for this bloody great pool,' said Dr Amin. 'I was getting quite used to

227

Water Bugs

splashing around with you in the birdbath… it has some nice memories.' Dr Amin looked at Mary-Jo and smiled not altogether innocently.

Mary-Jo moved next to him. 'There's no reason why we can't create good memories in this pool too,' she said, putting her arm around his waist and squeezing his spare tyre. Then she became serious.

'By the way, what happened to the last payment?'

Dr Amin gave Mary-Jo a playful kiss on the nose, not wanting to spoil the relaxed mood they were in.

'Received in the bank today. That makes $20 million we've got over the past twelve months. Who's a clever boy then?' Dr Amin suddenly looked pensive. 'But there're still a few things I really don't understand.'

'What do you mean?'

'Well, for a start, that chap de Gruchy just disappeared into thin air. We had all those discussions about setting up our account, and then just as it is beginning to work, bang, he goes.'

'Perhaps he retired.'

'No… far too young. And what's more, no one at the bank knows anything about him. It's as though he didn't exist. Hartono is as mystified as I am.'

'I'm sure there's a completely logical explanation. Banks are funny places.'

'Perhaps you're right. But it's the same with that arse-licking younger Fang. Just disappeared. The only people I talk to now are his old man and the sugar suppliers in London.' He went quiet for a bit and then had another thought.

'And if I think about it, I haven't heard from that chap Smith at Clyde and Clyde for ages. He's gone quiet as well. Someone told me that he had decided to do something completely different after a rich aunt died and left him a fortune. But then Hartono reckons it's all something to do with that Thai uncle that got shot. But I can't see the connection myself…'

'You know, you worry too much about other people,' said Mary-Jo sternly. 'We've been doing much better since you started worrying more about us. The President is happy with the way you solved the sugar problem and we have twenty million in the bank.

Water Bugs

I don't give a shit about disappearing bankers or Chinese traders. And neither should you.'

'I suppose you're right,' said Dr Amin slowly. Even after all these years he still couldn't get over Mary-Jo's forthright American manner. She was so different from any of the Indonesian girls that he might have married. He had certainly come a long long way since the first time he had waved goodbye in Surabaya to the small wiry Javanese man dressed like a circus clown. What would the father have thought about his son if he had still been alive today?'

'I suppose you're right... but...'

'But what?'

Amin took a deep breath. What would the funny little Javanese man in clown trousers have said if he had ever found out that his son had used his education for personal enrichment? But there was no point in upsetting the pleasant evening. The deed was done and he would have to live with it forever. He would be better off keeping his thoughts to himself.

'Oh, nothing really.'

Dr Amin put his arms around Mary-Jo and pulled her to him. He kissed her gently.

'Come on. Let's create some more good memories...'

$\star$

The two men from the Ministry for Internal Security looked at each other, smirked and removed their headphones. During the nine months since their Ministry had installed Dr Amin's new pool they had discovered a considerable amount about the new entrepreneurial activities of the Minister of Agriculture. He was significantly less of a security risk now that he was on board. It was much better this way.

For the moment, however, the only sounds that the bugs in the wall of Dr Amin's pool would pick up, although entertaining, would be of little additional professional interest to the security services.

They would be better off seizing the chance of finishing early and enjoying a cup of sweet, thick Javanese coffee before going to

Water Bugs

their homes.

'Let's call it a day,' said the older man.

'Great... perhaps you can tell me some more about what you did as a student?' said Osman, as he began switching off their monitoring equipment and preparing to leave.

Printed in the United Kingdom
by Lightning Source UK Ltd.
103931UKS00001B/19-21